Hold Your Horses

PRICKLE ISLAND ZOO
BOOK FIVE

ALI K. MULFORD

Ebook: 978-1-923184-21-3

Print: 978-1-923184-26-8

Hold Your Horses

Ali K. Mulford

Dear Readers,

A lot has happened in the Lachlan family since you last checked in! I wanted to let you know that Hold Your Horses takes place five years into the future from the events of Book 4, Crocodile Tears. The younger Lachlan siblings are getting older and there's lots of new additions to Prickle Island Zoo (both animal and human alike!).

I hope you enjoy this new adventure!

Happy Reading,
Ali xx

PRICKLE ISLAND ZOO
KEY
TOILETS
FOOD
SHOPPING
FREE WIFI
GIFT SHOP + ENTRY
ENTRY
VET HOSPITAL
CAFÉ
PLAYGROUND
REPTILE HOUSE
THE PECKISH PEACOCK
SAVANNAH
AVIARY
BABOONS

N
W
E
S
FARM
KANGAROO POINT
RAINFOREST WALKTHROUGH
GIBBONS
MEERKATS
PORCUPINES
CARNIVORES
INSECT HOUSE

Evelyn Lachlan (she/her) CEO of Prickle Island Zoo

Hawk Lachlan (he/him) Carnivore Keeper

Lark Lachlan (she/her) (Moved to New Zealand)

Finch Lachlan (she/her) Head Veterinarian

Dove Lachlan (she/her) (Moved to France)

Heron Lachlan (they/them) Hoofstock Keeper

Crane Lachlan (he/him) Reptiles and Inverts

Wren Lachlan (she/they) Primates

Hannah Murphey-Lachlan (she/her) Birds and Farm

Frankie Benedetti (she/her) Head Chef

Aya (she/her) Food Prep Manager

Mateo (he/him) Gift Shop Manager

Chapter One

Heron

"It's the end of an era," I said with a sigh as I slung my arm over my twin's shoulders and stared at the renovated monkey house. The building had been our home for the last five years—something we'd dreamed about for far longer—and now we were moving out.

"It's like I blacked out and half a decade disappeared," Crane mused, giving thoughts to my own words. "It feels like just yesterday we were terrorizing Dove back to Mom's house, and now she's married to a freaking movie star."

I let out a chuckle. "Mom's birthday calendar is getting so filled up, we're doing cake every other week at this point."

"Yeah, we really don't need to do a cake for the ones that live overseas." Crane shrugged. "But she insists on video calling and blowing out the candles."

"And when have we ever said no to cake?"

"Exactly."

I gave one last wistful look at the house. I imagined it felt like saying goodbye to a college campus—only a home for a season before getting passed on to the next generation of ne'er-do-wells. "Well, I hope the new interns love it."

"Remind me next time to renovate the buildings while we're still living in them so we can enjoy it," Crane added.

"Good idea," I replied, slapping my twin on the back. "*So*, you want to come fix the boat with me this weekend then?"

"You already know my answer."

"As long as I buy pizza and beer then yes?"

"Yep." Crane's shoulders shook with quiet laughter. "I still can't believe you're living on a *boat* now. And everyone says I'm the crazy one."

I eyed my twin. "Living on a boat does not even make the top 100 of crazy things we've done."

"Touché."

"It's going to be weird there without you though," I admitted a little more quietly.

"Yeah." Crane's brow furrowed in thought. "Maybe I should build the shed up a few floors so I can see it from my place."

"I think we can manage ten hours a day apart."

Crane was already not listening. "I dunno. Maybe I'll point one of the kangaroo CCTV cameras out toward the harbor . . ."

I leaned my shoulder into him and he leaned back, a quick, silent acknowledgment that I'd be fine.

Crane and I had shared a room for most of our lives, mostly out of necessity. Having so many siblings meant sharing for everyone, but even when we'd moved to the monkey house, we'd still been under the same roof, with only a chain-link wall and heavy curtain separating us.

Now, Crane was going to be living in the old groundskeeper shed by the volunteer house—a surprisingly charming, little wooden building that had been mostly abandoned since we'd built the giant metal shed by the kitchens in the early 2000s. With Crane's renovations, it was the epitome of tiny-house chic. He had managed to squeeze a bathroom in and loft the bed above an all-purpose room below. Still, there was no way both of us could've fit.

"The shed will be a fun, new adventure," Crane said as if giving himself a pep talk. Despite his gusto, I knew he was stressed about his current living situation.

"It'll only be until next year, and then you'll be off on your conservation adventures," I added with a nudge.

My twin was ready to fly the proverbial nest. It was time for him to have more life experiences than our little island could provide. At some point in puberty, he and I had hit a fork in the road and our interests had split. And while we still liked many of the same things, thought the same words at the same time, and spoke through grunts and facial expressions alone, I wanted to stay on Prickle Island and Crane wanted to travel and see the world.

As the morning light filtered through the trees, I knew Crane was thinking the same thing: how the two of us had always thought we'd end up in each other's shoes and at some point we'd split off, diverging in opposite directions. I was supposed to be living a cool, queer, artsy life in the city. He was going to take over the carnivore team when our eldest brother, Hawk, took Mom's position as CEO.

As if summoned by my very thoughts, Hawk's old truck announced itself with a sputter before he rolled around the corner. He drove so slowly that his wife, Hannah, and my nephews, Simon and Max, strolled alongside it instead of riding in the bed. Simon had definitely inherited the Lachlan go-get-'em genes and, at five years old, was already dressed in full khakis, ready to start the day with his zookeeper parents. Max was only just starting to walk and already I knew he would be another troublemaker, him and his brother causing the next generation of Prickle Island Zoo havoc. Crane and I would teach them well.

"Hi, Uncle Crane! Hi, Heihei!" Simon cheered, waving exuberantly to us.

When Simon had just been starting to babble, he'd dubbed me Heihei because Heron was too much of a mouthful. It was also the name of the chicken in *Moana,* and everyone thought it was hilarious that even my nickname was a bird's. But I loved being Heihei. It was the perfect gender-neutral moniker for me, neither aunt nor uncle, just Heihei.

"Hey there, troublemaker," I called affectionately as Crane gave Simon a crisp high five.

It was sweet seeing our nephews romping around the zoo, even cuter when Lark brought her daughters, Lila and Hazel, over from Aotearoa New Zealand too, the four of them tearing around the zoo like a rambunctious troop of howler monkeys. And now that Finch and Frankie were talking about having their own kids, I knew it wouldn't be long before there was a gaggle of the younger generation making mischief for all of us.

"Wow," Hawk called, admiring our freshly painted shutters. "It looks like a real house now."

"The bedrooms even have sheetrock walls instead of chain-link," Crane proudly declared.

"Why didn't we do that sooner?"

"Too much work. None of us cared enough to take the time." Crane shrugged. "We had toilets, a toaster, and a fridge, so good enough."

"Yeah. True," Hawk replied with a laugh.

"The new keepers won't know how good they have it," I added with a chuckle. "We should've all signed the original concrete or something. Every one of us has called this place home."

"Except Wren," Hannah chimed in as she hustled to grab

Max and swept him up in her arms as he steered off a path in the wrong direction. Honestly, I needed to throw my nephews around more. Hannah had guns for days from lifting those two.

"Wren is never leaving Mom's house," I countered.

"I thought you'd never leave this place," Hawk said to me. "And now you're living on a freaking boat in the harbor. Are you sure you aren't having a mental breakdown or something? Boat life really screams quarter-life crisis."

"I'm not having a quarter-life crisis." I rolled my eyes. "I just have cooler sleeping arrangements now. Less chain-link, more ocean sunsets."

"Let them have their cool-kid, boat-life phase," Hannah called from the bushes, where Max was currently inspecting an oddly shaped stick.

"Yeah, no one else is allowed to leave," Crane said, pointing at me and then Hawk. "My money was always on Dove taking off, and now that she's jet-setting around the world with her movie star husband and Lark is living her homesteading dream in New Zealand, that's it. No more Lachlans leaving the zoo."

Hannah snorted.

"What?"

"The lady doth protest too much, me thinks," she said, winking at Hawk. *So it isn't just me who's noted Crane's growing wanderlust.*

"I'm not going anywhere," Crane shot back defensively.

"I thought you were applying for that conservation show next year," Hannah chided.

"That's not *leaving*," Crane countered. "I'm just going to do some conservation work, and then I'll be back in my new house."

"House is very generous," Hawk added, and Hannah laughed. They really were the one-two punch of older sibling taunting.

Crane's jaw tightened in hilarious frustration. "It's a tiny house."

"Yeah, yeah," Hannah said, waving a hand at the wording.

We all knew Crane wouldn't last in the shed for long. It wasn't insulated for one thing, didn't have a shower, and was as leaky as a sieve. But I wasn't about to point that out when my boat was a rusty, discarded relic that would probably have to be sold for scraps in a matter of years. Neither of our living situations were going to last. But my plan was to save up until I could buy a proper boat, one that actually still had engines and I could cruise around the island in. I'd been squirreling away my zoo wages for a long time, but a nice boat was still an expensive investment, especially when adding in all the maintenance costs and mooring fees. But I was determined to make my seafaring dream a reality one day.

Crane nudged me. "You could still come with if you wanted," he suggested, and I realized he was still talking about the conservation trip he was planning next year. "Applications haven't closed yet. There's still time."

"The last thing I want is a camera shoved in my face, no thank you." I tipped my head to Simon, who had collected a bouquet of fallen leaves while Max was trying to eat one. "Plus, who will wrangle all this chaos with both of us gone?"

"I think you will find that the two of you are the source of most of that chaos," Hawk called. He tapped the side of his truck. "Right, I'm off to the ferry to grab the new crew."

Hannah wandered over to the truck with Max on her hip, Simon a pace behind. She gave Hawk a kiss, to which Simon made a "blech!" noise, and Hannah dutifully covered their son's eyes before giving Hawk one more lingering kiss. It was kind of ridiculous how much Hawk and Hannah still had those puppy-love looks in their eyes. Weren't two kids supposed to ruin the romance?

Maybe the secret was having so many built-in babysitters

around. And I was completely biased, but my siblings had the cutest kids. Simon and Max were adorable, and Lark's daughters were already hilarious badasses at the age of four and two respectively. Lark was pregnant with her third, keeping Mom incredibly happy with the rush of grandchildren.

"I've got to get up to the giraffes," I announced, hooking my thumb uphill. "Debra keeps breaking into the silage and nesting in it."

"Oh, Debra." Crane sighed. "She's desperate to lay some eggs. I think you need to just bite the bullet and dance for her."

"I am not doing a mating dance with another bird," I bit out. "I already have one bird wife and that is plenty."

"So loyal."

"So what's one more?" Hannah guffawed. "It would be good for the breeding program if she laid. Think of the species, Ronny!"

"Ugh," I groaned. "One of you can do it."

They all instantly touched their noses, and I rolled my eyes again. With a muttered curse that I was determined my nephews wouldn't learn until at least the age of seven, I headed up the hill to start my day by dealing with a sexually frustrated stork.

Chapter Two

Hollis

"Why did I do this to myself?" I groaned to the whipping wind as the ferry bobbed across the sea. "I don't know anything about horses."

I leaned on my forearms, staring down at the waves over the balcony. Normally, I loved the smell of salty air and the ocean breeze on my face, but it currently did nothing to quell my rising anxiety. What had I done?

"Horses have got to be close enough to zebras, right? I've worked with zebras and gazelles before, even a couple of donkeys at the children's farm in the last zoo . . ." I let out another grumble, dramatically flopping my arms onto the railing. "Yeah, Hollis, I'm sure equestrians would really appreciate you thinking donkeys and horses are the same thing."

I stared down at my thick jeans and pink button-down shirt,

already knowing that if I put on the cowboy hat in my duffel bag that I'd look like I was cosplaying some sort of rancher Barbie. The clothing was practical, comfortable, hardy work clothes, but the hat? I'd bought it in a panic, thinking it would sell the lie. "A lie that you're trying to steer people away from asking you about, Hollis," I grumbled. "I really need to watch some more YouTube rancher videos STAT."

I pressed my lips shut, realizing I was the stranger muttering to herself at the front of the ferry. The charming little blip of an island slowly pulled into view, and I prayed once more that I'd be able to steer any coworker small talk away from my childhood. Maybe we'd all be too busy to chat anyway? Thank God for my resting bitch face. Still, I was sharing a house on-site with two other summer interns. There would probably be some amount of chit-chat involved. Ugh! I hated small talk, but I was determined to fight my introverted ways and not spend all summer hiding in my room. No more wearing headphones and reading a book during my lunch break like I had at my last job . . . and the one before that, and one before that.

It'll be fine, I coached myself, remembering not to speak aloud this time. *Fresh start. New job. One little white lie about my childhood. Yep, it'll be fine. And if it isn't, I'll just move on to another place like I always do.*

I shook out my hands, nerves clawing up my throat.

Most people probably didn't start a job thinking of their exit strategies—something I should've considered before I'd lied on my resume. They were going to fire me the second I opened my mouth. People from Wyoming had a twang, right? Or maybe they didn't. I was twang-less with a vague New Hampshire accent. Hopefully, it was non-regional enough no one would question it.

My contrived background was my perfect ADHD cocktail of rebellious, impulsive, and the dopamine hit of white lies. I'd known I shouldn't have done it, but I'd hit the submit button anyway. All of my previous job references and academics had been true. *That counts for something, right?*

I had a dozen real, glowing references, but every time I got offered a job, it was always in a city where the rent was astronomical, and I didn't want to share an apartment with seven other zookeepers to be able to afford it. My introverted self would've imploded. But the jobs at smaller zoos in quieter towns were long-held and highly competitive. So it had been fate when I'd seen that the internship for Prickle Island Zoo was both well-paid and came with room and board. *Bingo!*

My phone buzzed, and I looked down at text after text from my increasingly irritated mother. She'd been sending me passive aggressive links all month, ever since I'd been diagnosed as both autistic and ADHD—something I'd suspected for nearly a decade, since my school guidance counselor had suggested seeking out a diagnosis. But my mother wouldn't hear any of it. I was a straight A student. I was "quirky" but "normal." And the more I learned about my brain, the more I realized both my parents were probably also neurodivergent and in denial about it. My father would rather chew his own arm off than be confrontational, so he just agreed with whatever my mother said.

Ever since my younger sisters—twins—had gone off to college, my mother had been up my ass with a vengeance. Her latest conquest? Finding me a partner. She didn't care their gender, age, credit score, anything. She just wanted me to get married and have babies immediately now that she was an empty nester. And whenever I would try to remind her that I was only 27 and she needed to chill out, she would remind me that I'd never had a single long-term relationship and she had a "right" to be concerned.

Apparently, she thinks giving birth to me gives her all sorts of motherly "rights."

But considering how well the diagnosis conversation had gone, there was no way in any circle of hell I was going to tell her I was asexual *and* never wanted to be a parent on top of that. While I was technically panromantic and liked the idea of having a partner, I accepted the fact that trying to find someone who fit the bill was pretty much impossible.

It just wasn't in the cards for me. My needs were too specific, and I still felt a little fuzzy about accepting them myself, let alone explaining myself to a romantic partner. I'd tried dating men and thought that maybe that was the problem. I'd tried dating women and non-binary folks, and it had still always ended badly because they had sex drives and I didn't. I knew it probably would've been easier if I had just loudly and proudly declared myself as ace from the start, but it had taken me a long time to even figure that out. I was opaque to myself. It wasn't until my last girlfriend had suggested it that a lightbulb had gone off.

But that breakup had been three years ago and had sucked so terribly, I never wanted to go through one ever again. No more. I didn't want to be constantly second-guessing whether I was being a good partner and if I was giving enough of what they needed, and then forgetting that what I wanted was also important . . . Ugh! Why did existing with other people have to be so complicated?

I'd tried for a long time to mold myself into the right kind of partner to please others and found I'd burn myself out pretending to be what they wanted, so now, finally, I'd decided I'd rather be alone than exhausted all the time. Those were apparently my only two options.

I'd never have my Lizzie Bennett or my Mr. Darcy. I would be a spinster. The fun aunt to my sisters' eventual children. The reliable friend who'd pick you up at the airport at 6 am. That was who I'd be. Another role not quite suited for me, but one I found more palatable than any of the alternatives. And hopefully this little zoo in the middle of nowhere would be the perfect place to hide out from the rest of the world and all of my shortcomings . . . that was if they offered me a full-time job after the summer and didn't ever figure out I'd lied about being a rancher from Wyoming.

"Why, Hollis!" I groaned to the roiling white sky. *Stupid impulse control.*

I'd been furious at my mom when I'd filled out the application and had decided that I'd add a little *sparkle* to my backstory. That ended up being a completely reinvented life of growing up on a horse ranch out west instead of in a little fishing town in coastal New Hampshire.

I dropped my head in my hands.

"Hey!" a deep voice called from behind me, and I whirled. "Are you Hollis? I'm John."

A handsome, thirtysomething man with killer dimples and bright green eyes extended his hand out to me. He had sharp, angular features and the friendly ease of someone who had doors open for him just by smiling. I quickly ran through the list of "John"s I knew, and when I came up short, he added, "I'm one of the summer keepers." He tipped his head to the chameleon-shaped bag tag on the duffel beside me. "I saw your name in the email list and just assumed. Not that many people named Hollis, I figured."

"Oh!" I extended a hand, and he shook it as I reminded myself to perform interest. Men got so easily offended when they thought I was blanking them. "It's nice to meet you, John."

"You too," he replied, being a little too friendly in a way that made my hackles rise. *Lord, help me, he seems like a hugger.* He was the kind of guy who treated everyone like they'd been his best friend for years. John shot a look to a man sitting at the other side of the ferry with broad shoulders, wearing a wind breaker and Ray-Bans. "And I'm guessing that must be . . . Diego?" He called the name and the man's head whipped up.

Dark hair swept into his sharp brown eyes as he scrutinized us for a second before recognition dawned on his face and he waved. "Zoo?"

"Zoo!" John called back and instantly went in for a hug.

I knew it! He is a hugger.

Diego shot me a "What the fuck kind of uppers is this guy on?" face as he looked over John's shoulder, and I stifled a laugh. *Oh, I think Diego and I will get along just fine.*

John kept a hand clapped on Diego's shoulder as Diego wandered over to the side of the ferry and joined me at the railing.

Diego pursed his lips as he sized us up. "So, you two are the competition."

"Competition?" I asked.

"There are three of us," he reasoned, sweeping the folder in his hand around in a circle. "And only two permanent jobs at the end of the summer. One for the bird team and one for reptiles."

"I thought we were all going to be swings?" John asked.

Diego shrugged. "We are, but I will be making sure they know how good I am at birds and reptiles specifically." He lifted his stubbled chin. "I've worked in both before. You?"

I grimaced. I'd wanted to be on the reptiles team at my last zoo, but I'd been beat out by a chirpy, extroverted girl with a perfect swishy ponytail and too-wide smile. She and John would've gotten on like a house on fire.

"I'd pick you for more of a hoofstock girlie," Diego added as he swept an assessing gaze over my attire.

I felt a blush burn across my cheeks. I knew the outfit was too much.

While I looked like equestrian Barbie, I was internally a little cave gremlin who just wanted to hang out with snakes and spend the day misting lizards and tweezer-feeding geckos medicated mealworms. The reptile job would be the one I was gunning for. I just really hoped it didn't involve talking to people . . .

"I'm pretty much a jack of all trades." John put his hands on his hips and took a deep breath of sea air like he was posing for a flavored water commercial. "Maybe we'll all be so good that they'll offer us all jobs." John gave me an apple pie, baseball on the Fourth of July sort of breezy smile. "You're a shy one, aren't you, Hollis?"

I flashed a tight, uncomfortable smile that bordered on a snarl. "Yep."

John, who still had one hand on Diego's shoulder, put his free hand on mine. "I'm sure we'll pull her out of her shell in no time, right, Diego?"

I laughed, using the motion to step out of John's touch without making it a big deal. Diego gave me another sarcastic look, so quick I didn't think John spotted it. Men like John tried to commandeer every conversation and friend group. He was already acting like he was the leader of our trio, and I suspected because he was 6'4" and had a sharp jawline, no one had ever corrected him.

"I might go grab a coffee from the cantina," Diego said.

"I'll come with you, bud," John cut in.

Diego pointed at me. "Do you want one?"

I shook my head, appreciating the out.

Diego winked at me, and I mouthed the words "thank you" to him as the two of them walked back inside. I really didn't want to share a house with a guy like John, but hopefully the work would keep me busy and I could hide out in my room when I wasn't. Diego seemed nice enough though. Hopefully, the two of us could form an alliance and vote John off the island. That was how internships worked, right?

As Prickle Island drew closer, carved in more detail against the horizon minute after minute, I let out a long sigh. "Yep." I groaned. "Everything's going to be fine."

Chapter Three

Heron

I knew nothing about boats, I realized, as I looked around the vessel, picking up a neon-pink bra that had been wedged into the sun lounger cushion. I grimaced at the lacy thing and tossed it in the garbage bag that was already heaving under the weight of my cleanup efforts. I probably should've watched at least a few YouTube videos about boat ownership before I'd decided it was a good idea to accept this thing.

The Farrier, as it was named, had been left in a post-party state of debauchery by one of the Holloways' Spring Fling guests. With an array of Champagne flutes and discarded designer clothes strewn about, it was like a rich, New York elitist glitter bomb had gone off all over the custom leather. I pinched the collar of a wine-stained shirt (*that probably cost more than my entire wardrobe*) and put it in the "sell" pile. *The*

Farrier's owners had taken their souped-out engines with them when they'd abandoned ship, which had prompted an entire police investigation. But apart from some cocaine residue, no crimes had been committed aboard, and the owners had just signed the title over to the marina and paid the astronomical fine like it was a parking ticket. Turned out, when you had that much money, you could just decide you didn't want a tens of thousands of dollars toy anymore and leave it for someone else to deal with.

Without engines, *The Farrier* was going nowhere until I bought new ones, which I definitely didn't have the money for. But considering I only wanted to use it as a place to sleep for now, it seemed good enough. It was better than Crane's shed, at least, and gave me a little privacy from the rest of the Lachlan pack. I'd had our family friend and local mechanic, Petey, take a look at it, and he'd said it was in good condition despite the wear but would eventually need to be dry-docked for some repairs.

"It'll be fine," I said aloud as I picked up a diamond tennis bracelet and added it to the "sell" bag. I'd let my siblings pilfer through my findings, and Wren had volunteered to sell the rest. We would probably make some decent money off the treasures that had been discarded like Solo cups on deck.

Oh, the lives of the rich and famous.

"I can be a boat person," I added to myself, and the boat beneath my feet groaned as if it were laughing at me.

I'd always been obsessed with the water. *My fish child,* Mom had called me when she'd have to bribe me off the beach after I'd spend eight hours in the water as a kid. I liked being rocked to sleep by the gentle lapping of the waves. I'd always found the ocean soothing. The marina was in a sheltered inlet of Prickle Island, where the storms never destroyed the docks, *and* it was less than a five-minute walk up the steps to Kangaroo Point with my keycard. It would be perfect. And a nice quiet reprieve from my constant sibling interruptions—

A knock on the hull jolted me from that thought, and I clambered to the side to peek over the railing to the dock below.

"Ahoy there, matey!" Finch called, saluting me with a tattooed hand as she climbed aboard. "Frankie sent you this." She passed me a basket brimming with baked goods from her wife and head zoo chef. "I think she's decided you living on a boat means you'll never eat again."

"You'd think with Lark about to pop and Dove and Deacon moving to France, that me moving onto an old boat wouldn't be such big news," I said with a laugh.

Finch's phone buzzed and she looked down to read aloud, "Have they fixed the leak yet?"

"So, Mom's still freaking out too then?"

"It's Mom." Finch shrugged, her piercings clinking with the movement. "She has enough freaking out energy to split seven ways . . . well, ten, nearly eleven with all the grandchildren, and adding in the partners of all the kids—"

"Yeah, I get it. Evelyn Lachlan's well of worry never runs dry." I rolled my eyes. "And you can tell her that the leak is just from the door to the kitchen when it rains, not in the hull. The boat isn't going to sink."

"I don't think the specifics will make her worry any less, Ronny."

"Yeah." I rubbed a hand down my face. "Just tell her I fixed it already."

Finch gave me a thumbs-up. "Honestly, I think she's pretty supportive of you having a little more adventure in your life." She pilfered one of the muffins from the basket and popped the whole thing into her cheek like a hungry chipmunk. "I think she just worries that you're isolating yourself down here."

"I *am* isolating myself down here," I stated, waving my

hands out to the deep blue ocean dotted with distant islands. "I've been living in a Lachlan family cuddle puddle my entire life, and I need a bit of space."

"But you love our smothering," Finch said sarcastically with a pout then laughed. "Nah, if any of us understands, it's me. The apartment above the vet hospital was the best investment ever. I love having some peace and quiet at the end of a long day, well, as quiet as above a vet hospital can be. Then I met Frankie, and suddenly there was one person I never wanted peace and quiet from."

"So you don't think I'm going through a quarter-life crisis by moving out here?"

She squeezed my shoulder and jostled me to and fro. "This place is the perfect distance from work and town. You can still pop in when you want to *and* get away when you want to. I think it's great. Just make sure not to give Crane a key to the jetty."

"Good point," I said with a laugh, appreciating how my eldest sister understood me.

It was one of the many things I was grateful for about having a big family: there was usually at least one of them who got where I was coming from. Always someone to confide in, always someone who would support me no questions . . . and always someone to mercilessly tease and harass me to counterbalance all of the love and support.

A sudden question snagged my attention. "Wait, so how did *you* manage to get down here?"

Finch held up a carabiner crammed with keys. "I used to date a girl who babysat a sailboat for the Westworths. Gosh, that was probably . . ." She looked up to the cloud-filled sky, counting. ". . . over ten years ago, but I still have a copy of the key."

"Very slick," I teased. "And I should probably tell the marina owners it's time to update the locks."

"Okay, I'll leave you to your newfound peace, sib," she said, giving me a quick bear hug before clumsily disembarking. "Enjoy the muffins, and . . ." She looked skyward again. "Maybe stash them below deck before the seagulls eat them."

"Good idea," I replied, mirroring her salute.

The ferry horn was low and sonorous, echoing across the waves and catching our eyes. On it, I knew three new keepers were on their way. Crane, Hawk, and I would be taking up the mantle of training them. Mom seemed intent on giving us more of the team lead responsibilities, shifting some of the head keeper tasks off Hawk. She hadn't said as much yet, but I knew she was making moves for her retirement, giving Hawk more of the CEO tasks, the handover years in the making. Though I had a feeling Mom would never really fully retire, it was good for Crane and me to not be seen as the unreliable kids of the family anymore.

"Do you think they'll be good ones this year?" I asked, staring at the crowd lining the ferry bannister.

"I hope they're all troublemakers," Finch answered with a grin, and I shot her a look. "What? You and wrecking ball have mellowed out too much for my liking these past few years, and the nephews are too small to raise hell yet. And Wren's always been a homebody. I think it's time for some new blood to shake things up. Maybe some wild cards are aboard."

Everything felt blissfully calm for the first time in a long time. The zoo was thriving, all the siblings were doing well, we were well-staffed, and the visitor numbers were steady. The last thing we needed was to have our lives "shaken up."

I grimaced at the ferry. "God, I hope not."

Chapter Four

Hollis

John, Diego, and I were given the keys to what appeared to be a very recently renovated house, wet paint still drying on the shutters, the smells of vinyl glue and freshly unwrapped furniture wafting through the air. It was a truly gorgeous, albeit somewhat unconventional accommodation located right next to a giant steel warehouse, greenhouses, and an industrial-sized composter. Uphill and upwind of the compost scent though, thank God.

Our house had similar trim that matched the old, Nantucket-style house on the hill—one that had apparently been in the Lachlan family for generations, built by their great-great grandfather himself. The whole place had a wonderful vibe about it, something both historical and modern, where things had been clearly added decade upon decade in their own stylings to make it the zany amalgamation that it was today. I liked all of the grooves and details of a place, a well-worn history filling it up, every scuff and dent a new story.

After a safety briefing led by a friendly though brusque head keeper, Hawk, we were given leave to roam the zoo and get acquainted with the space before we were invited to a staff dinner at the restaurant located at the center called Peckish Peacock.

The information binders we'd been given were robust. We'd already been sent PDF versions, but when they'd handed us laminated copies upon arrival, I wasn't going to admit that I had a hole-punched copy of my own in my duffel bag, nor that I had already memorized everything inside it. I wanted to seem hard working but not overly zealous, just the right balance of competent and reliable.

After the tour, I hastily abandoned Diego and John to go explore on my own. I sighed, spreading out my arms and embracing the afternoon quiet after all of John's nattering. The gentle rustle of bamboo in the breeze and soft caws of far-off gulls were punctuated by the whoop of gibbons and the squawks of parrots. I was instantly charmed. Every zoo I went to seemed to have its own heartbeat. Some were sleek and modern, others warm and rustic, small and intimate, epic and sprawling, bright and colorful. As I wandered around, I felt like I was introducing myself to a person, becoming acquainted with the pulse of Prickle Island Zoo.

The exhibits were beautiful, lush, and thoughtfully designed for both animals and visitors alike. Said wildlife was clearly well cared for, in good physical conditions, and with an abundance of species-specific enrichment that I had already memorized the rotating schedules for. Today, for example, I knew the meerkats would be getting cricket-filled foraging boxes. When I turned the corner, I was delighted to find them tearing the boxes to shreds and burrowing inside to hunt their hopping meals.

The place had a lighthearted and eccentric feel about it too, a sort of playful cheek to the porcupine playground and interactive designs. Still, it was balanced with a degree of professionalism that impressed me. Judging from the extensive onboarding protocol and Hawk's health and safety briefing, the Lachlans took their jobs incredibly seriously, even if they had fun while doing it, and that put me at ease. No one wanted a cavalier health and safety briefing when working with wild animals.

I meandered up toward the top of the zoo, enjoying the quiet paths and little, winding routes that I was sure made the place feel intimate even on the busiest days. Evening time after visitor hours was always my favorite time to be in a zoo. The animals were awake and active past their afternoon feedings and the paths were shady but still warm from the midday sun. I took in another deep breath, absorbing the sea breeze and loamy earth. This place was the perfect combination of ocean air and crisp forest. I splayed my hands as I trailed them through the bamboo hedge, up to the savannah viewing platform.

I spotted one zebra who had managed to slip between the enclosure and visitor fence, but I remembered from the debrief that that zebra's name was Jailbreak and he would wander back home by sunset.

"Hello, buddy," I said to him with a wide smile.

His ears twisted toward me for a brief moment before he returned to munching the hard to reach grasses bordering his exhibit.

So long as he stayed on that side of the fence, all was well. I really didn't want to have to make an escaped animal radio call on my first day—

And with that damning thought, I spun around and came

face-to-beak with a towering male ostrich. This feathered escapee was definitely not in the handbook.

"Aw, come on, seriously," I muttered, staring at the big guy, his black-and-white feathers billowing as he splayed his wings wide and flapped them at me. "You better not kick me, you smug mother-plucker."

I held up my hand, instinctively ready to shove him back by the neck if he attempted to charge me. I'd worked with enough emus to be used to that maneuver, but this guy was much bigger than an emu and could probably still kick me regardless. And while I was grateful when he eventually tucked his wings back in, I still edged away a step, just in case I needed to vault over the fence and join Jailbreak.

I spied the egregious fence gate swung open. Unlatched, it led to the service area of the savannah, and I had no idea how this ostrich had managed to skirt around the hot grasses between the service area and the exhibit, let alone unlatch the gate, but here we were. Animals accomplished the most surprising things. And sometimes when spooked would bolt through all sorts of barriers. And ostriches were certainly grade A bolters.

I grabbed the radio off my hip and tried to remember my new call signs. Why did every zoo have to do it slightly differently?

"Swing two to . . . uh, savannah team?"

The ostrich cocked his head at me like he, too, was embarrassed for my blunder.

"Stop it," I whisper-hissed at him, but he just mindlessly snapped his beak in the air, probably wondering if I had any food with me.

A voice answered on the other end. "Hoofstock, go ahead."

Shit. It was hoofstock, not savannah. The perturbed ostrich clicked his beak again and I swore that he was laughing at me. A blush burned across my cheeks.

"Heyyy." *Oh my god, Hollis, stop sounding so squeaky. You're supposed to be a tough ranch girl, remember?* With that pep talk, I straightened the pearlescent buttons on my shirt and put on my newfound persona of competent zookeeper who was definitely going to get this job. "We have a male ostrich standing in the middle of the visitor pathway by the zebra lookout. There is a gate open to the service area at the southern end of the savannah exhibit."

"Roger," the voice replied. "If you can just walk Beaky to the gate, I'll be up in a minute."

"Roger." I clipped my radio back to my belt. "Beaky?" I asked the bird. "What the hell kind of a name is Beaky?" The ostrich snapped the air again. "Okay, okay. Now, how exactly am I supposed to *walk* you to the gate? It's not like I can put you on a leash."

I'd done all sorts of crazy things as a keeper, but taking an ostrich for a walk wasn't one of them. I looked around once, twice, as if there would be some sign explaining "how to walk an ostrich" but had no such luck. Taking a few steps backward, I cocked my head at Beaky and sized him up.

I rubbed nervous hands down my freshly issued khakis. Like many hurdles in this job, I would just have to figure it out as I went.

"Okay, come on, make me look good on my first day, please," I whispered, walking backward and beckoning with my hand like an air traffic controller.

I really, *really* hoped the entire Lachlan family wasn't watching me on some CCTV footage somewhere. Maybe this was new staff member hazing? Seeing how I would handle the situation?

Bolstered by the sudden urge to prove myself, I rolled my shoulders and narrowed my sights on Beaky. I'd already messed up the call signs. I couldn't be the new girl who was also associated with a bungled ostrich escape. I needed this job.

With my hands tentatively stretched out, I started to move between Beaky and the path that led farther afield. I was incredibly grateful when Beaky took a step toward me and then another, seemingly already knowing we were heading back to the gate. A lot of animals only needed the barest encouragement. They knew where home was as well as the rest of us.

Beaky took another step and then another, continually checking that I was not, in fact, holding a bucket of feed. But the unflustered bird seemed to give me an "oh, this is what we're doing?" look and kept moving at his leisurely pace toward the gate.

"That's it," I reassured him, my pulse steadying as I took another step backward. We'd just about made it to the open gate and I was so focused on Jedi mind tricking the ostrich in front of me that I didn't pay attention to a recklessly planted hedge. The back of my boot caught the lip of the sidewalk, and with an embarrassing yelp, I tumbled head over heels into a shrubbery.

Get up, get up, get up! I thought, flailing in the all too sturdy bush.

What in the name of robust foliage was this? I was Velcro-walled into the hedge no matter how much I bucked and wiggled. This was such a disaster. It was like trying to get out of one of those gymnastics foam pits. I was trapped, tipped halfway upside down in bush that was neither rigid enough to push off of nor flexible enough to fall through.

Something caught one of my failing hands. At first, I thought maybe Beaky had taken pity on me and was trying to rescue me himself, but then I realized it was another hand. I was hoisted up by a tall zookeeper who appeared to be holding in laughter. But before I could get a good look at them, they took a step back, their boot slipped over the planter of succulents, and they started to tumble backward. I tugged up on our still clenched hands and steadied them, yanking them back to me, their chest brushing against mine, their chin skirting across the top of my head.

"Thanks," they said, clearing their throat.

"You too," I replied, hooking my thumb to the hedge behind me as if it weren't obvious what I was referring to.

"I'll talk to the grounds team about making this path wider." The keeper took a half-step backward, careful to avoid tripping this time, and met my gaze. "Too many hazards this way."

They had long, honey brown hair pulled atop their head in a loose bun, an easy smile, and a permanent twinkle of mischief in their piercing blue eyes. *So this must be Heron.* I'd read about them in my onboarding packet. But nowhere in the document had it said they were a striking androgynous mixture of masculine and feminine, stunning features that seemed worthy of the front cover of a fashion magazine. They had a steady, almost soothing calmness to them that I found frequently in people of this profession, but it was streaked through by playfulness that was intriguing too. That dimpling of their cheeks made me feel like I wasn't the first person they'd hoisted out of a hedge.

I realized I was still hanging onto their warm, calloused hand and I played it off as intentional by shaking it. "I'm Hollis, by the way. It's nice to meet you."

"Heron," they replied. "Welcome to the team."

I looked around to find a camera facing the giraffe feeding area. "That . . ."

"Can't see this hedge," they assured me as they put a hand on the back of Beaky's neck and guided him the last stretch through the gate.

Ah, so that's what "walk him" meant.

Heron latched the gate and squatted down to inspect it, frowning at one of the rusting hinges that seemed to make it bow in the middle. I couldn't help but stare. Something about the way they moved was mesmerizing, fluid, like they were underwater. Everything I did felt like shaking and frenetic, sharp and rapid, whereas Heron was so confident and purposeful, like each action had been choreographed. It was an alluring appeal, something in me recognizing how different they were to me, maybe part of me yearning for their steady ease when I was a ball of nerves.

My heart was racing so fast, my anxiety refusing to let my pulse slow. I bounced on the balls of my feet and shook out my hands again, trying to still my telltale trembling.

Heron didn't seem to notice as they inspected the gate. "We're going to need to replace this before Beaky has the bright idea to gallivant around the zoo at night again."

"Can I help?" I asked eagerly. "I feel like I've already landed on the wrong foot." I looked back at the hedge. "Or on no foot for that matter."

Heron's laugh was bright and warm, their countenance reminding me of a clear summer's day. Where I felt like my personality was the darkest part of winter, cold, abrupt, never soothing or feminine enough. *If only I could bottle up a bit of their ease.*

"Nah, I've got it, thanks," they said, and my stomach sunk a little. "It's your first day. You go explore the zoo. I promise we don't have that many rogue animals around here."

"I believe it," I said. "Your health and safety briefings are quite thorough."

Heron smiled, and I tried to blame my quickening pulse on my nerves again. "Yeah, I think every single one of Hawk's specifics is tied to an actual story."

"Well, I look forward to hearing about the meerkat one then."

Their lips pulled even wider, making the dimpled grooves in their cheeks deepen. "Maybe over pizza tonight at the Peacock."

"Okay." *Come on, Hollis, stop being so awkward!* "Uh, nice to meet you."

I gave an even more awkward half-wave to Heron and fled uphill farther into the zoo, moving as fast as could be constituted a walk and not a run. I was probably just incredibly overstimulated after a long day and a lot of information. I just needed to go calm down somewhere . . . Yep, those dimpled cheeks were playing no part in my racing pulse at all.

Chapter Five

Heron

The Peckish Peacock was at its best at night, when all of the trees were lit in soft pinks and purples and the patio glittered with twinkling Christmas lights. Frankie had curated a full Mediterranean dining experience, and it was hilarious to see all of the new summer staff—keepers, front of house workers, tour guides, education team—all stumble up to the restaurant, expecting to be greeted with a bunch of cardboard boxes of takeout and instead finding an artisanal feast of brick-oven-cooked pizzas.

Frankie was excited for the first guests of summer. The eagerness to try out all of the dishes she'd been perfecting in the quiet months practically radiated off her. This was her season as much as it was the visitors', and she'd spent weeks fussing over tonight's menu.

Crane and I sipped Frankie's heavenly sangria, guarding an entire carafe between us, a far finer fare than the beers and tequila shots that had once been our drinks of choice. Finch and Frankie came out with wave after wave of delicious food, the grazing tables getting stormed and picked clean like a swarm of leaf cutter ants to a freshly fallen tree.

Hannah had plugged her phone into the sound system to play a funky playlist that was just as eclectic as she was. Apparently, Simon had requested every song from *K-Pop Demon Hunters*. Still, "How It's Done" was a banger and had everyone dancing and singing along in a tipsy chorus.

"So?" Mom asked, milling around with Max on her hip. He tucked in adorably to Grandma Evie's neck as he held his stuffed red panda to his chest, already nearing his bedtime. "What do we think of the newcomers?"

"They all seem good so far," I said, appraising the trio of new keepers from across the crowd. They were easy to spot, still all in their new, unstained uniforms like nervous freshman at a new high school. "All very qualified. It'll be hard to decide between them."

"Yeah, at least no one's fallen into a hedge yet," Crane quipped, and I gave my twin a glare. I knew I shouldn't have told him, but there was no keeping secrets from him either. He could sniff them out a mile away.

Secondhand embarrassment flooded through me again. I'd really bungled that introduction with Hollis. I'd been so awkward, practically monosyllabic, and she'd fled from our interaction like she couldn't get away from me fast enough. I just hadn't been prepared when I'd hoisted her out of the hedge, and then when she'd caught me, the sight of her had hit me like a crashing wave. She was beautiful, yes, with long, wavy brown hair and eyes like the ocean before a storm, but it had been the sharpness of her gaze that had really put me off balance. It was like she could stare straight into my soul, like something in her had recognized something in me instantly, and I didn't know what to do with that unsettling feeling in my gut. I should've tried to strike up a more casual conversation or . . . I'd replayed our run-in so many times over the last few hours, trying to think of what I should've said instead. Maybe she just found me off-putting. It was hard to tell from such a brief interaction.

At first, it had been a funny moment, turning the corner to see her half consumed by a hedge like she'd been trying to disappear into a shrubbery dimension. But then I'd helped her up and she'd immediately had me tongue-tied. She had sharpened focus that had words lodging in my throat, cutting, assessing, like she could see the very thoughts floating in my head. And I'd fumbled so badly, so caught off guard by her, that all I could offer her had been a dopey smile and few misguided quips.

Luckily, she was going to be on Crane's roster for the first week of the summer, so that left him with plenty of time to win the medal for "Most embarrassing Lachlan sibling."

"Well, I'm going to get the boys to bed," Mom announced. "It's a sleepover at Grandma's tonight! Yay!" I didn't know who was more excited, Mom or Simon, the two cheering in gleeful unison. Max was already asleep and drooling on Mom's shoulder, his red panda toy wedged under her armpit, safely secured.

I was honestly grateful that Mom had been so swept up in her grandmothering that she had stopped being so aggressive with her matchmaking efforts for the rest of us. It had been five years since Dove and Deacon's romance had rekindled and she hadn't tried to arrange anything for the remaining three unwed siblings.

I thought part of her realized that life was happening so fast. One day, even Wren, the baby of the family, would have a life of her own. And I thought seeing how quickly her grandkids were growing up had made her slow down a little and take it all in.

"Don't you have to give a welcome speech?" I asked Mom as she took Simon's hand in her free one and started steering him away.

"I'm passing the torch to Hawk this year," she said over her shoulder.

My eyebrows shot up. Wow, she really was serious about stepping down from her role as CEO. It had been a long time coming, her slowly moving all of her duties on to the rest of us, hiring more staff, and relinquishing more control. But I'd thought my mother would never fully retire, and here she was, passing off her beginning of summer welcome speech. It felt like a marked occasion.

Next year, she was planning on traveling for the quieter half of the year. Crane was going on conservation leave. Dove was moving with Deacon from New York to France, and even though they'd kept a little cottage on the island, I had a feeling it was only a matter of time before they were having little French babies and we'd see them less and less too. At least she was coming to dinner next week before they left. They were technically on the island now but had offered not to come to the staff dinner because we all knew what happened when Deacon came to an event. It stopped being about the zoo and started being about him, and while he'd leveraged his fame into lots of conservation money, it still was a distraction, and I was sure they wouldn't mind a night to themselves regardless.

Hawk and Hannah bombarded Simon with goodnight hugs and gave gentle kisses to Max to keep him from stirring, although a chorus of howler monkeys probably wouldn't wake him. Hawk's hand slid around Hannah, and she folded into his arms, watching as Mom toddled away with their sons in tow. When they walked out of sight, Hannah lifted on her toes to kiss Hawk, the two barely able to stop smiling long enough to smooch each other.

"Gross," Crane said from behind me. "They're definitely about to sneak off and go bang."

"Yep."

Crane slung his arm around me. "What do you say we snag another pitcher of sangria and get drunk at the meerkats like old times, hell raiser?"

I sighed wistfully. "If by drunk you mean have one more and then go to bed at a reasonable nine o'clock, then yes."

Crane clicked his tongue. "When did you get so old?"

"The same exact time as you did," I countered, swatting his hand when he reached for a pitcher.

He gave me a stubborn look and swiped it up triumphantly, and I rolled my eyes. How long were we going to play these games? All of the shenanigans were starting to wear me down. They'd been fun when we'd been teens, but we were nearly thirty, and Crane's sense of adventure had never dulled or matured. It felt more and more each year that we were two distinct people, more different than we were similar, and I felt like I was just going along with his antics because what else was I supposed to do?

"Eh!" Frankie shouted, a flashlight suddenly in my eyes. "Put. The. Sangria. Down."

Crane's and my shoulders drooped in unison. "Some things never change," he muttered. "We know you have more pitchers," he called to Frankie. He held the other side of his and lifted it toward his mouth.

"Crane Attenborough Lachlan, I swear to God, if you put your mouth on that!" Frankie shouted, tossing a dish towel over her shoulder and storming over.

"You'll what?" Crane teased, lifting the pitcher higher and sticking his tongue out.

"Come on," I said, pulling the other side of the ceramic

handle. "We don't need to do this tonight." Crane pulled harder. "Let's just put it back." I pulled more.

"When did you become so fucking boring?" Crane gritted out, his words stinging more than they should have.

"Why won't you grow up already?" I growled back and yanked harder, just as Crane let go, sending the pitcher careening downhill and dousing a staff member head to toe in sticky, sweet wine, a wedge of orange tangled in her long, wavy hair.

And when I saw which staff member it was . . .

Chapter Six

Hollis

It took me a second to register what had just happened, as if my brain were trying to deny what my body was feeling, but no. I was really soaking wet in stinking, sticky fluid. One second, I'd been making my way to the edge of the crowd, trying to get a moment of fresh air out of the throng, and the next I was covered head to toe in reeking, cold wine.

My shoulders bunched around my ears, raised like a cat in snow, and I scrunched my face, wishing I could close my nostrils at the assaulting sting of alcohol. "What the hell?"

I looked up, glaring, only to find a sheepish-looking Heron holding the handle of a now empty pitcher. The man standing next to them, who I assumed was their twin, Crane, was holding a fist to his mouth, trying to stifle mocking laughter.

Well, great. Just great. Of course it had to be them.

A million iterations of the last five minutes flashed through my mind in rapid succession. Had Heron's twin goaded them into doing this? Was this a prank? A joke? Had they already determined that I was the keeper that was going to get the boot and this was just their way of egging me on to quit before my contract ended? And the worst question of all: why, of all people, did it have to be the keeper who only had to pull me out of a hedge to make my pulse lodge in my throat?

Heron's mouth bobbed open and closed several times before they finally twisted toward their twin and pointed an accusatory finger. I didn't know what to believe.

I'd already been incredibly overstimulated by the end of the day in a new place, hungry but not able to eat because it meant battling through the others to reach the grazing table. The music was too loud, the lights too bright, and the press of too many people was starting to make me nauseous, and then this.

I just wanted to be left alone to work with my animals. I didn't want to do this crowded socializing thing, but the sangria really was the icing on my meltdown cake. Tears started to prick behind my eyes and I had to fight them back. The last thing I should do was cry on my first day. But I hated feeling sticky. Wet clothes on my skin made me feel like a thousand beetles were crawling under it. My vision narrowed and the acid in my empty stomach burned up my throat.

As my hands began to shake, I tried to recalibrate, as if this were just a normal day of mucking into a messy job. I was used to being wet in my khakis from cleaning and hosing down enclosures, covered in all manner of wild animal bodily fluid and excrement, but that was for work Hollis. Work Hollis could handle the mess and grime. I'd built an association with the uniform and the sensory input. But this sensation was new: sticky, sweet, cold, citrusy, and reeking of alcohol. Worse, everyone was watching me and laughing like some sort of over-played school cafeteria trope that suddenly felt all too real. My senses were assaulted and I was so damn angry for once again being made to be the center of everyone's focus, when all I wanted to do was be in the shadows.

Crane gave me a tight look that bordered on apologetic, though he couldn't quite wipe the smile from his sangria-splattered face. And I could see the moment he decided to make things right in the worst way possible, like a light bulb flicking on behind his eyes.

"Food fight!" Crane shouted and grabbed a tray of finger food and started pelting the volunteers with it. They squealed and darted toward the buffet table.

And then suddenly the whole picnic area was whizzing with food. Frankie shrieked as her canapés went flying, and Finch pushed her way through the crowd, smacking Crane on the back of the head and yanking the tray of food from his grip. But it was too late. The melee had begun, and food was being splattered across the crowd as I inched farther and farther away, every movement making wine squelch in my boots and more clothes stick to my body.

Then suddenly, Heron was flying toward me with a dish towel, patting me down. "I am so, so sorry!"

"Don't." I snatched to the towel from their grip, my skin burning at every place they pushed that wet fabric into it. "It's fine," I muttered, moving farther away from them and those big, beseeching blue eyes.

"Enough!" Hawk's voice boomed over the microphone. He stood looming over the crowd, his face pinched and angry. "Chef Frankie has worked incredibly hard making this food for you all. Stop throwing it or this will be the last time you get a team meal." He glared around at all the sheepish, mostly teenage volunteers and twentysomething, front of house staffers.

The delineation in age was pretty clear. All the younger ones were caked in food, all the older ones still clean with rapidly sobering expressions. Embarrassment burned hot in my cheeks as I inched away from Heron. They looked at me, hands hovering halfway in the air like they wanted to help and didn't know how. *Curse them.* I didn't want to be the object of anyone's attention, least of all theirs right now.

"Please just leave me alone," I gritted out.

Their normally breezy expression faded, and with a stoic nod, Heron turned and walked away, making my gut plummet with every step.

Way to go, Hollis. Making enemies on the first day is a new record.

I looked over to find Diego looking me up and down, a smile on his lips he couldn't seem to hide as he waved over the tableau in front of us and gave me a knowing look.

I gave him thumbs-up. *Yep, first day is going terribly.*

To his credit, John ran over with a bar towel he must've snagged from somewhere and offered it out to me instead of attacking me with it like Heron had. "Are you okay?"

"Oh, uh, thanks, John," I said, wringing wine from my hair. "I'm just gonna go have a shower and get changed."

"Do you want me to walk you back to the house? I can get—"

"No, no." I held up a hand, waving away the offer. "You have fun. Thanks, though."

I started marching away, giving Heron one last glare before heading off. Unfortunately, with the aid of the microphone, I could hear Hawk's shaming speech all the way back to the monkey house. I neared it before his scolding finally morphed into the welcome speech he'd clearly prepared, and I could hear the effort it took for him to try and hide the frustration in his voice.

And even though I hadn't personally volunteered to be doused in sangria, I still felt somehow responsible for ruining the evening. Either way, I'd be marked by this moment the whole summer—the girl who'd gotten *Carrie*-d on her first day. And I hated most of all the stupid butterflies that had danced in my stomach earlier for the same keeper who had thrown me into the wine-coated spotlight. Clearly, those butterflies had terrible judgment and couldn't be trusted.

I kicked off my soaked boots and peeled off my sticky socks, frowning down at them. "I'll deal with you later," I told the inanimate objects, my lips pulling into a pout. "Shower first."

Maybe I'd made the biggest mistake of my life coming to this place. Maybe it would be more of the same. Maybe I would be too alien and awkward to fit in here, too, and they could already tell that I was just plain different and were not so subtly trying to find a way to tell me to go.

I walked straight into the shower with my clothes on, setting my phone on the sink edge and playing my music loudly so that if anyone followed me home, they wouldn't be able to hear me cry.

Chapter Seven

Heron

I'd like to say it had been a long time since my siblings and I had been lined up in my mother's office, being scolded for something we'd done . . . . but that would be a lie. Six months, maybe a year since the last incident? But in the last few years, the shenanigans had become more increasingly incited by one person in particular. I wasn't about to snitch on my twin though, it was like sibling code, so I'd take the berating right along with him.

Still, I was starting to get really fed up with Crane. Especially now. Hollis didn't deserve what had happened to her. If I wasn't sure if she hated me before, she definitely did now.

Please just leave me alone. That had been one hell of a sucker punch, no matter how much I'd deserved it.

I had barely been able to sleep, replaying the look in her eyes when she'd dismissed me. Angry. Embarrassed. I could tell she'd been holding back tears, and that had wrecked me worst of all. It had been an accident. I hadn't meant to hurt her feelings, but she'd seemed so upset by everyone's attention, most of all mine.

I'd waffled between seeking her out to apologize again and obeying her clear wishes. I didn't want to dance around her all summer either, watching her from afar, wishing I could set things right between us. I hated the tension when coworkers didn't like each other, but this was the first time I was involved. Maybe I should bring her some sort of peace offering. Then again, if I approached her uninvited, she could probably kill me with her wrathful glare alone.

Luckily, I hadn't had time to decide which path to pursue. The cowardly one had been chosen for me when I'd woken up early after a restless sleep and had immediately been called to Mom's office for a team meeting.

Mom marched up and down the line, stopping in front of Crane as if in knowing. "How old are you again?"

"Twenty-seven."

"Oh really, I could've sworn you were still seventeen," she said tightly. "You certainly still act like it."

"Look, the lady—"

"Hollis," I cut in.

"Hollis," Crane amended, eyeing me like we were going to talk about that little interjection later. "Heron and I were just messing around and we took it too far," he brushed off, and I noted the way he said "we." Another thing we'd be hashing out later. "We messed up, and Hollis got sangria on her and she looked so embarrassed by it, and so I thought I would pull a Finch and rescue her—"

Finch guffawed from where she sat in the corner chair,

arms tightly folded. Frankie leaned against the wall beside her, looking like she wanted to pull a *Sweeney Todd* and bake us both into her next meal.

"You do not have my finesse, wrecking ball," Finch scoffed. "I would've whipped up a dozen rumors and saved Hollis from any perceived embarrassment without letting the staff think it's acceptable to pull a Lost Boys from *Hook* and ruin all of that perfectly good food."

Frankie looked between Crane and me. "You two are not having any of my pastries for a month."

"Or sandwiches," Finch added, and my mouth fell open in horror.

"I was trying to stop him from licking the pitcher!" I protested, the dam finally breaking as I pointed a finger childishly at Crane. When my twin gave me a shocked look like I'd somehow betrayed him, I hissed, "She's going to take away the sandwiches. The sandwiches, Crane! I was willing to take the fall for a month without her cinnamon rolls, but I will literally die if I have to go a month without my caprese and avo smash."

Hawk rolled his eyes at that, and as if she had eyes in the back of her head, Mom whirled on him.

"And you," she said, pointing at Hawk, and his eyes widened in surprise. He might've been pushing forty, but when Mom did that finger point, it still filled all of us with icy dread. "When I agreed to let you handle the welcome speech, Hawk, I expected it to be a *welcome* and not a half-hour-long reprimand." Hawk opened his mouth, but she kept going. "Yes, I heard the whole thing while I was putting your boys to bed."

"But they—"

"Food fight or no, you set this whole summer off on a bad foot with that whole lecture you gave. Where was the first week spirit? Where was the morale?" She gesticulated wildly. "You have to work pretty damn hard to make people hate working at a zoo, but I think you might've actually succeeded. Who wants to work hard for a grumpy old man, hm?"

"Yeah, just ask the Madigans." Finch huffed under her breath.

"Not now, Finch!" Mom barked, pointing at her eldest daughter without tearing her gaze from Hawk.

The Madigan family had been our sworn enemies since before I could remember. Our parents had been best friends with the owners of Madigan Mountain Zoo back in the seventies, but after a mysterious and sudden falling out, our dad and Gaz Madigan had hated each other, which was saying something because apparently our dad had loved everyone. Rumors had abound over the years over what the split had been about, but no one knew for certain, and Mom didn't seem like she was going to inform us any time soon.

After a decades' long reality show, Madigan Mountain Zoo had fallen on hard times after Gaz and his wife, Beverly, had split. And after, Gaz's drama had been splashed all over trashy tabloids, a trail of one-night stands, bar fights, and drunkenly accosting paparazzi, and they'd lost their show. Now, it seemed the Madigans' eight zookeeper children were all scrambling to get back in the spotlight by whatever means necessary. But the mention of them had quieted in our family. It felt a little like punching down since they'd lost everything. Still, every once in a while, they were brought into the heat of an argument.

Mom pinched the bridge of her nose as she pointed between Crane and me. "I want you two to start acting your age, please," she pled, then turned to Hawk and added, "And I want you to think about what kind of legacy you want to leave behind for your sons."

Hawk rocked back on his heels at that.

"Oof," Crane muttered to me.

"Brutal," I whispered back.

He leaned his shoulder into me, and I leaned back, all of the steam and anger in me instantly ebbing.

It had been nearly two decades since our father had passed away. Hawk had been a teenager at the time and still idolized our father, we all had, but Hawk especially since he had the largest memory of him. Now, Hawk was a big part of running the family zoo, just like his father and his father's father and so on. Even with all of us pitching in, that was a lot of weight to bear.

"I understand," Hawk said tightly.

"Good." Mom nodded. "Then get back to work."

We all turned to the door, and when she said, "Not you, Heron," my gut plummeted.

Part of me wanted to reach for Crane just like I had when we'd been little, shove him in front of me, and make him fight my battles for me. Crane would always defend me, even to the scariest animal in the zoo: our mother. It made all of my building frustration toward him ease.

Crane mouthed, "Sorry," and the rest of my siblings gave me apologetic glances before abandoning me to an angry mother by myself. I didn't know how she did it. My mom was the kindest, most caring woman in the world, but no one brought the hammer down like she did either. I supposed with seven kids, she'd kind of been forced to. Telling Hawk to think about the legacy he wanted to leave to his sons was a perfect example of her knockout punch, and now I was braced, waiting for her to decimate me with something as well.

Mom slid into her desk chair and steepled her fingers as I waited for her to speak. "How's the boat?"

"Good," I hedged, picking at my purple-painted fingernails behind my back.

"Good," she said with a nod. "Dove and Deacon are coming to dinner tonight."

"Okay?" Nerves coiled in my stomach.

"They have an interesting proposal for this new show they're doing. A lot of really important conservation work is going to happen through their charity, and I want you to hear them out and consider applying."

"Mom, I don't want to be on some reality TV show—"

Mom held up her hand. "You have the rest of your entire life to be a sailboat hermit," she dismissed. She took her glasses off and rubbed a weary hand down her face. "I feel like Crane never grew up and you grew up too fast."

"I can see that." It surprised me that she did, though. I'd been feeling it more and more the last few years, the echoes of where Crane and I had diverged, but to have her point it out so acutely was impressive.

"You need a little more of his adventure and he needs a little more of your wisdom."

I let out a hum in agreement. "A lot more."

"You two could go together," she added. "It's going to be like *The Amazing Race*. They're pairing keepers up in teams and . . . I mean, I know it'll be hard for you when he's gone. Even if he drives you up a wall. I think a little travel would be good for you both."

"I feel like I have plenty of adventure here."

Her face softened and I could see the moment she resigned defeat. "Okay, will you at least consider it?"

"I'll consider it." Consider *being the operative word.*

"Thank you." She nodded, and as I turned to the door, she sucked in a breath that I already knew was going to say the thing she'd wanted to tell me the whole time. "Oh, and I've put Hollis on your roster. I think after the Crane incident, it would be better if you show her the ropes."

I opened my mouth to protest, but Mom gave me that look that had me closing it again. There was no room for negotiation on this one. I would be strapped with Hollis for the next week whether I liked it or not.

"Wonderful," I said tightly as I pulled the door closed behind me.

As I trotted down the steps from Mom's office, I braced myself for the black cat personified to stare daggers into my soul so sharp that I could die from those blue eyes alone.

"Great start to the summer."

Chapter Eight

Hollis

I didn't know who was poking pins into a tiny Hollis doll, but fate was currently being a real nasty bitch to me. My anxiety of doing a shift with the sangria-throwing twin, Crane, had been tempered by the fact that I'd be on the reptiles team. Getting to spend the day with boa constrictors felt like a pretty decent silver lining, but that morning, I'd been unceremoniously informed that the roster was switching and I would be put with Heron instead.

Crane was bad enough, but men were simple and I had a knack for making them avoid me like a high-pitched dog whistle only they could hear. Heron was another kettle of fish entirely. That steady smile, those easy blue eyes . . . It was a therapist's sort of calm, one where I felt like they could weed out all of my thoughts just by looking at me hard enough. *Nope.*

Calm people can't be trusted. I'll take the flailing, anxious ones, thank you.

Worst of all, I really didn't like surprises. They threw my whole world off-kilter. I'd really been looking forward to getting to know all the zoo reptiles, especially since I'd spent all night studying their names, feeding schedules, and medical histories. I would've studied the savannah animals instead if I'd known. Plus, I'd game-planned scenarios to avoid any awkward conversations with Crane, and now it had all been upended.

I knew the job required flexibility, and within the confines of my schedule, I was actually quite adaptable. But when it came to surprises of the human kind, I was incredibly rigid. And Heron Lachlan was not the sort of person I wanted to be surprised by.

This job had gone completely off the rails. I'd already dealt with an escaped ostrich, had sangria thrown on me, *and* been devoured by the sturdiest hedge in all of hedge-dom, and now I was being paired off with the hoofstock zookeeper who looked at me with a friendly kind of pity, like they knew I was a hot mess and I didn't belong.

When Heron trotted down the stairs from their mother's office, they barely gave me a cursory glance before hooking their thumb uphill and saying, "Change of plans. You're with me today."

Diego and I had barely a second to exchange confused glances before I was running after the long-legged keeper to the golf cart. And while I'd managed to remain calm and nod with a tight smile, internally I was screaming: *What mirror did I shatter? What ladder did I walk under? What hex had I accidentally enacted to have this bad freaking luck?*

The ride up to the giraffe enclosure might've been one of the most awkward silences of my life, and I was a gold medalist in making silences awkward. Heron kept shooting me quick smiles and opening their mouth as if to speak before looking like they swallowed a bug and keeping quiet. Maybe they were allergic to my darkness. Most people were.

Or . . . maybe Heron was really the evil twin. I still couldn't decide if what had happened the night before had been a rogue accident or the twins trying to sabotage me, but judging by Heron's stilted silence, I was beginning to think the latter. But then again, I had a way of always thinking the worst.

Pull it together, Hollis.

At the very least, I knew from the way Heron's face pinched that they didn't want to be roped with me as their swing keeper. But John, Diego, and I needed to learn the ropes, and the first three weeks of summer would be us shadowing the permanent keepers and having them sign off on tasks. And the task I was dreading most? Doing the visitor talks. And unlike the different animal teams, all the keepers had to be able to deliver all the talks. Great.

Apparently, today I had to give a tiger talk, which included hand feeding the zoo's Bengal tiger, Ruby, through the mesh at the visitor pavilion. Public speaking was like a literal nightmare already, but now knowing that Heron, not Crane, would be the one evaluating me seemed to make it a million times worse.

A group of tigers is called an ambush. I started rehearsing again in my head as the golf cart pulled into the savannah service area and parked behind a giant mound of silage. I silently took one of the buckets from the back of the cart and followed Heron inside the building.

Once we moved through the two sets of gates, the room opened up into a long, narrow kitchen, hoses and squeegees mounted in neat order along the wall. To the far side were poles separating the kitchen and a covered barn three stories high, with peeks of the open savannah beyond. The legs of a giraffe passed by me, so close that I could reach out and touch them. I marveled at the size of the eager animal waiting for her morning food. The poles were spread out far enough that

Heron and I could easily squeeze through, but all of the animals on the other side were too big to pass into the kitchen and steal each other's breakfasts. Enclosures didn't need doors when the animals were giraffe-sized.

I started cleaning without any further conversation or prompting, getting lost in the easy routine. So when Heron finally did speak, I jolted in surprise.

"Hollis?" Heron asked.

"Yeah?" I called, leaning the broom against the wall.

"This is Dot," they said, waving to one of the female ostriches who had her head stuck through the poles, snapping at Heron to feed her. "And this, as you know, is Beaky," they added, waving to the male ostrich who'd made me lodge myself into a hedge only a day prior.

"Yep," I said tightly, feeling the awkwardness radiating off me like waves. "I learned all of them from the information packet."

"I'm sure you'll be sorted on this team then." Heron nodded to the broom. "I saw you've already had a lot of ruminant experience at your last two workplaces."

"Uh-huh."

Dear god, Hollis, please say something other than grunting sounds. Something like: Why do you hate me? Why did you throw sangria on me? Why do you have to have such gorgeous dimples?

"Plus, growing up on a horse ranch," Heron continued, and all thoughts of dimples instantly evaporated. I knew they were trying to make small talk, but it was the last area of interest I wanted to go into. "You probably have a lifetime of animal experience."

"You're one to talk," I replied, trying to bring some levity to the conversation, but it sounded more accusatory. "Growing up in a zoo sounds seriously magical."

"I have nothing to compare it to," Heron said with a shrug. "But yeah, I think it was pretty magical."

Ugh. How did they do that? How did they speak with such effortless charm? I wished I had the tiniest crumb of that charisma. Everything I said came out wrong. Besides, I shouldn't want to talk to them, not after what happened.

"Did you always want to work in this area?" I asked, finding my groove as I filled a bucket of feed for the guinea fowl.

"Zookeeping or hoofstock?" Heron replied with a chuckle.

"Both."

"Well, the zookeeper job was kind of thrust upon me," they said, waving around. "I mean, my mom always welcomed us exploring different career options, but we all just kind of fell into animal husbandry at a young age. Now, I honestly can't think of anything else I'd rather do. I love my job. I love that no two days are the same. I love the new challenges it presents."

"I get that," I replied with a nod. It was the same for me. It was actually the perfect AuDHD job. In hindsight, I understood why I'd chosen it. It was the perfect balance of routine and novelty. Always keeping me on my toes but with steady reliability to its pacing too.

"As for hoofstock," Heron hedged. "I kind of fell in love with it in my teen years. I started off working more in Kangaroo Point. I love the wallabies and the dingoes particularly. I mean, it's not like I don't go see them everyday anyway, and I still often cover shifts out there, but yeah. The keeper who used to work hoofstock is basically like my honorary aunt and she was the one who made me fall in love with it."

"Where is she now?"

"She and her wife retired and moved to a little town in Vermont. They still have a hobby farm up there that turns into a Santa's workshop every Christmas." They looked wistfully at the wall as if remembering. "I hope we do a family trip up there this Christmas with my nephews."

"Well, with a few more zookeepers around, I think you'll be able to take more trips."

"I hope so."

We fell back into a silent routine. A lot of the day was the same as every other zoo I'd worked at, slightly different names to the routines and different techniques and schedules, but the bones of the job were the same: cleaning, feeding, observations, enrichment, etc. The role of animal husbandry suited me like a well-rehearsed dance.

Heron made it hard for me to hold the same amount of ire I'd had that morning, but still, they put me on the back foot, unsure of how to navigate around them. I didn't know if they were trying to be friendly or mocking me.

After we'd fed all of the birds and let the giraffes out into the wider exhibit to roam for the day, we did a permitter check, and I kept a keen eye out for any more rusty hinges.

"So, what's Wyoming like?" Heron asked as we strolled around the outer fence. "I've barely left this island, let alone seen much of the States."

"Oh, you know," I started. "Sweeping prairies, mountains, all that. What's it like growing up on an island?" They eyed me for a minute. "What?"

"Don't like to talk about yourself, noted."

"That's not what I . . . I mean, yeah." *Take the win, Hollis.* "I don't know. I guess I'd rather talk about my interests than my past."

Those blue eyes held mine. "What interests you?"

I scrutinized the fence as I thought about it, the feeling of Heron's gaze like free-falling. "Have you seen the latest breeding study on Almadran skinks?"

They lit up. "My older sister runs the organization that funded it."

"No way!"

"Yeah!"

"I thought the male sexual dimorphism was fascinating! It's unlike anything we've seen in other skink species. It's wild to think that they were never studied before and we almost lost them."

"Yeah . . . ," they said. "That was kind of my brother-in-law's doing."

"Oh, right," I replied, snapping my fingers. "I remember now. Your sister is married to that movie star guy. David or something."

"I love that you know more about Almadran skinks than you do about Deacon Harrow," they complimented, and that made some odd, floppy things happen in my stomach.

"I'm more of a Jane Austen buff myself," I said with a shrug. "Action movies aren't really my jam. I'll take promenades and candlelit balls and walking through the morning mist every time." I realized I was waxing poetic and quickly added, "No offense if you like—"

"None taken." They shrugged, those eyes making my stomach float into my throat again.

Seriously, what is wrong with me?

I didn't know why it irked me that Heron made conversation so easy. It shouldn't be something that I was angry about. Classic me. Instead of appreciating that I didn't have to talk about the weather or celebrities or sports, I was angry, as if Heron had foiled my great plan to hate them forever and make every interaction insufferable.

"Okay, what else can I help with?" I asked.

Heron looked around, sticking out their bottom lip as they contemplated. "Actually, we've already finished the morning routine. That was the fastest I've done it in years."

"Well, normally you don't have me with you," I taunted with a wink and then instantly blushed. What had gotten into me? I was so not a winker.

"Yeah," they replied, easy as that. "So . . . maybe let's just have an early lunch break? I'm guessing you want some time to practice your tiger talk?"

"Oh no." I groaned.

They chuckled. "You'll be fine."

I pointed a finger at them. "You don't know me well enough to make such bold assessments."

Their smile broadened. "I don't know. Skink enthusiast. Jane Austen buff. I think we're getting there, Hollis Kettring."

And now my heart was lodged in my throat right along with my stomach. Anxiously shoving my hands in my pockets, I turned to head back toward the golf cart when Heron reached out and touched my elbow. I paused and looked down to where their fingers grazed my pebbled skin.

"Hey," they said softly. "I should've led with this when I first saw you this morning, but you said to leave you alone and I wasn't sure if you wanted me to talk to you and I wanted to give you some space." I thoroughly enjoyed their rambling. It seemed to make me calm, as if balancing the energetic scales between us. "But I'm so incredibly sorry about the sangria accident last night." Their eyebrows knit together in a look of genuine apology, and it added yet another crack in the wall I'd built between them and me.

"How does one manage to throw a whole pitcher on someone accidentally? What exactly happened?"

"Crane and I were going to snatch a pitcher and go drink with the meerkats—"

"Naturally."

"As one does," Heron added with a laugh. "But Finch caught us, and Crane thought it would be funny to lick the pitcher to claim it as ours, and I thought it was childish, and so then I did the most childish thing imaginable and entered into a game of tug-of-war with my twenty-seven-year old twin that led to the pitcher flinging from his grip and dousing you in wine." They grimaced at me. "It was so stupid and I was so mad at him, and then he thought the food fight might cover any perceived embarrassment, and it was all really, really all so foolish. I'm so sorry."

"So you weren't trying to pull a *Carrie* on me on my first day?"

Heron laughed and shook their head. "Honestly, you're the most qualified keeper out of the three of you, and I'm really hoping that you'll fall in love with this place and the job will work out." They shrugged. "Who else am I going to nerd out about Almadran skinks with? John? I think not."

"Um, your entire family would nerd out with you about that," I countered. "Your literal sister funded the research."

"Yeah, good point." They rubbed the back of their neck, blush pinking their cheeks. "Alright, no more delaying. Let's go practice your tiger talk."

A begrudgingly smile tugged on my lips. "You see right through me, Heron Lachlan."

Chapter Nine

Heron

Hollis had spent her entire lunch break huddled in the shade of a picnic table outside the break room, pouring over her notes for the tiger talk. It was a blustering summer's day, not quite cloudy enough to deter visitors but windy enough that they might zip through the zoo faster than usual, so at least she wouldn't have a 300-head audience watching. My eyes kept finding her through the window, watching her replaying her talk over and over.

Even on the walk to the tiger exhibit, she continued the talk like a chant. Even as I helped her find the headset and battery pack to amplify her voice, she kept whispering her speech in her head. Now, as she stood in front of the crowd at the display glass, she looked like she'd rather be eaten alive by the tiger than have to talk to a crowd about one.

Since she hadn't been trained on hand-feeding Ruby through the grate yet, she would just be in front of the floor-to-ceiling glass—something I thought would bring her relief, but she seemed to be even more stressed at the realization that she would be speaking toward the crowd instead of with her back to them. Luckily for Hollis, a light sprinkle of rain had pitter-patted through five minutes before she was set to begin, dispelling the bulk of the crowd.

She looked adorably frazzled, but I knew she'd do fine if she shared her animal fun facts with the same gusto as she had with me. Her microphone sat askew on her head, giving her a cowlick of shiny brunette hair. Her rapid breathing played loudly over the speakers as I watched from the back. When her eyes landed on me, I gave her two thumbs-up, but that only seemed to increase her nerves further.

She cleared her throat loudly over the mic and rolled her shoulders back, summoning all the courage she could before she began.

"Hello, and welcome to Prickle Island Zoo's tiger talk. I'm Hollis, one of the keepers here, and today I'm going to be telling you all about our Bengal tigers."

There was a slight wobble of nerves to her voice, but other-wise she was doing a great job. It was her first time doing a zoo talk after all. My first tiger talk had been mid-puberty and I'd been a pimply, brace-faced tween whose voice had broken every other sentence. Compared to that, she had the confidence of a seasoned performer. Apparently, Hollis's last jobs hadn't required her to do any of the front-facing work, but here, we all took turns doing the talks, feedings, and visitor encounters. We needed all of the keeper team to be able to do them regardless of which section they were on.

Fortunately for Hollis, our two-year-old tiger, Ruby, was really putting on a show for the crowd, who oohed and aahed, watching as she would stalk around the bushes of her enclosure and then round the corner and pose, perfectly highlighted between the bushes and her heated cave like something out of a postcard.

She picked up the rabbit we'd given her as a treat and brought it right down to the glass so that everyone could watch her consume her meal. Visitors ran up to take selfies with her as Hollis kept going. It was much easier to give a speech when people were more focused on an awe-inspiring wild animal than you.

A few dutiful, elderly people kept watching Hollis and nodding, but most were too enamored with Ruby to pay much attention anyway. I gave her a "see, you're doing great" look, and she gave a tentative half-smile back.

"Did you know tigers not only have striped fur, but they have striped skin too?" she continued, and even got a few delighted looks at that fun fact. Her shoulders dropped another inch in relief. She was nearly at the end, just needed to upsell the visitors on lunch at the Peckish Peacock or to book in their own tiger encounter and then it was smooth sailing.

A cheeky seagull flew into Ruby's enclosure and landed beside her, clearly angling for some of her rabbit. One of the many blessings of having a zoo on a summer-vacation island was that the visitors' fries and ice creams at the beach were usually safe from harassment because the seagulls knew the hottest spot in town for a quick feed was at the zoo.

All of the animals were pretty used to seagull interruptions and usually ignored them . . . and just as I had that thought, faster than lightning, Ruby pinned the gull under her giant paw and bit its head off.

A gasp went up through the crowd, a few visitors even screaming as the seagull continued to flap for a few more seconds before being devoured—far more exciting fare than a run-of-the-mill rabbit apparently. Still, it was rather gruesome as a cloud of feathers flew up into the air. Parents grabbed their children and fled the area as I darted toward Hollis, who was now panicking herself.

"Oh well, circle of life, you know?" she croaked with an awkward laugh, looking frantically to me in the crowd for help. "We don't intentionally do live feedings, but nature finds a way, I guess. That seagull really had it coming, though, right? Talk about survival of the fittest. It's probably great enrichment for our tigers to practice hunting—"

"No," I groaned, waving emphatically to get her attention and making a cutting noise at my neck.

Her eyes flared at me. "Alright, well, that's the tiger talk. Go get lunch at our award-winning restaurant. No seagulls on the menu, haha . . . Uh, bye."

She turned her microphone off and removed it like it was on fire as an older woman with a spiky blonde "Karen" haircut stormed up to us.

"So you're saying you encourage your animals to kill these poor, defenseless birds?" she screeched.

"It came into the tiger's home and practically inserted its head into the tiger's mouth. It wasn't her fault," Hollis explained. "Besides, tigers are obligate carnivores and seagulls are assholes."

I had to stifle my laughter at that comment as I ran the last stretch to Hollis and practically leapt in front of her.

"What my colleague is trying to say," I shouted. "Is that this was a terrible incident that has never happened before in the history of the zoo"—I had no idea if that was true, but at least I'd never seen it happen—"and we will be doing everything in our power to ensure it doesn't happen again."

"Let's hope so," the woman said tightly. "Before you traumatize even more children. I *will* be mentioning this in my review." With that, she turned on heel and stormed off, probably to request to speak to a manager.

"I mean, these *are* wild animals," Hollis muttered. The

crowd dispersed as Ruby took her half-eaten seagull behind her cave where the visitors couldn't see. "Kids have seen nature documentaries before. We all grew up watching Discovery Channel, right?"

I turned to look at her. "I think future zoologists tend to watch those kinds of things more than others."

Her expression tightened. "I'm guessing I didn't pass, did I?"

"I think we're going to need to run that one again tomorrow." I attempted to break it to her gently, but her face crumpled in frustration. I wasn't about to admit that yes, it was because she'd said "asshole" in front of a gaggle of small children, but also because I was trying to find more excuses for us to see each other.

I could already read the disappointment all over her wide-eyed face and I really needed to say something, anything, to smooth over all this tension between us. I normally didn't put too much stock into what people thought about me. None of them were around long enough to matter. But Hollis was different. I didn't know why, but I needed her to like me, or at the very least not hate me, and I selfishly wished she wanted to spend more time with me too, whatever that meant.

Just as I opened my mouth to give my best awkward attempt at an invitation to work drinks at the Salty Dog, Ruby turned the corner holding the decapitated seagull in her mouth.

I pointed to a group of school children moseying down the lion trail in the distance.

"I'm going to head them off until Ruby finishes her meal," I told Hollis as I darted off down the path. "We'll debrief tomorrow, okay?"

"Yep," she said tightly, her eyes focused in the distance.

"You're replaying the whole talk in your head, aren't you?"

"Yep."

I was halfway across the space toward the lion trail as I called, "Well, snap out of it because however bad you think that went, I can name you at least a dozen times it's gone worse for me. It just means you're one of us." I loved the way her muscles eased, the way the whisper of a smile ghosted her lips as I added, "Welcome to life at Prickle Island Zoo, Hollis." And I ran off to stop a bunch of third graders from witnessing our tiger doing what tigers did best: causing mischief.

Chapter Ten

Heron

I should've known she wouldn't listen to me. When I caught up with Hollis the next day, she already had a ten-point checklist prepared of all of the things she'd done wrong during the tiger talk and all of the ways she would fix it for next time. It saved me trying to tap dance around the foibles, and I was impressed by her keen assessment, although I suspected she'd been stewing over her failure all day yesterday despite my reassurance. And since the storm clouds had brought in a deluge of rain and there were exactly zero visitors left in the zoo by the time of the tiger talk, we decided to postpone her redo until another day.

We whizzed through the morning shift again, falling into a steady, pleasant routine. Hollis and I had the exact same level of conversation energy and it was awesome. Most people either wanted to gab the whole day or talk about topics that bored me or didn't want to speak at all, but with Hollis, she was the Goldilocks of conversationalists, just right. We talked about the new insights in crayfish conservation, the cheetah protection dogs program, and our favorite social media channels, like the orphaned sea lion fish-eating school. She even liked watching Dropout TV—a passion Dove and I still shared, and we texted each other while watching new episodes of *Game Changer* wherever she was in the world. Hollis's hobbies were the greenest of green flags, and now I was angry at myself for ever perceiving her nerves as coldness.

Hollis's focus was incredible too. It was like she had tunnel vision for the work. I was beginning to worry that she would struggle on the visitor side of things, though. I needed to help her find a way to get over her public speaking anxiety. It was clear that she wasn't a people person so much as she was an animal person—something I could certainly relate to, but I'd been trained my whole life to engage with visitors too, so I'd smoothed out those rough edges through practice.

"What's next?" Hollis asked, following behind me as we wandered down the rainy path in the afternoon.

"I have a few more things to do, but I think that's it for us for the day." I checked my watch. "Four o' clock, wow, that's a new record."

Without the talks, no visitors to chat with, and an experienced keeper joining me on my shift, the work had raced by.

Hollis shrugged. "I guess I'll go swing around the top loop and grab some buckets. And then see if Aya needs a hand in the prep kitchens."

I gave her an approving nod, and we headed up the path together. Clean buckets were like zookeeper currency. She definitely was playing to win herself a permanent job by offering to clean them for other people. Still, I wasn't sure how well she'd fare with all of my siblings and their shenanigans, let alone all of the different visitor personalities. Customer service was a big part of the job in the summertime, and some of the difficult and unsavory guests required an abundance of patience that I wasn't sure Hollis had. I kind of loved when the snark slipped out though. She was normally guarded and tight-lipped, but occasionally she'd call seagulls assholes and it delighted me. I wondered if as she got to know me, she'd let those things slip more often, but if she swore like a sailor in front of visitors . . . well, it was certainly something my mother would take into consideration, even if I was eager to keep her there.

That thought made me pause. Did I want her to stay? I knew it wasn't just because she was a good staff member, but there was nothing there for me to grab on to. She seemed indifferent toward me at best, my opposite in every way, and it would be delusional to consider us friends . . . . Still, I'd known her for all of two days and didn't want her to leave. And I already knew it wasn't just the pleasant conversations and the similar interests, nope. The second I'd pulled her out of that hedge, I'd known I wanted her to stay, which was a damning thought because it wouldn't lead to anything good.

We reached a fork in the path, and I headed to the left.

Hollis stalled, considering my direction. "I thought we were done for the day."

"You are," I corrected. "I've got one more enclosure to visit." She stood there, clearly trying to figure out what I wasn't saying. "I have to do a shift standing over Crane's egg."

Her brow arched incredulously. "Your brother's egg?"

"No, not Crane, my brother, Crane," I amended. "Our white-naped crane, Crane."

"You named your crane, Crane?"

I cringed. "Uh-huh."

Her eyebrows lifted into her hairline as she folded her arms. "And no one thought that would be confusing since you have a sibling named Crane?"

"Apparently, it didn't occur to him. He was the one who named her," I said with a weary laugh. I started to wander off toward the marsh area and noted the way Hollis followed after. "Granted, we were three when she hatched, so really it's my parents' fault for letting us."

Her lip flickered and it was the closest to a smile I'd seen from her since we'd talked about fish-eating school.

"It's not the first time it's happened, naming an animal after someone," I continued, "and probably won't be the last now that Simon has taken up the mantle of baby animal namer."

She studied the fence line beside us as we walked, always noting things, always assessing. "I'll admit it was confusing when I first heard someone talking about Frankie and realized only halfway through the conversation they were talking about a macaw and not the head chef."

"Ah, yes." I let out a soft laugh. "That was Finch's doing."

"Maybe not the wisest choice on your parents' part naming their children after animals, considering you all work with them for a living," she noted. "But it's whimsical as fuck, I'll give you that."

I laughed in surprise. There was that sharp humor again. "Bit late to change their minds now," I said with a chuckle. "Besides, I kind of like the name Heron."

"It suits you," she added as we rounded the bend to Crane's enclosure.

I didn't know if that was a compliment or not but decided to take it as one. "So, you and Crane—the bird, not your twin—are like in an avian situationship?"

"You could say that." I shrugged. "She started initiating mating dances with me a couple years ago, and on a whim I decided to return it, and then she started laying and getting all clucky. We've just submitted a proposal to the breeding program director to see if we can try artificial insemination with her since she seems, uh, eager to procreate."

"Eager to procreate," she echoed, the flash of a dimple on her cheek. "I've worked at a few zoos where something like that happened. I suppose it's good to know they can never fire you," she added. "Not that they ever would at a family run zoo, but . . . being needed by a critically endangered bird that lives for so long . . . really ties you down to this place, I guess."

"Yeah. I guess so." I lingered at the gate. "I hadn't really thought about it like that."

I had no plans to move, no desire to travel, but if we did end up being part of a breeding program, Crane would need me to be there to help with our chicks, or at least be around during the spring and summer months.

"It must be nice to feel so connected to a place," Hollis mused. I swore I saw a hint of longing on her face, but I had no idea how to reply to that. Was that feeling something she wanted? Should I admit how lucky I felt? Before I could think of anything to say, she took note of the silence and said, "Well, congratulations, I guess. I hope you and your crane are very happy together."

I hung my bucket on the hook on the fence and entered Crane's enclosure. "Thanks."

She took one step away and then turned back. "Are you sure I can't help with anything?"

I studied her for a second as she folded her arms tighter, those pale blue eyes lingering on me expectantly. Was she just eager to go the extra mile to get a permanent job offer? Or was she looking to spend more time together? *Obviously the former, Heron. Pull it together.*

"I'm okay," I called back to her.

Still, she idled. "How long do you have to stay there?"

"An hour or so." I pulled out my phone. "It's okay. I normally just read."

"Oh, okay. Well, I'll leave you two lovebirds to it," she quipped.

Our white-naped crane, Crane, busied herself foraging as I took position over her eggs—our eggs technically. They were dummy eggs, but they made her happy, and we were hopeful that one day we would be able to work with the Smithsonian on a breeding program for her. Until then, she and I were childless, but still sort of life partners.

It wasn't until Hollis gave a final wave and started wandering back down the path that Hannah emerged from behind the wall to the gibbon service area like the ghost of zookeepers past. I lurched in surprise as she dramatically rolled her eyes at me.

She put her hands on her hips. "You really are an idiot, Heron Lachlan, you know that?"

"What?"

"She clearly wanted to hang out with you and you just blanked her!"

"She did not want to hang out," I countered. *Did she?* "I think she was just trying to be helpful, and I didn't want her having to hang around just because she felt like she had to. She just really wants this job."

"Hopeless." Hannah slapped a hand to her forehead before heading off with her buckets in tow. "And that's coming from me."

"She wasn't trying to hang out," I called again, but I was too busy egg-sitting to chase after her and belabor the point.

"Yeah, yeah." She waved a hand as she kept walking.

"I didn't misread the situation!"

"Of course you didn't, Sherlock," she called back with a final salute and disappeared down the hill, leaving me to stew over that exchange with Hollis, scrutinizing it like a Magic Eye picture I couldn't quite solve.

Chapter Eleven

Hollis

My first week at Prickle Island Zoo was going surprisingly well. My resting bitch face had successfully kept anyone from asking about my childhood in Wyoming, and the bout of summer thunderstorms meant I'd been spared from the redo of the tiger talk. By day five, I actually found myself looking forward to seeing Heron in the morning and catching each other up on all of our doomscrolling-induced hyperfocuses that had popped up overnight. I was still too skeptical to call it a friendship though. I'd been burned too many times before, assumed I was hitting it off with a new friend when that person was just being nice.

Still, a little blossom of pride filled my chest when Heron called us the "dream team" as we installed the new gazelle feeding trough in record time.

"Carnivores to all units, uh—" Hawk let out a long sigh, and Heron and I both instinctively turned our radios up in unison. That was either bad news or something that they didn't know how to break to you. "I just got a call from the Westworth estate. It appears two of their horses have gotten out of the stables and they would like some assistance getting them back into their paddock."

Heron and I exchanged confused glances as Finch jumped on. "Don't they have a fancy show horse groomer person who's in charge of them?"

"Yeah, apparently she's off the island today, and the rest of the staff is busy setting up for a *garden party*."

"Too busy to get their own damn horses?" Crane chimed in.

"Language," Evelyn and Hawk said over each other.

"Listen," Hawk said wearily. "It's not a work requirement, but while the zoo is ours, the Westworths still own the rest of the island—"

"And kissing their ass is still in our best interest," Finch said. "I know, Mom, language," she added, beating her mother to it. "I've got a gibbon on the table right now so I'm out."

"Yeah, I'm behind today too," Crane added. "We had a pipe burst in the rainforest walkthrough and I need to sort the drainage before the afternoon feeding."

I wondered if John wasn't being particularly helpful with that, judging by the tightness in Crane's voice.

"I guess it'll just be Diego and me on horse-wrangling duty," Hawk groused tightly.

"Hollis and I can join you," Heron jumped in. I tried to keep from looking stressed as they added, "We're already done with the morning feeds, and she's got a lot of experience in wrangling horses, so it should be easier between the four of us."

My stomach plummeted. *Great, I was finally having a wonderful time at my new job, and now I'm about to get fired for clearly having no fucking idea how to wrangle a horse. What did* wrangling even entail? Was I expected to lasso the freaking things? Was it like "walking an ostrich," for goodness' sake?

"Great, thanks, Heihei," Hawk said. "We'll drive down to the northern point and you two go on foot. It sounds like they're near the eastern bay."

"Roger," Heron replied, turning toward me. "Ready?"

"Heihei?" I asked. "Like the chicken from *Moana*?"

"Sort of, yeah." Heron chuckled. "It's what my nephews call me. Auncle is kind of a mouthful for a little kid, and when Simon started calling me Heihei, it just stuck." Those gorgeous dimples deepened as they smiled.

"Keeping with the bird theme, I like it."

Heron grinned as they locked the enclosure and tugged the lock twice. "Ready to round up some horses, cowgirl?"

I swallowed the frog in my throat. "Yep."

We darted off down the emergency exit, making sure to walk and not run through the areas visible to visitors. The last thing passersby needed was seeing a bunch of panicked, running zookeepers, and this was certainly not an emergency, especially on a small island with only one main road and more golf carts than cars. The horses would probably just be grazing on the drift grasses and exploring the beaches. Hopefully, they'd already tired themselves out on their adventure and it would be as simple as grabbing their reins and walking them home, looking like I'd done it my whole life. But knowing me, I was probably far more likely to end up kicked into a fancy rich person's hedge.

As Heron and I headed off down the back street that circumnavigated the Prickle Island shops, I started replaying every possible plan in my head, swinging wildly from just walking up to the horses, simple as that, to getting fired, to getting trampled to death and everything in between. And between my bouts of panic, I kept thinking about how attractive Heron was in an emergency. High intensity situations were the fastest way to reveal a person's true nature. There was something about their confidence, being both fast and calm . . . *Great, of all the things to make my stomach flutter, watching a zookeeper chase after pampered horses shouldn't be one of them.*

When we turned the bend, sure enough, there were two gorgeous white horses, manes billowing in the wind and looking more like something out of a toy set rather than real-life animals. But they had a crazed look about them too, like they were too beautiful and they knew it. These horses looked like if they were humans, they'd be trying to get me to be an ambassador for their yoga pants pyramid scheme. Their ears lay flat, and I knew enough about animal behavior to at least know that wasn't a good thing. A third little Shetland pony grazed between them, pawing at the sand and kicking at the grasses with its back legs.

Heron grabbed their radio. "You didn't say there was a pony too," they muttered to Hawk.

"If I had, you wouldn't have helped me," he countered, the radio reception patchier this far from the zoo.

I tried to hide my questioning look. "What's wrong with ponies?"

"You know what they say? The shorter the legs, the closer to hell," Heron answered before picking up their radio again.

"Oh." I snorted. "Yeah. Right."

"They're at Seafoam Bay," Heron added to Hawk. "We'll try to get them moving up the road, and you can cut them off up ahead."

"Roger," Hawk replied.

Heron looked at me. "I'll try to approach the horses and let you deal with the pony."

"Why?"

"You have more experience."

"Not with ponies, I don't." I balked.

"Just grab the lead rope and you'll be fine."

"Uh . . ." What the hell was a lead rope? The only pieces of equestrian gear that came to my mind was saddle, stirrups, and reins. After that, my knowledge was tapped out.

"I'm sure you'll be fine." Heron clapped me on the shoulder. "Weren't wild stallions on your resume?"

Were they? I couldn't remember. "Oh, uh, yeah."

They gave me a half-smile before trotting off toward the horses, and sure enough, Heron's movement spooked that sketchy looking pony and it bolted straight down the road in my direction.

"Dammit." I groaned, ready to leap behind a sand dune for cover. I splayed my arms wide to try and slow the thing down. "Easy. Easy, you demonic little turd," I called to it, not knowing what the hell to do.

The little shit bag ran faster, booking it down the street and closing the distance before rearing up in front of me, and I was certain I was about to be trampled to death when it came to a sudden halt. I instinctively grabbed for its halter, and to my utter surprise, the pony let me.

"Okay, okay." I panted, heart racing as I leaned down so my mouth was next to the pony's ear. "Listen, short stack, if you make me look good right now, I promise you a million sugar cubes, okay?"

As if in acknowledgement, the pony snorted. I took a step and the pony took one. I took another and it followed, as if resigned that now that I'd caught him and the jig was up.

"Alright, they're turning down the road," Hawk's voice called. "Make sure you've got the gate open."

"Roger," Diego replied.

The pony and I kept walking, listening to the two keepers quarterback the return of the horses. Heron came jogging around the bend, giving me a thumbs-up.

"See?" they called. "This is no sweat to a pro like you. Way to get 'em, cowgirl."

It was the second time in a matter of minutes that Heron had called me that. A warm blush crept across my cheeks at their pride in me, at their confidence that I could do it, at the nickname that so easily rolled off their tongue. Nobody had given me a nickname before. I secretly hoped this wouldn't be the last time they used it.

Chapter Twelve

Hollis

The rest of my first week was blissfully uneventful. The work was steady and enjoyable, the animals were fun and challenging, and John and Diego were too tired at the end of the day to really bother me much. Perfection. I'd settled into an easy routine after my first few days dancing around Heron and realizing they valued both my work ethic *and* I was pretty sure they enjoyed my company too. They'd called me "cowgirl" three more times, not that I was counting, and while I didn't necessarily consider myself buddy-buddy with anyone, I might make an exception when it came to them.

Nothing about the two of us should work. On paper, we didn't make sense as friends. Heron had this allure that was almost addictive, an easy warmth and calm and ease that I just wanted to be around. But I'd be shifting to Crane's team soon, and I had a feeling there wouldn't be any reason for us to spend time together anymore. We'd only talked as we'd worked, and once I was on someone else's team, we probably wouldn't talk at all.

I'd even convinced Heron to wait until I was trained on the tiger feeding to let me redo my tiger talk. On the plus side, I wouldn't have to face the crowd. On the downside, I'd procrastinated until the busiest day we'd had all summer. The sun was beating down, the weather a glorious late June day that had people pouring through the gates.

When Heron and I arrived at the tiger exhibit with the meat bucket in tow, there was already a press of people smushed up against the glass. Ruby walked back and forth in front of the feeding platform like a house cat to the sound of a can opener, making children squeal with delight.

Nerves clawed up my throat as we pushed through the thick crowd. Heron squeezed my arm, making me pause as they murmured, "Remember, it's okay to pause and take a beat. Everyone is looking at the tiger." Their thumb swept across my forearm. "Just breathe. You'll be great."

I nodded and left them in the center of the throng, while I unlocked the gate to the feeding platform and adjusted my headset one more time. Ruby was letting out adorably eager chuffs, rubbing her face against the wooden post next to the mesh of the feeding platform, clearly excited for her chopped pieces of raw chicken.

At least I could focus on her, give the tiger talk *to* her, as if she hadn't heard some iteration of it a million times before. If I looked only at the giant tiger, maybe the crowd wouldn't exist at all. *Yep, that's the head in the sand thinking that's going to save me today.*

A group of school children pressed up against the fence that separated the feeding platform from the main path, whispering and giddy, letting out little gasps every time Ruby walked past.

I took a deep breath before turning my microphone on. "Hello, and welcome to Prickle Island Zoo. I'm Hollis . . . ," I began, managing to force some inflection into my voice.

I was a fairly decent mimic, and I'd spent most of last night eating dinner in bed while watching YouTube vloggers to get the cadence right. It had been a mistake to spend all my time studying tiger fun facts. I already knew plenty. What I needed to study was public speaking. But whether I could replicate it with this many people watching, was another story entirely.

I grabbed a chunk of bony chicken and held it to the mesh. Ruby's head lifted to head height to gingerly take it from my hand.

The crowd reaction was incredibly satisfying, particularly the children who gasped with glee at every movement.

I picked up another piece of chicken, delicate chopped bones poking into my hands as I held it out for Ruby and she licked it up, the hooks on her rough sandpaper tongue practically taking a layer of my skin off.

One more piece of chicken. One more fun fact. And then I was done.

This is going so well. I have everyone on the edges of their seats.

With my newfound bravado, I decided for the last piece, I'd hold the chicken up high above my head and get Ruby to stretch all the way up on her hind legs and show everyone her impressive height, her giant paws gripping the mesh, her fuzzy white belly showing to the crowd. It was something I'd seen Hawk do during his talks and it was always a showstopper.

"And as you'll see . . . ," I said, lifting the last piece of chicken.

Ruby stood, awaiting another treat, and everyone gasped in unison at the size of her. The raw meat was slippery in my hand, and as I held it to the mesh, I almost lost my grip. Instinctively, I squeezed the gelatinous chunk tighter and pierced my pinky finger with a broken needle of chicken bone.

"Gah!" I exclaimed, flinching, and everyone behind me shrieked.

As Ruby took the last bite of chicken from me, it suddenly dawned on me what it must've looked like from the visitor's perspective. Me, holding my hand up to the mesh, a tiger's mouth on the other side *right* as I made a pained sound and flinched.

I turned to find a group of horrified school children looking at me and then my hand, probably expecting to find a missing finger.

"Sorry, sorry," I announced. "Just a pointy piece of chicken bone, nothing to worry about." I grimaced. "Surprise! Just a little skit we do around here to remind you to not poke your fingers into animal enclosures." I was rambling now. I needed to pull it together. "We've got to keep you on your toes, I guess." No one seemed amused by that. "Well, if you're in the mood for lunch like my friend Ruby here, make sure to check out our award-winning restaurant, the Peckish Peacock." Heron gave me a confident nod, like it was a good recovery, and then I had to go and ruin it by adding, "There's no pinky fingers in the food, I swear." I laughed awkwardly. The crowd was, again, unamused. "Thanks for coming to the zoo, everyone."

There were a few sporadic claps, which was honestly worse than there being none at all. And as the crowd filtered out, I spotted Heron rubbing a hand down their face.

"I'm going to have to do this again, aren't I?" I grumbled, and they looked up from between their fingers.

"Turn your microphone off," they mouthed, miming to the battery pack clipped to my belt.

"Shit, I mean, crap," I fiddled with the switch. "Aw, come on, for fuck's sake."

"Turn your microphone off, Hollis!" they called louder.

The slippery dial finally clicked, the red light turning off, and my shoulders sagged as my cheeks burned in embarrassment.

Heron walked over with a tight smile. "So that was—"

"You might as well fire me now. I'm really not cut out for this." I moaned. "I am a good keeper—"

"You are," they agreed.

"But I just don't know what happened. I panic and then the words just start flying out in word vomit, and then I feel like I need to scramble more to make up for all the fumbles and—"

"You know, I think I might have you shadow Hannah for the next one," Heron said with a knowing nod. "She knows a thing or two about controlling the word vomit."

I frowned, disappointment bleeding through me. I knew this was part of the job description, knew I couldn't just be a wild introvert and had to work with other people and talk to visitors. A zoo's lifeblood was the visitors, and it wouldn't exist without them, but I really, really wished it were someone else's job to deal with them. *I should've stuck to the original plan of being one of those wildlife workers who only rehabilitates bats in a cabin in the middle of the woods.*

Heron silently read my defeated expression and nudged me with their elbow. "Come on, let's take our afternoon break with the meerkats. They make everything better."

I perked up a little at that. It was true. There was nothing better to cheer up an animal person than some time with cute animals, after all.

We wandered up through the dispersing crowd. Our radios scratched and then Evelyn Lachlan spoke.

"Did someone just say the s-word, the c-word, and the f-word on microphone during the tiger talk?"

I let out another groan. "Even crap counted?"

"I'm afraid so, cowgirl," Heron lamented as they picked up their radio.

Man, word traveled too fast around this place.

Crane's voice came over the radio. "Yeah, and for once it wasn't me."

Heron pressed in the button to respond and gave me a wink that made my pulse race for an entirely different reason. "If it's any consolation, Mom, the c-word was the one that rhymes with trap and not runt."

"It still counts," Evelyn shot back.

I slumped forward, trudging up the hillside like a stubborn toddler, and Heron rubbed a soothing hand down my back.

"Yeah, I think we're going to need two doses of adorable meerkats STAT."

Chapter Thirteen

Heron

Hollis sat on a log in the meerkat enclosure, a meerkat perched on every conceivable flat surface on her body. Knees, forearms, shoulders, head. I gave her a few treats to give our meerkat mob and left her to cool off while I chatted with the visitors who wandered past, sharing meerkat fun facts and telling them about the enclosure design. Children's faces would pop up in the plexiglass dome on either side of the den, a tunnel beneath the exhibit that they could crawl through like a child-sized burrow. Eventually, the last of the stragglers headed off to the monkey talk, leaving Hollis and me in blissful, late-afternoon quiet.

Over the course of the week, I was beginning to recalibrate whether Hollis actually hated me or if she was just wildly intro-verted. I'd started finding more and more opportunities to invite her around, more things that needed fixing, more enrichment to prepare, inviting her along when I stood guard over Crane's eggs so we could chat about the latest conservation research articles. She always said yes, but I wasn't sure if it was because she wanted to be perceived as going "above and beyond" or actually wanted to spend time together.

You should just ask her! my brain screamed at me. Hollis seemed like the kind of person who'd appreciate my bluntness. It was me who didn't want the answer because if she was just trying to suck up to me, it would be crushing.

I should tell her I'm going to miss being on shift together, I thought as a meerkat burrowed into her pocket. Instead, I wandered over and sat on the stump across the stretch of sandy earth from her and said, "Candy and baked goods."

She looked at me without moving her neck, keeping still so the sentry could use her head as a lookout point. "What?"

"If you need to bribe Hawk while you're on the carnivore team with him, candy and baked goods always work."

"Oh. I thought I was on reptiles next?"

"Mom switched the roster around," I said apologetically.

I wasn't going to tell her it was because of her bungles with the tiger talks and that Mom thought that shadowing Crane next would probably only lead to more swearing and shenanigans instead of less. Not that Hawk was a particularly great influence himself, but anyone was better than Crane when it came to rule following. To be fair, I didn't think that Hollis was easily influenced. She just seemed to get nervous and panic. And considering Hawk's wife, Hannah, had once been the most chaotic ADHD keeper at the zoo, he definitely had more experience being a calming influence on stressed-out keepers than Crane.

"Okay. Thanks." A beat of silence fell between us, but then the meerkat scuttled off Hollis's head and she turned her whole body toward me. "I enjoyed hoofstock. A lot, actually."

"You sound surprised."

"I am," she admitted. "It wasn't my favorite team before, but with you . . . you make it fun."

Warmth spread through my chest at that. "I'm glad."

With you. Those two words did something to my insides. It made me feel like an excited, jumbled up mess. The thought of the two us . . . The truth was, she made everything more fun too. I got up earlier, excited to see her, found excuses to stay longer just to steal a couple more minutes . . . *with her.*

Just tell her, Heron, I demanded of myself.

I opened my mouth, summoning the courage to say that I would miss her, that maybe we could still spend time together . . . when a meerkat decided to dive beneath the hem of my shirt and crawl up my back.

I let out a squeal as I reached behind me, trying to dislodge the meddlesome critter, but as I stood, it became even more sandwiched into the small of my back and shirt. The tickling sensation of the culprit's claws made me make sounds I didn't know were in my register.

"Do you want help?" Hollis offered, rising and tentatively walking over to me with her hands out, a smile she couldn't quite contain on her face.

It wasn't the first time a meerkat had burrowed into my clothing, but something about it being trapped against bare skin on the most ticklish part of my side had me leaping about like an old-timey bandit from the Wild West was trying to "make me dance."

"Please! Save me," I called, half-sincere even as I put on my best damsel in distress voice.

I did a little wiggling shimmy, trying to dislodge the cheeky animal who was clearly trying to climb up rather than drop down.

Hollis stifled a giggle, the sound soft and breathy and beautiful, one I had yet to hear from her lips. And even through the tickling and scratching of fur down my spine and claws up my back, I started laughing too.

Hollis jumped straight into action, stealthy and calm even as her guffaw rose to meet my own. Tears were now spilling from my eyes with the force of my belly-shaking glee. My face flushed and my body shook as her warm hands dipped under the back of my shirt. Grabbing the meerkat and delicately extracting him, Hollis set him on a log, and the meerkat leapt out of her hands and back toward his burrow. My insides flipped as her fingers brushed across my sides, our chortling sounds echoing across the space as I turned to her.

She beamed up at me, eyes crinkling with delight for only a split second before she seemed to remember herself and dropped her hands from my skin, her face falling, and she instantly retreated a step . . . only to catch her boot on the stump behind her.

I saw it coming as if in slow motion. Before she even reached the stump, my hands shot out and yanked her back, pulling her into my chest. We stood there, flush for an instant, before I regained my senses and retreated a step. Even as I tried to get some distance, her hands still clung to my forearms, the haze not having cleared from her gaze as her lips hitched.

"You and I are constantly saving each other, it seems," I said with a laugh.

"We can take turns." Her light, adoring huff made something within me soften. "You rescue me from hedges and stumps, and I'll rescue you from flowerpots and sneaky meerkats."

"I like that idea." I didn't want her to let go of my forearms, didn't want this moment to end, but my radio blared and she released me. "Carnviores to hoofstock."

Hollis's expression tweaked, as if she were disappointed too, and I wondered what would've happened with a few more moments frozen together like that. How long would we have stood there, holding onto each other, staring in each other's eyes if we hadn't been interrupted?

I hated that empty pit feeling in my stomach as I turned away to pick up my radio. "Go ahead."

"Hey, can you swing by the office when you're done for the day?" Hawk asked. "I need you to sign off on some paperwork."

I sighed, the sound more weary than normal. "Roger, heading down now."

I wasn't about to tell Hollis that this radio call was inevitably about the tiger talk incidents or that Hawk needed me to sign off on the report that would have to be filed. And I definitely wasn't going to tell her that we'd had three separate complaints for her swearing on the microphone from upset parents. Hollis had been so defeated at the end of her talk. I was grateful that Hawk had only said "paperwork" over the radio at least.

"Thank you for the meerkat time," Hollis said as we headed back to the service area, checking our pockets and shaking out our clothes one last time just in case of a stowaway.

"I hope it helped," I offered.

Her eyes held mine, a sea of azure blue, an ocean I wished I could swim in. "It did."

We locked the enclosure behind us and moved through the airlock to latch that too, tugging on the locks in a habitual way.

"See ya." Hollis turned one way down the path and I the other.

"Hollis?" I called, and she looked over her shoulder at me, brows peaked in interest. "I'm going to miss having you on the hoofstock team."

Her smile was as beautiful as it was hard won. "If you offer me the permanent job, maybe I'll be on your team again. Who knows? Think of all the research articles I could rant at you about."

"I like your ranting." I chuckled, and her lips quirked again. "You fit in well here."

She snorted, her tension seeming to mount instead of ease at my compliment. "I appreciate it, but I don't fit in well anywhere."

It was such a throwaway comment, one she clearly had said to herself so many times, she didn't even second-guess it, but it hurt to hear.

She started to turn away as I called, "Hey." She turned. "You fit in here. With us."

With me, I added silently to myself.

I let that thought linger for a while, floating in the air between us. Her expression was a cool, impenetrable mask, and I thought for the hundredth time that she'd make a killer poker player. She offered a half-wave and left before I could get a read on her.

As I headed to Hawk's office, it felt like my chest had been filled with helium, like my insides were levitating. What was this giddiness? Never in my life would I think that I, Heron Lachlan, destined to be a lovable hermit, would be practically skipping down the path because a beautiful woman had smiled at me.

My feet stalled, my body rearing with the sudden halt. It hit me all at once: the way I felt about her was as a good friend, yes, but maybe there was a flicker of something more, and I had no idea what to do with that. My levitating mood soured as I came crashing down to earth.

It would only turn into a problem if she stayed.

Chapter Fourteen

Hollis

By the end of the day, I was exhausted. The work itself was great, but my mind was still so focused on the charged moment with Heron. The way I'd hung onto them like a crazed baby koala . . . My cheeks heated. The way I'd just glared at them when they'd told me I fit in . . . I refused to believe it. Heron was a charming, sunshine-y person who was just trying to be nice. That was all it was. I'd learned my lesson the hard way too many times that people didn't actually mean those things.

By the time I left, the sweet moment between us had curdled in my memory. The more I thought about it, the less favorably I pictured it. And now I'd arrived at catastrophe: I was certain they were mad at me, though I didn't know why. Worse, I felt like I was mad at them, and I also didn't know why.

Normally, I thought I was quite good at cataloguing my emotions, but this time I couldn't place it.

Anger. Heat. Sadness. Longing. What was it?

My mind kept flashing back to the way they'd caught me, the way I'd caught them, like we both put the other on the wrong footing. And the way it felt to be held in their arms . . . the way my heart raced when I could feel the heat of their skin against my hand . . . It was like something out of a Jane Austen novel, the chivalrous rescue, the two of us taking turns being the damsel, the electricity of just a single touch.

Where they were Darcy, I was Elizabeth. Where I was Brandon, they were Marianne. We waltzed together, push and pull, one of us taking on the opposite's role as if magnetized poles.

I'd always loved Austen books, loved stories that ended with marriage, where a kiss was the completion of a love story, where it felt like only a single burning look was enough to encapsulate an entire romance. And I knew that in reality, happily ever afters usually led to sex for most people, but in my fantasies, they ended with a kiss and nothing more. Heat and passion and yearning and love could still burn just as brightly without that kind of ending, and the physicality of holding hands or whispering lips held just as much power in me that sex seemed to for most people.

But of the few people I'd tried to discuss my sexuality with, most of them had seemed to view a relationship unconsummated as more of a friendship than a romance, no matter how I'd tried to explain that the feelings between a friend and romantic partner were most definitely not the same, that regardless of physical intimacy, there were different kinds of love. I had a capacity for romantic love, it seemed, but not a sexual one, and that left me in an odd middle ground that made me feel constantly misunderstood—though that was nothing new to me as someone who'd also grown up as an undiagnosed autistic girl.

These feelings I couldn't catalogue, the vivid flashbacks to hands and eyes and smiles . . . They were romantic, the same sort that made my stomach flip when I read Austen or watched a cheesy, adorable rom-com. And my first thought was: I wish I could take it back. I wish I could erase these feelings. Because they never ended well for me.

As I wandered back to the house, the skin on my arm tingled again as if Heron had permanently left a mark upon it. With a weary disposition, I trekked to the front door, only to find an overly jovial John on the steps, holding two beers.

He offered out a sweating cold bottle to me. "End of first week drinks?"

"Thanks." I took it, sitting on the steps beside him, suddenly too tired to enter the house or even take my boots off.

I couldn't wait to have a shower, get in my sweatpants, and hide in my room eating Ritz crackers for dinner. I was midway through a rewatch of the BBC adaptation of *North & South* and I was very much looking forward to zoning out for the rest of the evening ogling Richard Armitage in historical garb.

Instead, I cracked open the beer and took a long swig.

"Is Diego back yet?" I asked.

John clinked his bottle to mine in cheers. "I think he's still wrapping up with carnivore team."

"Should we radio to see if they need help—" I reached for the radio on my hip, and John's hand lightly covered my wrist and lingered.

I looked down to where his fingers grazed my skin. I laughed and shifted away, the feeling of his touch making me itchy, as if in allergic reaction. I made a mental note to buy an EpiPen and label it "John." That was normally how I felt when anyone but close friends touched me, like I'd just had poison ivy swathed across my body, nothing like the pleasant buzz of when Heron had caught me. How could the same type of contact feel so, *so* different?

I took another swig of beer, trying very hard not to think about that clear distinction.

"Let's have a well-earned drink first." John took another sip and stared down toward the strip of Prickle Island shops far in the distance. "Diego is probably having the time of his life chasing Hawk around. You know why carnivore keepers do it better? All that meat," he added with a suggestive wink and a husky chuckle, as if that were peak comedy.

I fought the urge to gag as I shuffled a little farther away. John didn't seem to notice.

I knew it had just been an innocent joke, knew John was trying to be a buddy to me with his bro-y humor, but why did *everything* have to be sex and innuendo? It was like as a kid, everyone had thought fart jokes were hilarious, and then one day we'd hit puberty and then sex jokes had been all the rage and no one around me had ever aged out of them.

The jokes, the drunken conversations, the constant desire to reference sex were some of the many things that had made me realize I was ace. How often everyone else around me seemed to think about sex, let alone want to have it was truly unfathomable to me.

For a long time, I thought that everyone else was just performing this interest for each other, that it wasn't actually real but for show. But no, turned out some people cared a whole hell of a lot about sex, and sometimes it felt like my make and model just hadn't been installed with the interest button at all. After a while, performing all of that interest for partners had slowly turned into resentment. I knew there were ace dating apps, knew there were other ways to find a partner whose priority wasn't sex, but I was so tired of being burned by people that the idea of never having to deal with another partner again seemed honestly appealing. And what if I fell in love with an ace partner and it still didn't work out? It would be a definitive confirmation that I was the broken one.

"Plus," John continued, leaning his shoulder into mine even though he had to stretch way too far. *God, was he still talking?* "It's nice for the two of us to have some time to ourselves for once, you know?"

For fuck's sake! I can't catch a break.

Alarm bells instantly rang out at that statement. I'd been in this position a million times before.

I honestly had no idea how to interact with men without them thinking I was flirting with them. If I didn't make eye contact, I was being coy. If I made too much, I was flirting with them. If I smiled or laughed, my intensity was misread as interest, and if I didn't, I was playing hard to get. It was *exhausting*. Men were the worst, but the signals got crossed with people of all genders. I really needed to buy a shirt that said, "not flirting with you, just autistic and conditioned to maintain intense eye contact."

Apparently, I'd gotten so used to every interaction with people of all genders being taxing that when it felt easy like it did with Heron, that stressed me out even more. I couldn't win.

"So . . . ," John hedged, and my stomach clenched. *Here it comes.* He took another sip of his beer, letting that "so" linger like I would just infer the question, but when I didn't reply, he finally asked, "Do you have a boyfriend?"

"No."

I fought the urge to storm into the house. Why did it always have to come to this? Why did everyone think that if you weren't paired off, that you wanted to be?

"Girlfriend?"

"Nope." As he scooted closer, I quickly added, "And I'm very happily single. And I don't date coworkers."

Neither was entirely true, but I found it was easier to shut it all down now. Guys like John didn't do well with any vagueness or potential for misinterpretation. It was better to say that I firmly didn't date coworkers and wasn't looking than to say I wasn't interested in him specifically. Not that there was any potential partner out there for me. I doubted someone was wandering around this little island who was looking for a sexless romance.

"Sorry, I wasn't flirting with you, if that's, uh, what you thought . . ." I internally screamed at myself for always apologizing in these situations. I had nothing to be sorry for. And yet, apologies seemed to take some of the sting out of it, making it seem like it was my mistake and not theirs.

John bobbed his head a little too aggressively. "Yeah, okay. That's all good. I was just asking."

He stood abruptly and walked inside, ego clearly bruised despite his assurances. I hung my head. I had zero finesse. I felt like there was a whole rulebook to being human that I'd never been given growing up. How did one let a person down gently? Was it even possible?

It was one of the many moments in my life when I wished I never had to interact with another human being ever again. And now I had *yet another* person that I had to dance around on Prickle Island. Honestly, it made me want to cry, and going to bed crying two nights in a row was completely unacceptable. I was a grown ass woman. I shouldn't be so overwhelmed by all of this. Why couldn't I have a job working with animals that involved zero people? Maybe I needed to be one of those fire lookout people like I'd seen on TikTok. I'd thought an island off the coast of Connecticut was fairly remote, but apparently not remote enough.

With that frustration milling about in my head, I shucked my boots, leaving them by the front door as I padded up the stairs in my socks to my bedroom. I flopped on my bed and pulled out my phone, only to find another string of text messages from my mother. I slung my forearm over my eyes and grabbed for my headphones to put on a D&D podcast and zone out until I could summon the energy to go have a shower. And all the while, Heron Lachlan's face kept flashing in my mind, smiling at me as I helped them fish a meerkat out of their shirt.

Chapter Fifteen

Heron

We sat around Mom's kitchen table, falling into the joyfully chaotic routine that was Sunday Funday Fondue Day. A giant pot of bubbling cheese fondue sat in the center, and the room was filled with the clamor and hubbub of the Lachlan clan all speaking over each other at once.

The weekly tradition had been a staple in our family's household since before I'd even been born, and I loved that even now, with all of us grown up, we all gathered each week for a family dinner. Even Lark and Logan sat on a laptop at the head of the table, drinking their morning coffees and chasing their daughters around in New Zealand as we all had dinner. The video was constantly moving to a different location as they chased the girls around or it would suddenly cut off because

Lark had to pee again. Being so close to her due date apparently meant she had to go every thirty seconds.

"She's been pregnant longer than an Alpine salamander," Crane whispered to me.

Lark's microphone turned back on, the sound of toilet flushing filling the background. "I can still hear you, wrecking ball," she called with her uncanny ability to hear even our hushed remarks over the general din of conversation.

Dove and Deacon sat at the table across from us, Dove deep in conversation with her best friend, Hannah, while Deacon regaled Wren with a story from his latest film set. They had scheduled their flights for tomorrow evening so they could join us one more time before they flew to France.

Crane and I were already training young Simon up to be a master of the weekly family game of "It's feces but what species?" He was going to be a pro. Plus, there was nothing funnier to a five-year-old than poo, so we were getting serious uncle and Heihei points from our nephew.

"I just don't know." Frankie dropped her chin in her hand, and my attention was pulled across the table. My brain had become accustomed to listening to three conversations at once, a skill I thought many big families had, or maybe it was just because we were all neurodivergent. "You hear all these horror stories about doctors swapping out their stuff or people lying on their applications, and there's just so much pressure to pick the right person. But then going the private donor route, that's a whole other can of worms. Like, how do you even approach someone about something like this . . . ?"

Finch slung her arm around her wife and kissed her temple. "It's going to be okay, baby. We'll figure it out."

Hawk blotted the pasta stains off Max's chubby cheeks. "You know I'd offer to be your donor, but I've already had the snip."

"That can be reversed," Mom chimed in, as if she'd already

been thinking about the same thing. Anything that meant more grandbabies was apparently fair game in her books.

Deacon choke-laughed on his fondue-covered bread and Dove smacked him on the back. "Mom," she chided. "You can't just tell your son to reverse his vasectomy so he can be a sperm donor for your daughter-in-law."

Mom shrugged. "I'm just saying it is a possibility if he wanted to."

"Don't you have enough grandbabies?" I asked, waving to the two pasta-stained grandsons and her very pregnant daughter on the laptop screen chasing around two more miscreants with all the gleeful chaos that was the Lachlan family genes.

"We need at least seven to replace all of you when you get too old to do the job anymore. Maybe twelve so that they can take days off," she advised in a teasing way and then held up her hands at the chorus of protests. "I'm not saying they all need to be zookeepers. I'm just thinking about the zoo's legacy."

I didn't know what compelled me, maybe Mom talking about legacy, maybe the moment Hollis and I had shared at the meerkats, maybe the nights staring at the leaking ceiling of my bedroom thinking about what I wanted to do next, but something had me setting down my photo of giraffe poop and announcing to the table, "I could do it if you wanted. I could be your donor."

"What?" Wren sputtered, interrupting Deacon mid-sentence to gape at me.

"I don't want to have kids," I said, giving Mom a warning look to respect that decision and not push me. "Yes, I'm certain." I was twenty-seven and had been surrounded by children my entire life, both within my family and all the families that frequented the zoo. The decision hadn't been a hasty one. I knew what I wanted, and while I loved all of my siblings' kids dearly, I knew I didn't want my life to revolve around raising my own. "It would be a nice thing to do," I added, and Mom's expression softened at that.

"It would," she replied.

"And it's not like doing it would negate having your own kids if you did decide you wanted them one day," Dove added. "Not that you do. Just saying. I think it's really sweet that their baby would have some of Finch's genes too."

I gave my sister a grin. Dove had always been on my team. She was the first person that I'd told I was ace. She, too, was demisexual and had been incredibly supportive of me in my coming out. Still, despite that, I hadn't told anyone else in the family. They already knew that I was trans and were super supportive of me as I continually updated my pronouns from he/him to he/they to they/he to they/them, letting me test the waters and explore my gender identity with unfailing encouragement. And while I hadn't explicitly told them that I was currently flirting with a shift, they/she, I knew that they'd have my back no matter what. Having queer older siblings had certainly helped pave the way for me as I grew into my identity and my understanding of myself. But it felt unnecessary to come out to them again as ace. I'd probably never have a partner, and it just felt like a whole new hurdle to explain myself about.

"You can't be a sperm donor without consulting me," Crane chimed in, pulling my focus back to the conversation.

"No offense, Crane, but you weren't in the running for consideration," Finch quipped, and my twin held a hand to his chest like he'd just been punched.

"Ouch."

"I absolutely do not need your permission," I replied to my twin. "I can choose to be a donor if I want to."

"But we're identical, so it's basically like my biological child too," Crane argued.

"Because otherwise you wouldn't have been related?" Finch asked, arching her eyebrow quizzically.

"And you would've been a real jerk to your niece or nephew or nibbling if it wasn't biologically yours, huh?" Hawk asked as Crane helped Simon unwrap a Hershey's kiss from the bowl on the table.

"That's not what I meant," Crane muttered.

"There's time to think about it," Dove said to Frankie, giving her a sympathetic look. "It's good to have options."

She groaned. "Time is running out."

"You're only 36," Dove countered.

"That's considered geriatric pregnancy already," Frankie replied. "We wanted to save up the money and have time together to ourselves first, and now it just seems like maybe we waited too long and—"

"I was in my forties when the twins and Wren were born," Mom replied in her normal, calming way. "Every person is different. Every family is different."

The table laughed as Lark and Logan's video footage turned shaky as they chased their two-year-old around the kitchen island.

"Well, the offer stands," I said with a shrug.

"Thank you," Finch mouthed across the table to me.

Aside from Crane, the rest of my siblings seemed surprisingly unflustered by the offer. We'd seen all kinds of families within our own zoo, both humans and animals alike. We were used to all sorts of different ways of rearing young and creating family groups. I kind of loved the idea that I could help my sisters in that way.

"Okay, what about this one?" Simon said, holding out a photo from Crane's phone that he had slyly passed his nephew.

"You've got to say the thing," Crane whispered to Simon, nudging him with his elbow.

"It's feces but what species?" Simon declared as he waved around the photo of what was clearly kangaroo poo.

All of us dutifully hemmed and hawed, making a show of it, guessing a few incorrect animals to his delight before circling around to the kangaroos.

Crane ruffled our nephew's hair. "We'll make a keeper out of you yet."

"Speaking of which." Dove blotted her lips and cleared her throat, pulling our attention to her. "We've had over three hundred applications for our new conservation challenge reality series. I think *Conservation Keepers* is going to be a hit show."

"That's just the working title," Deacon cut in. "Netflix is workshopping some catchier ones with test audiences right now."

"Why did you have to make it a reality show?" I grumbled. "It just feels so Madigan-ish."

Deacon leaned into the table to look at me. "We will be following the pairs of keepers as they compete in different challenges at conservation charities around the globe. Think more *Crocodile Hunter* less *Below Deck*."

"And the winner gets a million dollars to split amongst those charities and their zoo," Dove added, and everyone gaped at her. A million dollars? I didn't realize the show had that kind of budget.

"Viewers can vote and donate to the charities directly too. So even the contestants that don't win will get a really great fundraising boost," Deacon continued, practically vibrating with excitement. "This is how we raise awareness. This is how we get people invested in conservation, by putting faces to these organizations."

"It's such a brilliant idea," Mom opined.

I liked the idea of highlighting conservation charities, but still I wrinkled my nose. "So long as there are no fake animal escapes to boost ratings like the Madigans used to do. There's not going to be, like, *Real Housewives* taglines and melodrama, is there?"

"Oh, come on, please let there be a little melodrama?" Hannah pleaded. "Like, at least one of the pairs has to bicker all the time and another has to have off-the-charts chemistry."

"It's going to be entertaining while still keeping the focus on conservation," Dove said diplomatically.

"And *I'm* going to be the star," Crane announced proudly.

"Only if you have a good enough application," Dove reminded. "Are you sure you don't want to have another crack at your essay before the deadline?"

Crane's face twisted. "You're not going to include your own brother in your show?"

"Not if my own brother doesn't take it seriously and doesn't present himself as the best possible candidate," Dove countered. "No nepo-bros allowed."

Crane pouted for a second but said, "Yeah, and I respect you for it, dammit." He swirled a piece of bread in the fondue and took another bite. "Alright, I'll have one more attempt at the essay, and if it's awesome, you have to pair me up with the second-best applicant so that we can win this thing and bring it home for Prickle Island Zoo."

"Deal," Dove said with a wink.

"For Prickle Island Zoo," Hawk added, putting on his silly dad voice and raising a glass in cheers.

"For Prickle Island Zoo," the rest of us cheered.

Chapter Sixteen

Hollis

After my terrible run-in with John, I was resigned for the next day to be equally terrible. It was my first on the carnivore team, and I was prepared for it to be as awkward, clunky, and embarrassing as normal.

But it wasn't.

I had stilted relationships with my coworkers at the best of times, so imagine my surprise when Hawk and I seemed to instantly hit it off. He liked to work mostly in silence, which was perfect, valuing more someone who could get the job done than someone who could carry on a good conversation. And I suspected since he'd just had John shadowing him for the better part of the week, he was grateful for the quiet. Still, the times we did talk were easy. It was as if he already spoke my language, and I wondered if it was because he was Heron's brother and Heron and I seemed to be birds of a feather.

You fit in here. With us. Maybe that hadn't just been a nicety after all.

A lot of the volunteers and other staff members seemed to think that Hawk had a grumpy, surly disposition, but I didn't see that at all. He had quiet focus. He was driven, sure, but whenever his kids and wife showed up, he turned into a goofy teddy bear. I didn't think the guy had a grumpy bone in his body.

The carnivores were interesting, albeit far smellier than the hoofstock animals. Nothing like starting the day off cleaning up day-old raw meat riddled with maggots to really get the blood pumping. No poop stunk like carnivore poop either. But neither of those things was the reason I missed hoofstock, nor was it the savannah animals, but rather the person who took care of them.

Heron had an addictive sort of magical buzz about them, as if the EMF meter in my brain started beeping whenever I got within a single pace of them. I just wanted to stay near to them, just wanted to keep that buzz tingling across my skin. And I missed our conversations too—something I never thought I would miss. I didn't like talking to people. But turned out, it had to be the right person, Heron mainly, and especially about our special interests, which varied from wildlife research to K-dramas to watching makeup review videos even though neither of us normally wore anything other than tinted SPF.

"Did you see that article about those new anti-poaching dogs at that rhino charity?" I offered to Hawk as we squeegeed the viewing windows inside the cheetah enclosure.

"You sound just like Heron." He chuckled to himself. "I haven't seen it, but it sounds interesting. Ronny isn't catching me up on the latest research as often these days now that they've moved to their boat." Hawk didn't sound particularly pleased about his younger sibling living on the water.

"What kind of boat is it?"

Hawk paused the squeegee halfway down to arch his brow at me. "What kind of boat is it? I don't know, like, the floats on water kind."

I let out a half laugh at that. "Is it a sailboat, a fishing boat, a catamaran, a bowrider, a deck boat, a cabin cruiser?"

"I have no idea what half of those mean." Hawk shook his head. "How do you know so much about boats?"

"My dad," I said with a sigh.

My dad had bought his dream boat the year I was born—an ocean clipper with a stepped hull, furling mast, self-tacking jib, and large hull portholes that streamed sunlight into the customized mahogany interiors. She'd been named *The Wyoming* and held a special spot in my heart. My happy place, *The Wyoming* had been the location of all my favorite child-hood memories. Every single weekend and school vacation, we'd take the boat out and sail around the coast. The best sleeps of my life had all taken place aboard. It had been the one time when I hadn't felt anxious, when all my thoughts had been lulled by the rocking waves and rustling wind. I'd been very confident that *The Wyoming* had been my dad's favorite child too, his prized possession, and the only topic he ever could carry on a long conversation about. *But no, my dad was definitely not neurodivergent, nope!*

"I didn't peg you as a boat person," Hawk said, pulling my thoughts back from my memories.

"No?"

"I didn't think there was much of a sailing culture in Wyoming."

My face instantly flushed. "Oh, yeah, well, you know, there are enthusiasts everywhere, I guess."

Say something more convincing, Hollis!

But Hawk took the statement at face value. "Heron's boat was apparently very expensive about twenty years ago, but the previous owners abandoned it in the marina without its engines so it's basically just a floating bedroom for Heron, and not a very good one at that. *The Farrier*, it's called, the perfect name for you if you ever had a boat, huh?"

I gave Hawk a quizzical look. "Why?"

"Didn't you grow up with horses?"

"Yeah . . ."

"So, *The Farrier*."

"Because horses are fair?" I dragged the words out, trying to piece together what in the world he was talking about.

"No, farrier, like the person who works doing horse hoof stuff." He waved his hand around like that would help me work it out.

"Ohhhhh." I nodded vigorously. "Yes, of course."

Shit, Hollis. You don't have to be a horse expert to remember what a fricking farrier is!

I really needed to smooth out the bumps in my backstory. No more talk of boats. What was next, lobster boils and summer beach trips?

I decided it was better if Hawk and I returned to our silent work. Talking only led to trouble. But I did make a mental note to go to the top of the zoo where I could peer down at the marina and see if I could figure out which boat was *The Farrier*.

Animal research nerd *and* boat life enthusiast? Damn. Heron Lachlan very well might be my perfect person. That thought made my stomach clench.

It's just a crush. A stupid, fleeting crush, I coached myself, as if that would do anything.

I really wished I could turn all those dopey, heart-eyed hormones off. It would make my life so much easier. What was the point of even having crushes if the person I had a crush on and I were entirely incompatible? But Heron and I *were* compatible, apart from one thing: the fact that I didn't want to have sex, not ever, not even for a partner I loved. Which filled me with guilt and shame because it felt selfish and wrong to not want to give that to a partner. But I was so damn tired of trying to please other people at the expense of myself.

I wanted to claim it, say it with my whole chest: I didn't like sex. I didn't like the sensations, I didn't like the body fluids, I didn't like the sounds, I didn't like the logistics of trying to figure out how to move and sound and act and the facial expressions I should make, and the whole thing was a literal nightmare. I didn't like any of it. I didn't want to touch myself when I was alone either. Even though the sensation of an orgasm was fine in the moment, it made my stomach feel sick and restlessly anxious from being so overstimulated afterwards. Some ace people were like me, but still, I often felt like I was in my own little corner of the ace spectrum that made me incompatible with just about everyone.

Why, dear sweet queer goddess, couldn't I be aromantic? Why must I long to be compatible with someone when I knew I never would be? There was no one for me.

Not even gorgeous animal nerds who lived on boats.

Chapter Seventeen

Heron

John was only beneficial for one task, lifting heavy things, and that would've been good enough were it not for his mouth. The guy never shut up, not for a single second. He nattered away about everything, especially the dullest things. Man, did this guy love dull topics, and it made me miss Hollis more and more with every passing second.

It would be crazy to text Hawk and ask how she was doing, right?

I'd completely tuned John out as I hosed down the crush after weighing Scarlet, when I heard Hollis's name on his lips.

I released the hose nozzle, quieting the room so I could actually hear him. "What?"

He had a broom covered in clumps of hay slung over his shoulder, scattering more behind him than he managed to clean up. "Yeah, I know, right?" he said, looking like a zookeeper chimney sweep.

"No, sorry, I didn't hear you," I corrected. "What did you say about Hollis?"

"She said she doesn't date coworkers," he informed me. "What a rule. Every zoo I've worked at was like an episode of *Love Island*. Everyone hooks up with everyone. Maybe she's religious. Do you think she's religious? I mean, she's from Wyoming. Does that mean anything?"

Jesus, he really never shut up. And for all his rambling, he still never got to the fucking point. What I really wanted to know was how his conversation with Hollis had come about. It didn't seem like a very Hollis thing to do to just offer up that information out of nowhere.

Had John ambushed her with questions about her dating life? I could imagine her saying the first thing she could to get him to back off. John didn't strike me as the sort of guy who could take a hint, considering I'd turned the music up to ear-splitting levels, cranked up the pressure washer, made us do our food prep next to a flock of squawking parrots all in an effort to drown him out, and the second the sound had stopped, he'd still been going.

"She also told me she wasn't flirting with me." John snorted. "Can you believe that? As if I didn't already know that. I mean —" He waved himself up and down as if he were a Greek statue and not just a normal, oafish looking man. "I *know* when women are flirting with me. She's an odd one, isn't she?"

"I think she's great," I said instantly, anger cresting in me like a wave.

It was unprofessional under the best of circumstances to speak about a coworker like this. I also found it kind of disrespectful the way John treated me all bro-y, something I suspected he wouldn't do if he had any respect for my gender. John saw me as a cis man, that much was clear. It suddenly made me unsettled, like maybe I should've shaved that morning, my five o'clock shadow signaling that I clearly wasn't as fem-presenting as I wanted. The difference between who I was in my mind and who I looked like in the mirror had never felt more disconnected than when men like John treated me like "one of the guys."

John rolled his eyes. "God, you sound like Diego. You two are both obsessed with the black-sheep ones, aren't you?"

"It's the ones who aren't odd that we look out for around here," I added pointedly, which was the closest I'd come to menace in a long time. I wasn't particularly good at defending myself, but for some reason, when it came to Hollis, I didn't think I could hold my tongue.

"Did you see that gift-shop worker with the green hair?" John held his hands up to his chest, miming two giant breasts.

"John," I cut in, about ready to implode. "Take the buckets down to the kitchen and wash them. I'm going to take the logbook down to the education room."

"Oh, I was hoping to shadow while you—"

"Unfortunately, we're running behind," I declared, turning off the hoses and opening the back gate. "If we're faster tomorrow, we can do it."

"Oh, okay. Sounds good, man."

Man. Awesome.

I balled my hands into fists by my sides. I wasn't a man. I was non-binary, for fuck's sake. It shouldn't matter how I looked. It wasn't that hard to not punctuate every sentence with man and bro and just treat me like a human fucking being.

But instead of sticking up for myself and putting him in his place, I said, "See you tomorrow." And I practically fled out of the enclosure as John gave me a thumbs-up. I knew I needed to be better about defending myself, but I hated confrontation, and I always ended up crying in arguments, and then it made it even harder to have the other person listen to me because I would be blubbering angry tears.

Maybe I should send him a strongly worded email and CC my mother in. *Yeah, that'll show him—hiding behind my mom's skirts.* I shouldn't let someone like John carry on speaking the way he'd been, though, either. But my face flushed and my vision swam and my ears rang, and I couldn't bring myself to do anything other than get myself out of there. If it had just been me he'd been disrespecting, I might've not fished out my phone, but thinking of what he'd said about Hollis and the front staffer had me dialing Hawk.

He answered on the second ring. "Hey. What's up?"

I was out of breath, holding back the angry tears welling in my eyes. I sniffed, trying to hide the wobble in my voice as I kept thinking of all the things I should've said to John. "I don't want you to hire John."

"What, why?"

"He's just . . . I . . . He's . . ." I let out a frustrated breath, trying to find the words. A sleazeball? A douchebag?

"Ronny, what's going on?" I heard Hawk's chair squeak as he stood, concern filling his voice. "Are you okay?"

"I'm fine. Really," I replied, pushing more calm into my voice. The last thing I needed was Hawk storming off and punching the guy on my behalf, no matter how satisfying that would be. "I just don't think you should hire him. We don't want him sticking around after the summer. He's . . ."

"Not gelling with the company culture?" Hawk offered.

"Yeah."

"Okay," he hedged, clearing his throat. "I'll take that into consideration."

"Thank you."

I had a feeling Hawk was in the presence of other people judging by the corporate jargon, but I appreciated the support, nevertheless.

"You okay?" Crane asked, intercepting me as I cut across the reptile house. "You're all red and blotchy. Did you eat one of Frankie's curry puffs? Because those are seriously spicy."

"Yeah, I . . ." I pulled up short when Hollis rounded the corner behind Crane, carrying the carnivore team buckets. "You're right. It was just the curry puffs. I, uh, gotta go grab something from the boat."

I veered off at a sharp right-hand turn, abandoning my current plan and heading home instead.

Chapter Eighteen

Hollis

The evening summer air swirled around me, the sun only just now starting to dip toward the horizon as we neared the longest day of the year. I let my thoughts wander along with me as I drifted back to the house. A takeout bag swung in my loose grip, holding a greasy burger from the Salty Dog that I was looking forward to eating alone in a baggy T-shirt while I watched ASMR videos of people camping with their dogs.

Yep. This was the good life.

I was starting to find that balance. The days filled with staff and visitors were countered with my quiet solo dinners where I didn't need to hear anyone chewing and I could just decompress with my latest comfort show. John and Diego had given up trying to invite me out, and I was old enough now that I didn't feel guilty for introverting without explanation or apology. I'd finally accepted that I needed alone time at the end of a long day. It made waking up and being around people during work hours much easier, and I was starting to relish the duality of both. I actually really liked people in controlled and limited doses, so long as I had my quiet time too.

This might work, I thought. *Maybe I will be able to do this after all.*

It was during my sparkly reverie about what life on Prickle Island could look like that something snagged my attention and those whimsical thoughts blew away like clouds on a windy day. I halted abruptly, spying the last two people I ever thought I'd see spilling out of Johnny's Rockin' Candy Emporium: my parents.

"No!" I exclaimed, wishing I could melt into the pavement right then and there.

All of the lightheartedness I'd found over the last week evaporated. In the machinations of daily zoo life, I'd completely forgotten that I'd lied to my employer. *Shit!* Did I really think I could bury the truth of my past forever?

The answer: yes.

I was quiet and standoffish enough that people normally left me alone. I'd gotten by at one job for nearly a year before the guest services team had even asked my name. Another job had nicknamed me Eeyore—a cutting moniker that had unfortunately stuck. No one had been asking my favorite color or what shows I was watching . . . No one until I'd moved here and met all of the Lachlans. It was like my whole life, I hadn't known I'd been speaking another language, and then I'd come to Prickle Island and they were all fluent in it. The relief was incredible, the sense of feeling seen and understood growing day by day. I hadn't thought I'd actually make friends with the people here and want to talk about my life with them. And now, I was going to be in such deep shit.

Goodbye good job, goodbye belonging.

"Mom, Dad, what are you doing here?" I rushed down the street toward them and ushered them into the shade of the awning, as if that would do anything to hide us.

"We wanted to come see you at your new job," Mom said with a practiced smile that she always used in public. "We had a long weekend and we thought we'd drive down. We're staying at this gorgeous little B&B—"

"And you didn't think to tell me first?"

Mom waved away my concern just like she did with everything. "I know you don't like surprises but—"

This was one of the many things that a psychologist had spent *years* helping me work through. My dislike for surprises wasn't just neurotypical distaste. It threw my whole routine out of whack—the system I'd created to feel safe and capable of navigating a hostile world. I liked to rehearse my routines, recheck my calendars every morning, relive my plans throughout the day so that I knew what was coming and when. It made me feel steady, anchored, even in an unpredictable reality. When those plans were suddenly—*and unnecessarily*—disrupted, it made my whole brain turn to static. My skin felt like it was crawling and a wave of nausea crested within me, my body wishing I could bolt from my parents as I reeled.

"It's not a big deal, hon," was all my mom said to reassure me.

"Oh, okay, great then," I snarked, rubbing my eyes and trying to ignore the pricking sensation that preceded tears. "Well, if you say it's not a big deal, then I'll just notify my entire nervous system."

Mom rolled her eyes and gave Dad an exasperated look, like I was the problem. "You are so dramatic."

Angry is what I am. So angry that she had once again put me in this position. I bit down on the inside of my cheek as my eyes welled, refusing to cry in front of them. Then they'd just call me sensitive and lecture me about needing a thick skin, as if it were just a switch I could flip, as if I could just rewire my entire brain. No. Tears were the last thing I needed.

"Listen," I said, focusing on steadying my breathing as I tried to recalibrate. "I'm really happy to see you." I hid my grimace as my parents bought the lie. "How about we all go out to lunch tomorrow? I know a great place and—"

"You're not going to show us around your zoo?" Mom blustered.

"It's not *my* zoo," I amended, hoping she'd get caught up in the semantics. She loved correcting my details, after all.

Mom laughed and waved like I'd just been telling a hilarious joke. "We still want to see it."

"I'll be working." I tried desperately to keep a leash on my mounting frustration. My mind had already played out the end of this conversation a million different ways and none of them had ended particularly well. "I unfortunately won't be able to show you around while I'm working, but lunch—"

"You can take a break to show your parents—"

"I can't take a break!" I erupted, and Dad gave me a chastising look like *I* was once again being dramatic. I lowered my voice. "I'm doing a three-month internship, and at the end of it, only two of us get a job, and I need to be proving myself to them and—"

"Isn't it a family run zoo?" Mom countered. "I'm sure they'd love that you are taking time off for your family. It shows you understand their company culture."

I hated that she was probably right. Still, the last thing I needed was Dad wandering around giving my coworkers updates on *The Wyoming* and showing them pictures of the new cockpit leatherwork like he was more of a proud parent to the boat than he was of his own child.

"Listen, I love you both very much and I'm excited you're here. I just—"

"Hollis, hi!" I knew who it was before I even turned, and my stomach plummeted through my boots. Evelyn Lachlan, matriarch and CEO of Prickle Island Zoo, emerged from the flower store we were hiding in front of, a bouquet of daisies balanced on her popped hip.

"Hollis?" Mom muttered as Evelyn waved warmly and wandered over. "Why is she calling you Hollis, Holly?"

I cringed at my real name on Mom's lips. I hadn't been Holly since I'd been twenty-one and freshly graduated from college. The name Hollis had just felt so much more exciting and quirky and different than the twenty other Hollys in my grade year. It better embodied how I saw myself too. So unbeknownst to my parents, I'd changed it to Hollis on my first ever job application—an unpaid volunteer position at a local wildlife park—and had listed it as my preferred name on forms and documents ever since. It was how I denoted time: the people who knew me as Holly and the people who knew me as Hollis.

"Please, please just play along," I whisper-hissed, and Mom rolled her eyes as if she expected nothing less from me. I turned to Evelyn and offered a too-broad smile that I had a feeling mirrored my mother's own. "Mrs. Lachlan—"

"Evie, please," she corrected me.

"Evie," I amended. "These are my parents, Tom and Sheila."

"Oh my goodness," Evie said, delighted, as she swapped the bouquet of flowers to shake both their hands. "It's a pleasure to meet you. How long are you in town for?"

"Just the long weekend."

"Oh, well you must come over to our house for dinner on Sunday," Evie offered. "We do a big family fondue dinner, pasta, salad, all sorts. My daughter-in-law is a chef and she does the most amazing garlic knots and cakes. Oh, and we should get you on a giraffe encounter while you're here—"

"Oh, that's alright," Mom replied. "We're not really animal people."

My chest constricted as Evie furrowed her brow, looking between my parents and me.

"But don't you live on a—"

"Dinner would be lovely!" I cut in, my heart beatboxing in my throat. "Thanks so much, Evie."

Evelyn Lachlan was pure class and gracefully allowed me to pivot the conversation away from the awkward exchange. I knew my face was beet red as she said, "Wonderful! I look forward to getting to chat more. We'll see you at my house at six." She looked at my parents. "Enjoy your stay on Prickle Island."

The three of us waved with grimacing smiles as she wandered off. I waited until she had ducked into the bakery and was out of earshot to turn to my parents and say, "We don't like animals? You seriously had to say you don't like animals to one of the most preeminent conservationists in the entire country?"

"What?" Mom shrugged. "It's true. You kids always wanted pets growing up, but I knew it would be me picking up the poop and sweeping hair off the floor and having to feed them every day." She wrinkled her nose, and I held in the desire to reply that doing those tasks was literally part of my job now. "Not interested."

It took everything in me to not inform my mother that her bluntness was yet another perfect example of her neurodivergence manifesting, also her lack of consideration of my needs, her inflexibility in her plans, the fact that when I'd gone in for a hug upon greeting her, she'd taken a step away as if hugging your mother was inappropriate, and a bunch of other inane rules that she had decided were how things "should" be done.

"We are going to come up with some sort of stomach bug for you two," I informed them, my mind racing to come up with a solution. There was no way I could let them have a whole conversation with the Lachlans. "And you are going to kindly decline the dinner offer and then go home."

Mom narrowed her eagle eyes at me like. "What mess have you gotten yourself into this time, Holly?"

And there was the disappointment. Great. That was parent disaster bingo for me. The prize? Another year of being the least favorite child.

I was twenty-seven and they still viewed me as a perpetual fuckup. It didn't matter that I was smart and hard-working and dedicated. I was the "difficult one," and that was the brush they'd always choose to paint me with.

"I think fondue sounds nice," Dad said, his only contribution to the conversation. And I hated that Mom and I gave him the same exasperated look. "Maybe we should do a cheese night out in Milton Bay this summer."

Longing tugged behind my navel, and I wished I could go along for the trip, but I also knew that meant enduring a weekend stranded on a boat with my parents. I couldn't exactly ask my dad to let me take *The Wyoming* out on my own, and I already knew he'd never let me, even if I could manage it solo. Not his baby.

Maybe I should charter a boat just to get that longing out of my system? *With what time and what money?*

Mom snapped her fingers in front of me, instantly knowing when I was zoning out.

"What?"

"We are not going to lie to bail you out of whatever mistake you've made this time," she declared. "We were invited to dinner and you accepted, so now we have to go." There was that rigid thinking again. I knew there was no talking her out of it. My mom would rather chew her arm off than play hooky. She was a rule follower to a fault, and that meant we *had* to go.

I groaned, rubbing a hand down my face.

I was in such deep shit.

Chapter Nineteen

Heron

I wandered down to the education room that abutted the lemur enclosure. Using my keycard to open the building, I grabbed for the right rusty, old key on my carabiner to unlock the office door that had been built into the side of the lemur exhibit. I could see visitors on the other side, but they couldn't see me with the one-way glass camouflaged to look like plants. A crowd was watching two of the young lemurs playing toward the front of the exhibit, others pointing excitedly when they found more of the troop in different spots around the space.

But there was one lemur in particular that I was hoping had heard the click of the office door opening.

Sure enough, Henry the lemur came over to the window and waited for me to open it. This office was always closed as an external air lock to the enclosure. The window had technically meant to be permanently sealed when the enclosure had been built on to the preexisting building. But every zoo had its secrets and this window was mine and Crane's. When Crane had been finishing the enclosure, he'd left one window unglued so we could sit in the office pretending to do desk work and really spend time cuddling Henry instead.

The now elderly lemur, Henry, waited patiently for me on the other side of the glass. He pressed his fluffy face to the forested decals, needing to press up directly to the tinted window to confirm that I was, indeed, inside. He'd become one of our hand-reared black-and-white ruff lemurs after he'd been rejected by his mother. Even now, reintegrated into the group, he still liked to come down for the occasional cuddle and armpit scratch. All of our lemurs were friendly, but Henry was special. He wasn't as flighty and far more eager for human affection than the others. It made him a great animal ambassador, and he was a popular feature of the education team's programs, coming out to sit on a perch during class visits and wandering around the circle eating grapes out of the hands of excited school children.

But when Henry had the choice of who to go to, he always picked me, and for that, he was my favorite animal at the zoo. It was something special, not only when keepers had their favorite animals, but when animals had their favorite keepers too. And even though I wasn't on the primate team, Henry and I were still besties.

I sat in the desk chair and turned on the computer monitor as my alibi before reaching up and unlatching the window over my head. Henry hopped through before I could even relatch it. I unzipped my polar fleece halfway and Henry climbed in, snuggling between the warm lining and my cotton T-shirt. I booted the old computer at the desk and started inputting the morning observations from my physical logbook into the digital files while Henry slept in my jacket.

My fuzzy hot water bottle fell asleep instantly, as if he'd been waiting for this opportunity to nap all morning. I decided I would stay and work through lunch, needing to do something to keep my mind distracted.

I missed Hollis.

I shouldn't miss someone I'd only known a week, someone who was still right here, someone I could see whenever I wanted if I just asked her to hang out sometime. But would she want that?

"Stop," I groaned aloud to my spiraling thoughts.

My mind deflated more and more as I sat there. The feeling of Henry's little chest rising and falling against mine was my only comfort.

Longing grew in me as I tapped away at the keyboard. A strange kind of loneliness I couldn't quite name. I wished I could cuddle up with someone in the evenings, watching TV shows, talking about our days, sharing the latest animal research study, and info-dumping our latest special interests with each other. I liked the idea of sharing my life with someone, even though I felt like I had enough people to share it with already. But now, with Dove in France and Crane most likely going away next year, I was beginning to feel lonely even surrounded by family. Maybe lonely wasn't the right word. Maybe there were different kinds of loneliness. Maybe I'd suddenly unlocked a new one—something I hadn't ever known to be wary of before right now.

The door to the office jostled open and Mom poked her head in, giving me only a split second to hastily zip up my fleece and duck behind the monitor that half-obscured me from the door.

"I thought I saw the light on," Mom said as she gave a little wave to me. "Are the computers in the break room not working again? I think we might need to ask Kirby to come look at them. She told me the last IT guy really ripped us off."

"Did he rip us off, or did he have a lot to fix because Kirby messed up the entire computer system thinking she was a programmer after watching one YouTube video?" I countered.

"If it's not the computers, then what are you doing in here?"

"I was just putting my obvs in and the other monitors were taken up in the break room by summer staff members. That's all."

She nodded. "Okay." She nearly ducked back out when her head popped back in and she added, "Oh, just so you know, Hollis's parents are going to join us for Sunday Funday Fondue Day."

"Her parents?" I asked, surprised. And that surprise made Henry jostle in my sweater. I cleared my throat to cover the sound, twisting so his little hand didn't peek above my neckline. "I didn't know they were on the island."

Mom shrugged. "Visiting for the long weekend."

"Okay," I hedged. "And why did you think I should know about it?"

Her eyes narrowed, and I couldn't tell if she was detecting a hidden lemur or certain unspoken feelings for Hollis. "Why wouldn't I tell you?"

"I don't know."

Her eyes narrowed. "Okay."

"Okay."

She started to duck her head out again when our radios went off. "Primates to all units," Hannah said. "Whoever has borrowed Henry, please return him before the summer camp visit at 2 pm."

Mom looked at me in silence, like she was waiting for me to confess. But our staring contest was interrupted by a fluffy tail emerging from the neckline of my fleece.

She picked up her radio. "Roger, Heron's got him."

I gaped at her. "How long did you know?"

Mom gave me a maternal if not slightly patronizing look as she said, "The second I saw the light on in the office."

And with a grin, she shut the door and left me to my lemur therapy.

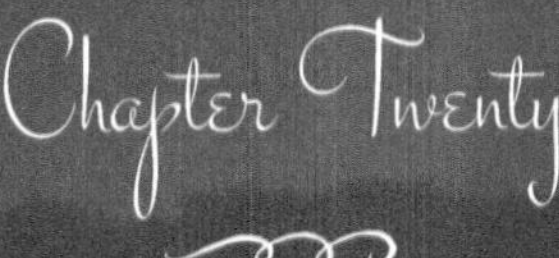

Hollis

I was coiled like a live fucking wire sitting between Crane and Heron with my parents across from me. I kept staring daggers at them as I ducked and dodged around everyone's attempts at polite conversation with them, plying them with food and wine, attempting to keep them quiet.

My dad mentioned *The Wyoming* only once, and his quiet mumbling meant that I could translate it to mean the state and not the boat. Still, the mental gymnastics were exhausting, especially with the weighty, disapproving stare from my mother all evening.

Fortunately, I had the mayhem of the Lachlan family to rely upon. Even with Dove and Deacon now gone for France, the table was brimming with people and food. Frankie's garlic knots were seriously to die for, but even for all its deliciousness, the food soured in my stomach with all the added nerves.

"How are you liking the carnivores?" Heron asked, leaning in to me, and my skin warmed with their closeness.

"It's good," I replied, still listening in to the conversation across the table just in case I needed to jump in.

"Yeah," Crane chimed in, leaning in from the other side. "But you're *really* excited to be on the reptiles team with me, aren't you?"

"Yep," Heron said, leaning an affectionate shoulder into mine, and it made me buzz with their proximity again. "She has reptile nerd written all over her."

I laughed as I nodded down to the chameleon-print dress I was wearing. "How can you tell?"

"Ah, to be seen is to be loved." Crane clinked his glass with mine. "To the reptile nerds."

"You always were obsessed with lizards," Mom added, jumping into our conversation. "You brought all sorts of random creatures into the house when you were little."

"Now *that* I can certainly relate to," Evie said, raising a glass of wine to the room.

A smattering of wine glasses and vintage soda bottles lifted in the air.

"You always said you were going to be a scientist," Mom continued, and my cheeks burned. I hoped I could slow her down. "Remember when you decided to dress up as Jane Goodall for Halloween that one year?"

"My daughter's middle name is Goodall," Evie added merrily, giving me a wink.

"Not Jane?" Mom suggested, and my attempt to kick her under the table went rogue and I kicked Hawk instead.

"Sorry," I whispered.

"Don't worry about it," Hawk replied.

Heron leaned into me again, and I secretly hoped that they

were doing it on purpose, finding the proximity just as addictive as I did. "Happens all the time at this dinner table."

"What's your middle name?" I asked them.

"Hanna."

"As in Jack Hanna?"

"Yep."

"So it must just be a zookeeper thing," Mom said with a laugh. "See, honey? They're all quirky," she added, and I felt it coming before I could stop her. "It doesn't mean you're atypical or whatever."

"Mom," I gritted out. "Please don't."

"Oh no," Finch chimed in, blotting her mouth with a napkin. "We're all neurodivergent." She looked up and down the table. "Yep, over half of us are officially diagnosed, but of course, self-diagnosis is also valid."

"This is a very neuro-affirming household," Evie added with a grin.

"You can't be serious," Mom said, and I tried to kick her again. Heat rose in my face as I battled between the urge to cry or flee or scream. "You all seem fine. You can have friendly conversations. You have jobs. You—"

"That's actually—"

"Everyone has their problems," Mom bulldozed over Evie. "It doesn't mean—"

"Mom—" She was literally insulting every single person sat around this table, and now she was cutting off and raising her voice to my boss. My face burned, my heart raced, and my vision began to tunnel like I might pass out.

I knew it was deep denial and shame and her inability to see how inappropriate this outburst was, but I had not a single shred of sympathy for her in that moment, not as she'd stormed into my life determined to ruin it.

My mom's brows dropped low as she pounded a fist on the table, looking incensed by the accusations that I could be anything other than the child she had decided I would be. "You don't know what you're talking about. My daughter is normal—"

"Hey!" Heron barked, and the entire table attempting to talk over each other and appease the situation froze. I'd never heard them angry, never heard them raise their voice, never seen them lose that easy calm as they rose to standing and glared at my parents. "If you're going to insult my entire family and yours, maybe it would be better if you leave."

"Heron," Evie said gently, forcing more calm into her voice to pull Heron back into themself. "It's alright."

"It's not alright," they growled, keeping their gaze glued to my mother. "It's not alright to say these things to your kid. It's not alright to do this to her, let alone in front of everyone like this. It's *not* alright."

Mom's mouth fell open. "Excuse me?"

"Come on, Mom." I stood, tears welling in my eyes, desperate for this moment to end. "I'll walk you guys out."

Shame and embarrassment burned in me anew. I walked them to the door and mouthed, "I'm sorry," to Evelyn, stealing one heartbroken look at Heron before heading out.

Apparently, I didn't need to spill any secrets to ruin my life. Nope. My parents had managed to do it without any talk of horse ranches, just their own ableist nonsense. I wanted to rage at them. I wanted to tell them that they'd screwed me over. That they'd insulted my employer. That they'd deeply hurt my feelings, but I couldn't summon the will to speak.

When the flood waters of overwhelm rose in me like this, everything shut down except the ability to get from point A to point B. The world was a thing happening to me, not something I was a part of anymore. I just let their words wash over me, unable to argue or defend myself as I walked them to the back gate and used my keycard to let them out. I let the weighted door clang shut in between us, effectively locking my parents on the other side. Mom was still ranting, but she sounded under water to me. I couldn't even make out her words. I turned and walked away as she shouted after me for a minute, her voice piercing but unintelligible to my ears. I just needed to get away, somewhere quiet and safe.

I wandered through the zoo, grateful for the silence and the nature and chill on the ocean breeze against my cheeks. I plopped myself down on the bench beside Kangaroo Point, dropped my head into my hands, and cried. That wave of emotions finally crested and roared toward the shoreline, purging itself out of my throat. Burning, salty tears dripped down my cheeks and collected like rainfall around my boots. I didn't know how many minutes passed before my senses started to come back to me, the lap of ocean waves, the rustle of the trees, the chirp of crickets.

Then, I heard the scuffle of boots, and when I looked up, Heron was standing there.

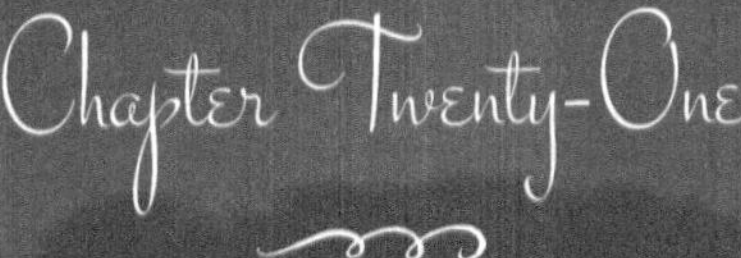

Chapter Twenty-One

Hollis

Heron bit their bottom lip, hands in fists by their sides, but as soon as my watery eyes met theirs, they asked, "Is it okay if I give you a hug?"

I didn't have the words but nodded. Normally, I wouldn't want someone to touch me when I was melting down, but Heron was different. They felt like a safe space, someone the walls around my mind always seemed to come down for.

In one swift movement, Heron sat beside me on the bench and wrapped me up in their arms. Their strength surprised me, the firmness of the hold like a swaddle around me, and I hadn't realized how cool my skin had become until I felt their warmth. How good it felt to be wrapped in their arms. That steady pressure, that anchoring to the world, to my senses, to them.

It was like they knew exactly what I needed in that moment,

knew exactly how to spool me back into myself. I'd never once let anyone help me come back down like that, had never even known what to ask for, what I needed. So whenever the world got too much and I felt like imploding, I'd flee to a quiet, safe space if there was one or a public bathroom at worst and find my way back to myself on my own.

But this was so much better.

Here, wrapped up in their strong arms, their chest rising and falling against mine in slow breaths that seemed to coax mine to slow as well, I felt the tension ease more and more, the spikiness of my senses dulling, the assault of emotions steadying until I could finally speak.

"I'm sorry my parents are such assholes," I murmured into their fleece-clad shoulder.

Their arms lifted and fell in a silent laugh, making my cheek bob along with the movement. "I'm sorry your parents are assholes too." A long pause passed as their hands splayed across my back. "But you're welcome to borrow my family whenever you'd like."

We chuckled, our bodies shaking against each other. Grips loosened, my hand circling Heron's back and theirs sweeping up and down mine in comforting strokes. But as my senses came back to me, so did my nerves. And as we held each other, my anxiety found a new foothold. I started to think that maybe this intimacy might somehow be misconstrued.

Maybe they'd think of it as meaning something it didn't. Maybe I'd have to explain myself to them. Maybe I needed to more firmly explain to them that despite having a crush, we couldn't be more than friends. But all of those thoughts kind of silenced as Heron said, "I'm watching this TV show right now where comedians are put in a room and they aren't allowed to laugh."

"What?"

They released me and shifted to lean against the bench. "It always makes me feel better watching it."

"Oh."

"Do you want to maybe have some tea and watch YouTube videos together for a while? I mean, most of my siblings have more fun forms of comforting each other, but mine's pretty subdued."

My lips twisted into a grin. "What are these fun forms you speak of?"

Heron smiled as they shook their head. "Finch would take you out drinking, Crane would want to do something adventurous like parasailing, Wren would bring a craft activity that would take over eight hours to complete . . . and I'm more of a movies and snacks kind of comforter." They scrubbed a hand down their face. "Oh my god, I sound like an insane person. I'm sorry. I—"

"No," I cut in at their adorable, sudden bout of panic. "That actually sounds perfect."

"Great." They stood and took one step toward the exit at Kangaroo Point. "Is it weird that I live on a boat?"

I wasn't about to tell them that I'd always wanted to live on a boat, that my happiest memories and best sleeps had all happened on a boat, so instead I just shrugged and said, "No, I think it's really cool actually."

"Thanks, I normally don't like bringing people down there but . . ."

"Oh, well, I don't need to—"

"But you're different somehow," they cut in, their words coming out faster as their embarrassment mounted. And something in their nerves rising seemed to make mine ease, as if we were a seesaw and when they went up, I came down, the two of us balancing each other out. "I don't think of you as regular people. I mean!" They quickly scrambled to add, "I mean that in a good way."

"Well according to my mother, I'm normal," I teased. "The highest compliment." They chuckled. "But thank you. I feel like you're different in a good way too."

I didn't mean just in general. I wanted to clarify that they were different to me, that there was something special about Heron Lachlan that seemed to counter and compliment me in just the right way and I couldn't explain it. But saying something like that would only lead to bad things, so I kept my mouth shut.

Heron's anxiety seemed to ease at my compliment though. They took out their keycard from their jacket pocket, and I followed them out the gate. We climbed down the steps to a little hidden wharf tucked around a bay, sheltered in the side of the island just below the southern edge of the zoo. I twisted, looking back up to the fence line of Kangaroo Point, and wondered if the wallabies and kangaroos had a glorious view of this harbor from their enclosure.

"Wow," I whispered, descending the steps to the moonlit bay. "This place is beautiful."

A smile bloomed on Heron's face, and we wandered the rest of the way to their boat. It was an older Oceanis model with a spacious cockpit and a covered table large enough to fit eight comfortably, two sun loungers on either side of the companionway. *The Farrier* was written in scrawling gold along the hull and had matching, gaudy gold embellishments in the upholstery and furnishings that had clearly been designed by a rich person trying to show off. Still, it was a beautiful boat, but I couldn't help but think how little it reminded me of Heron. I felt like they were much more suited to something like *The Wyoming*—rustic, timeless, beautiful.

"Gorgeous," I said as Heron climbed aboard.

"Do you know much about boats, cowgirl?" they asked, extending a hand down to me and helping me up the steps.

"I . . . Nope," I quickly amended, relishing the feel of their hand in mine. I wasn't about to admit I'd grown up in a little fishing town, surrounded by boats, and that learning to sail had practically been part of the elementary school curriculum. If ever there was a time to admit it, now would probably be it, but still, I didn't want to ruin this moment.

Instead, I just followed them below deck. "You're not going to murder me, are you?"

Great way to not ruin the moment, Hollis!

Heron shot me a mirthful look. "There are more creative ways to kill you than on my boat." They said it with a laugh and then hastily added, "Which wasn't meant to sound as threatening as it did. I've been watching too many true crime documentaries, sorry. No, I'm not going to murder you is probably what I should've led with."

"Well, now that you've said it, it must be true," I quipped as Heron descended the stairs and looked back up to me.

Still, I lingered at the top of the stairs as they turned on the light, illuminating what was little more than the cramped quarters of a bedroom. A rumpled duvet lay at the foot, a wooden bench seat across from it strewn with clothes, and suddenly the intimacy of the moment gave me pause.

A question burst to the front of my mind: what if this was actually a booty call?

Shit, shit, shit!

Come back to my boat? Come on, Hollis! They were obviously asking if you wanted to hook up!

How many times had I done this to myself? Misread a situation as innocent, missed the innuendo entirely, the signals only obvious in hindsight.

So I hooked a thumb behind me and did what I always did: bailed.

"Actually, I'm getting kind of tired, so I think I'm just going to go to bed."

"Oh, okay." *No, kill me now.* That crestfallen look on Heron's face was exactly the kind of thing I was trying to avoid. "Yeah, it's been a long day. Do you want me to walk you—"

"No, that's okay!" I said in a too-merry voice. "I've got my key card. Okay, bye!"

"You're sure you're okay?"

"I'm fine! See you tomorrow!" My voice was high and squeaky as I raced off the boat and back down the wharf to the steps.

My bungled exit had been awful and embarrassing and I'd have to avoid Heron for the rest of my life, but it was still a million times better than me bailing when they leaned in to kiss me. I couldn't bear to know if that was what they had wanted to do, didn't want to reach that precipice even as a voice in my head screamed that we'd already well and truly passed it.

My insides felt shredded with nerves. I wanted to drink tea and watch videos and fall asleep rocking to the gentle waves of a boat in a quiet bay with Heron's arms wrapped around me and then mine wrapped around them, us taking turns being the one to hold the other. And maybe Heron wanted that too, but they'd want more.

At first, they'd say no, it was fine and that they didn't care. Then at some point, they would care and the resentment would start to grow. It always played out that way. And I wouldn't do that to them. So instead of just being honest with them, like a coward, I'd run.

Chapter Twenty-Two

Heron

It was clear that Hollis was avoiding me the next few days. Whenever I tried to run into her in the break room or at the end of the day, she would suddenly need to be somewhere else. At some point, I just gave up. Something had spooked her, and I guessed it had been me coming on way too strong, trying to befriend her, offering for her to come back to my boat? That had crossed a line.

Maybe she felt embarrassed after being so vulnerable? And then instead of walking her back to her house, I'd invited her to a second location. Talk about stranger danger. She'd asked me if I was going to murder her and I'd joked that I had better ways. Really smooth.

I thought we'd had a moment, several moments. *All* the moments were a "moment" with her. But now, Hollis was opaque to me. An answer was sitting right in from of me that I couldn't quite grab. I just wished she'd tell me. The way she'd fit into my arms, the way she'd melted against me, the way she'd trusted me with her hurt . . .

No, I couldn't think about it.

That whole night had been a shit show, and I needed to just write it off as a weird day. Apparently, Finch had seen to it that Kirby got Hollis's parents kicked out of their B&B, telling them that they had to leave that night. "Unexpected maintenance" had been the reasoning. The B&B owner had kindly said not to worry and that they could suffer the one-star review. Knowing Hollis's parents the little I did, the one-star review might've happened regardless.

It had definitely been overkill, but that was what happened when you messed with one of us. Not just the Lachlan family, but the island as a whole. Prickle Island was a small community and we took care of our own. And Hollis was one of our own. She might be a black-cat introvert, but she was *our* black-cat introvert.

Just the thought of her made me sad all over again. One thing that was definitely not helping my shitty mood? Fucking John.

He'd taken the staff-wide email about workplace conduct and inappropriate comments with a grain of salt, as if the whole thing hadn't been drafted specifically for him. At least he hadn't made any more comments, but still, the relentlessly chatty optimist was driving me crazy. Normally, I was considered the sunshine energy of the zoo team, but this guy was seriously deranged.

And just when I thought the day couldn't get any worse, in an act of pure melodrama, the skies opened.

As the day wound down, Hawk jumped in to help us finish up. There had been barely a handful of visitors, everyone deciding to come on a better weather day, but still it had been a slog. Everything was slower on rainy days. The animals were reluctant to be moved, the enclosures took longer to clean, all weather gear needed to be put on and taken off as we moved about our tasks, and by the end, my socks were soaking wet and my mood was as gray as the clouds roiling overhead.

It wasn't until Hawk and John started heading off toward the kitchens that I had one flash of good luck in the shape of Hollis running up the path toward the meerkats.

"What the . . ." My voice trailed off, but the others were too far ahead to hear me.

I spied Hollis again, darting down the outlook trail to escape the rain. Knowing that there was nowhere to shelter in that direction, I ran from the zebra barn to rescue her from the deluge.

But as I neared the meerkat lookout, I didn't see anyone. My mind spun like a sudden bout of déjà vu. What did I think had happened? That she'd run into the bushes? That she'd been raptured? I didn't know. But I started searching the hedgerows and bamboo just in case she'd slipped on the wet rocks and had become lodged in a rigid topiary or something again. It wouldn't be the first time fishing her out of the foliage around here.

But then, to my great relief, I saw a flash of brunette hair peeking from the fisheye dome that popped up into the meerkat enclosure. The mob of meerkats was nowhere to be seen, having taken shelter in their den from the rain, but apparently Hollis had panicked with the sudden sprinkling of hail and had decided to take cover in the children's tunnel.

The wind whipped up faster and it stole my breath away. Unseasonably icy, it chapped my cheeks as the storm blustered through. The trees above me groaned, and I realized I was at serious risk of being clonked on the head by falling debris if I didn't move quickly. Maybe Hollis had had the right idea after all.

I dashed through the sudden puddles that filled from the torrent of rain, too quick to drain into the gutters. Skidding over and wheeling my arms, I dropped to a crouch and duck-walked my way into the tunnel. It had been designed for one child at a time, but the two of us just managed to squeeze in.

When Hollis saw me, her wide-eyed panic morphed into a red-hot embarrassment. "Of course you saw me," she said with a groan.

"I wanted to make sure you were okay," I offered. "Here." I took off my rain jacket and passed it to her. I had a T-shirt and polar-fleece vest on underneath that were soaked through. In my haste to get to Hollis, I'd forgotten to zip up my rain jacket. I'd surmised after the sangria incident that having wet clothes sticking to her might be a sensory nightmare, so when she opened her mouth to protest, I added, "I'm already drenched anyway. Better you have it."

She accepted it, frowning down at the navy-blue bundle in her lap. "I'm trying to decide where this ranks on my most embarrassing zoo moments list. Above or below getting Velcro-walled to a hedge."

"Believe me when I say, your embarrassing stories are tame compared to my family's." I snorted. "And I'm sorry to have to burst your bubble. I was just worried since there's no shelter this way."

"There's some," she said with a grimace, waving around her before slipping her arms into my jacket and zipping it up. It was too big for her, the hood dropping all the way down to her nose and the sleeves swallowing her hands. "I guess I didn't learn where all the rain cover in the zoo was fast enough. The weather was so good the first week that it spoiled me, but I should've been prepared for a summer storm."

"I thought you and Hawk were done for the day," I countered, pivoting to sit shoulder to shoulder with her. The slick nylon of my jacket scratched against the high-vis strips along the sides of my polar fleece as we shuffled in farther from the tiny hail balls that plinked onto the plexiglass above.

Hollis swept a lock of dripping wet hair off her face.

"We finished early, so I thought I'd help out with that new meerkat enrichment I was telling you about," she said. "It had been overcast all day, but I wasn't prepared for how quickly it changed from drizzle to a full-blown storm."

"The island has a way of shifting quickly."

"I'm learning that." She pursed her full lips together and nodded.

My eyes snagged on a raindrop trailing down her cheek and dripping off her chin. I had the sudden urge to reach out and swipe it away. Instead, I shoved my hands in my pockets—a maneuver I was barely able to pull off in the tight space.

"Maybe we should head off," she suggested, shuffling away from me.

I wondered if she wished I weren't there and I still didn't understand why. We seemed drawn to each other, both finding excuses to seek each other out and talk, but after her parents' visit, it had all just suddenly stopped.

We both jolted at another flash of lightning followed by a rolling rumble of thunder. "Maybe we wait until the storm isn't directly overhead before we leave."

"Maybe," she said with a half-laugh. "I'll help you do a permitter check once it's passed. I'm sure there will be fallen branches."

It shouldn't have been a charming statement, but I found myself smiling at her regardless. "I'd like that."

I'd like that? It's not like she asked you on a date, Heron!

We sat squeezed in our little fishbowl, watching the storm through the dome above.

Finally, I broke the silence. "I'm sorry I was so awkward the other day," I said. "I meant to comfort you, and then I think I made it weird by inviting you back to my boat—"

"I was the one who misread the situation, sorry," she cut in quickly. "I do that sometimes. I thought you meant tea and YouTube, not *tea and YouTube*."

I gave her a questioning look. "What does the latter mean?"

"Like Netflix and chill, I'm guessing?"

"Oh. Oh!" I replied, recognition lighting me up as I attempted to twist toward her in the cramped space. So *that* was what had happened. "No, I literally meant like drinking tea. I have a selection of different herbal ones I'm slowly working my way through. I wasn't, uh, trying to . . ." I wheeled my hands, letting her fill in the gaps.

"Flirt with me?" she replied.

"I mean . . ." I rubbed the back of my neck. "In that moment, no, but I guess I was kind of flirting with you. I just, not in the way you think. I . . ."

Oh god, was I really going to tell her this? I didn't want to. Not with the way I was feeling about her, not with the butterflies dancing in my stomach, not with the sudden thoughts of her and I cuddled up in bed together. But I had to say it. Better to stomp all over my heart now than feed any more of this dangerous fuel to the fire.

"I'm, uh, ace. Asexual," I amended, worried that she might mistake what I was saying for the name of a zoo animal. "Well, I guess, I mean, I'm panromantic asexual. It means—"

"I know what it means," she said with a nod, letting that statement linger there.

I nodded, and we just sat there in silence for a while, anxiety making my stomach clench. If she didn't say something soon, my insides might explode. I braced for a comment or rebuff or maybe further questions, but none came.

When I stole a glance at her, her cheeks were pink and she was grinning to herself. I eyed the way she nibbled her lip, and when she spotted me, her face straightened as if she'd been caught in a daydream.

"Why are you smiling?" I asked, my eyes crinkling in mirror to hers.

When she looked at me with those storming ocean-blue eyes, it felt like free-falling. I was totally unprepared to be the object of her attention.

Everything in my world seemed to tilt on its axis as she said, "I'm ace too."

It took me a second to even register what she'd said. Something like disbelief and joy warred within me. I wanted to wrap my arms around her again, to tell her that I'd been thinking about her constantly, that she made me giddy and I loved all the ways we seemed to fit together, but instead my radio blared.

"Reptiles to hoofstock."

I fumbled my radio before picking it up with trembling hands. "Go ahead."

"Hey, uh, it can probably wait until the storm passes, but . . ."

"What is it?"

"Uh, yeah, I'm up at Kangaroo Point," Crane said sheepishly. "And, uh, just thought you should know that your house is floating away."

"What?"

I frantically started crawling back out the tunnel as Hollis guffawed and crawled out behind me.

"To be continued," I shouted over my shoulder and ran.

Chapter Twenty-Three

Hollis

Just as I suspected, the harbor was in full view from the top of the steep hill at Kangaroo Point. I watched from the fence line as Crane and Heron, along with a Prickle Island local named Petey, towed Heron's boat back into the bay. It was too far and too thick with rain to see their facial expressions, but I suspected Heron's brows were pinched in concern, the worry lines deepening across their forehead, even while their cheeks dimpled as Crane cracked jokes to cheer up his twin.

I pulled the heavy-duty rain jacket tighter around me, the scent of Heron still imprinted in the lining. Soft and floral with a hint of earthy musk, the perfect combination of masculine and feminine, a heady mixture that felt so incredibly them.

Taking another deep breath, I waited as my storming thoughts disappeared under the whoosh of wind, waves, and pitter-pattering of rain. I appreciated the stellar quality of this zoo's rain gear, the hood deep enough to shelter under without getting my face wet. Some places issued gear that was barely a step above a plastic poncho, but this was excellent quality, rubber-covered zippers, cuffed wrists. A whole day could be spent working in the rain without being soaked through.

It was probably not the most appropriate time to be thinking about such things, but my mind was all over the place —splintering in ten different directions—but the loudest thought kept pulling me back with resounding emphasis? Heron was ace.

I'd met another ace person. At a zoo. On a tiny island.

But none of that mattered compared to how much I liked them. Not their job or their hobbies or even their sexuality. I liked the way everything in me eased whenever they were around, like all my muscles sighed, and I felt like I made sense to someone. Finally. At last. They made my mask slip, made me want to make theirs slip too. And the way they looked at me, like I was exciting and not annoying or odd or "quirky," but someone exceptional?

More than a fleeting crush. Definitely. The hug the night of my parents' visit had solidified that.

I didn't know what magical star I'd wished upon or what good karma I'd done in a past life, but this alignment of cosmos was ridiculous. And instead of delighting in my good fortune, all I could think was: if it feels this good, then it's definitely going to go wrong.

A list of panicked options flashed in rapid succession through my mind:

I should tell Heron I'm not interested in them.

I should tell them I have a crush on them.

I should flee the island and never return.

I should lie and tell them I'm aromantic.

I should give them a chance to take everything back.

There I went again. The old walls fortifying to protect my heart. I was sabotaging my happy ending before it had the chance to sabotage me, thinking of all the ways it could go wrong. It was terrifying to meet someone at last who made me feel like no part of me was lacking. I'd had partners who loved me before, but there had always been something holding us back. I couldn't bring the physicality they'd needed or I'd been too brusque with my opinions or we just hadn't gelled right and I'd always felt like I was this misshapen, oblong, neither square peg nor round hole, and at some point I'd just come to accept that.

But now, I'd met someone who understood and excited me and fit me so perfectly that they could really, *really* hurt me.

Because what if it all went wrong? Wouldn't that be a million times more terrible than thinking I was just not meant to have a person?

I didn't know the answer.

Rain tapped across my hood, the wind cupping my ears as I held my shaking hands in tight fists in my pockets.

I heard barked shouting coming up the path from below me. Realizing from my vantage point on the path, I was invisible to them, I shrunk closer to the chain-link, keeping my eyes on the choppy water and the dingy towing the motorless motorboat back to the wharf.

"Mom, come on, you can't invite her," Hawk was shouting to be heard over the rain.

"I invite her every year," Evie shouted back with an incredulous laugh. "And especially now when half her family is hiding their faces from those dirtbag tabloids."

"As they should."

"Hawk," Evie chastised.

"It is wrong to invite her."

"She is my friend," Evie countered. "Whatever petty family

bullshit happened is in the past. Let's try to be kind to the Madigans for once, Hawk."

My eyes bugged. First at Evie swearing and second that she was suggesting that she was still friends with the Madigans after their family had basically run itself into the ground with dirty schemes, scandals, and bad practices.

I remembered watching their reality show when I'd been in high school. It hadn't been exactly as riveting as the old reruns of *Crocodile Hunter*, nor had it been as wildlife focused as Attenborough documentaries, but I'd watched it anyway because I'd wanted to be a zookeeper one day, just like them.

Madigan Mountain had had all the chaos of animal husbandry that I'd come to know and love within my own career. They'd definitely made up storylines, reshot things in different lightning, and carefully placed branded logos for sponsorship money. No one else who'd watched the show had seemed to notice when their hair would be different one shot to the next, but I'd always spotted the continuity errors. Still, it had helped me daydream about running off to a zoo one day and working in the wild animal field. I bet *Madigan Mountain* had spawned an entire generation of zookeepers.

It had been sad when Gaz and Beverly had gotten divorced, and sadder still when the patriarch that I had thought was a tough but loving father figure had turned out to be a grade A douchebag, and then all the stories had started spilling out in the tabloids about the family of ten, feeding the media for nearly a year before the show had been canceled, and then they'd all disappeared from the limelight, apart from trashy paparazzi photos of Gaz.

I wondered how many of them even lived at the zoo anymore. Was the zoo even solvent? Could they afford to care for all their animals without the funding from the show? I wondered if they still had their tortoises, Mark and Shania. I'd thought the names were hilarious when I'd been a kid. They'd been at the Madigan Mountain Zoo my entire life and might very well outlive me.

I realized Evie and Hawk were still going, though their shouting had died down, but in the sudden pause in the rain, I could hear them bickering.

"Bev is my friend, Hawk. You don't have to accept that, but I'm allowed to have friends that you don't like," Evie said, cutting Hawk off. "And I'm still in charge of the gala guest list."

"Dove and Deacon are flying back for it."

"As they should," Evie replied. "What's your point?"

"Isn't it going to be weird to have Bev there considering Deacon once slept with one of her daughters?"

I audibly gasped, and the two of them paused, forcing me to shrink farther down the fence line. My ankle wobbled on the steep incline, and I eyed a wallaby next to me and held a finger to my mouth. Wallabies weren't particularly noisy creatures, but this was the biggest gossip of the century and I couldn't be revealed eavesdropping on it.

"They were teens when that happened," Evie said with a laugh. "It's water under the bridge. I even flagged it with Dove and Deacon already and they didn't care."

"But—"

"I know you don't like it, Hawk," Evie said with finality. "And I know you are loyal to your father and I respect that about you. But you don't know what you're talking about when it comes to the Madigans. Hasn't Gaz's behavior these last five years shown you enough? How many headlines have you seen him in?"

"Plenty," Hawk spat. "And that stupid fucking son of his, Fox."

"Eldest sons," Evie scoffed sarcastically. "And how many headlines have you seen Bev in in the last five years, hm?" A long pause. "Exactly. Maybe be careful before you paint an entire family with the same brush," she scolded. "How would you like it if you and Crane were lumped into the same persona." She laughed, and I assumed Hawk had made a face. "Case and point."

"Hannah told me not to push you on this," Hawk muttered.

"And you should've listened to your wife," Evie replied. "She's clearly wiser than you."

I looked down to see the wallaby was now standing directly between my legs, sheltering in the awning of my raincoat.

I let out a little squeal at the cuteness and quickly snapped my mouth shut, remembering I was trying to be stealthy. Waiting, waiting, no response. They must've walked away. But just to be safe, I stayed there being a wallaby umbrella, watching the boats navigating the choppy ocean back to the marina, as I reeled with all of my new revelations.

Chapter Twenty-Four

Heron

I paced nervously back and forth in front of the old monkey house. I imagined my brother making a commemorative sign to place beside my trodden path. *Here lies the spot where Heron Lachlan was too chicken to knock on a door.* What was I supposed to say? Just because I liked her, didn't mean she liked me. And just because we were both ace, didn't mean we were compatible either. It was a spectrum, after all, and would probably require some sort of conversation at some point in the future . . . assuming there would be a future. But she'd seemed interested in me, hadn't she? Or maybe I was just projecting.

I slapped my palm to my forehead. This was a disaster.

Never in my life had I felt so upended by another person.

Normally, I'd ask Crane for advice, but this was *definitely* out of his purview. My twin had a charm that couldn't be falsified, a bravery I couldn't summon, and as the token straight of our family, I had a feeling all of his advice would involve some sort of crazy antics that I could never pull off. I wished Dove weren't traveling. She and Deacon were flying in for the gala, so maybe I could wait to talk to Hollis until after Dove arrived?

I quickly ran through the list of siblings: Hawk, nope. The fact he'd managed to nail down someone as great as Hannah with his surly attitude had been an actual miracle. Finch, hell no. She was like a lesbian Casanova and in no way would have good advice for me. Lark was all the way in New Zealand, and while I was certain she would have a seven-point plan for me within twenty-four hours, that wasn't the kind of help I needed. Dove and Crane, I'd already written off, which only left—

"Hey."

As if summoned from my mind, Wren appeared, standing at the intersection of the path from the main house and the greenhouses. She watched me curiously, the epitome of a keeper doing observations on a wild animal with unpredictable behaviors. I almost expected her to jot it down in her logbook.

She cocked her head and folded her arms. "What are you doing?"

"Pacing."

"That I could gather. *Why* are you pacing?"

I threw my hands up in the air like an exasperated Muppet. "Because I don't know what to do."

She eyed me and then the monkey house and then me again, a smile stretching her lips. "And does that not knowing what to do at all involve a certain horse girl who might be inside the house right now?"

"Shh!" I hissed, whirling around and rushing her back down the path as she laughed.

It wasn't until I secured the greenhouse door behind us and we were locked in a sweltering room filled with ripening tomatoes that I said, "How did you know?"

She gave me an incredulous look. "Being the quiet one means being the most perceptive," she said. "And I see the way you look at her and the way she looks at you."

"She looks at me?"

"She does," Wren confirmed with a smile. "Also, the way you exploded at her parents was very uncharacteristic for you. You're like one of the gibbons being overprotective of their mate."

I rolled my eyes. "So my feelings are gibbon-level obvious then?"

"They are to a primate keeper," she said with a smug grin. "And she clearly feels gibbon-level feelings for you too, if that makes it any better."

"I don't know if it does."

"Listen, I'll admit I've never had gibbon-level feelings for anyone. Well, except for maybe that one summer for Chappel Roan . . ."

I let out another grumble. "What do I do?"

"You ask her out on a date," Wren replied like I'd lost my mind. Her eyes lit up. "Ooh, ask her to the gala. That's super romantic."

"We're both working the gala."

"Still, you're dressing up, aren't you?" She swatted my arm, her eyes going wide as if she were building the fantasy in her head even as she spoke. "You could dance together. That's really sweet. Doesn't she like Jane Austen novels? Yeah, you definitely have to ask her to dance. And bring her flowers!"

I pinched the bridge of my nose. "When did you become a hopeless romantic? You're supposed to be, like, twelve."

She folded her arms and frowned at me. The logical part of my brain knew she was twenty-four, but it still felt like she was running around after Crane and me with her hair in pigtails and a red panda stuffed toy her a pink, plastic backpack. I reached for a tomato, and she swatted my hand away. "Those are for the monkeys."

"It's quality assurance." I balked. "You sound just like Mom." She smiled, and I added, "That wasn't meant to be a compliment."

Even at twenty-four, I was still waiting for Wren to go through her rebellious phase. She was the only one of us who never fought with Mom, never tested boundaries, never pushed back. She busied herself with craft projects and dated the occasional summer staff member but kept it all very beige and low-key, never any drama, never any water works or heartbreak. Consciously uncoupling and all that. I didn't know what to do with her. I was still waiting for her inevitable implosion one day, but for now, she made a good point.

"How did you know Hollis liked Jane Austen novels?"

"Because unlike the rest of you, I listen," she replied. "I think she'd like something deeply romantic. You know, sweep her off her feet. And let her sweep you off yours in return." She gave me a knowing look. "You deserve feet-sweeping too."

I didn't give Wren enough credit. She really was the wisest of all of us. She knew I didn't want to fall into traditional masculine gender roles, that sometimes I wanted to woo and sometimes to be wooed, that I wanted someone who could move alongside me, shifting together like in some elaborate dance. I wanted someone who saw the feminine in me and embraced it, encouraged it even. I wanted it all.

I wanted it all—something I'd never admitted even to myself before. And here was someone so far out of my league and she seemed into me, and I knew I was going to mess it all up.

"Go ask her," Wren pushed.

"What? Now?"

"Yes, now," she urged, jostling me back and forth like an eager child. "The gala is tomorrow night. The time is now."

She opened the greenhouse door and practically shoved me through.

"I . . ."

"Be brave," she encouraged, giving me another eager shove.

I didn't let her move me. When I decided to root myself to the spot, her shoves did nothing—classic older sibling. "I'll tell you what," I hedged. "If I go be brave right now, then you owe me one act of bravery in the future."

"I'll be brave if you be brave," she agreed, foolishly sticking out her hand.

I shook it, knowing that one day the right person was going to come along and she was going to regret saying that. Maybe I hadn't grown out of my sibling betting phase after all.

With the smugness of having clearly caught her out, I turned and marched back to the monkey house, bolstered as I knocked on the door. All my bravado quickly faded, however, when John opened it in only his khaki shorts and a towel slung around his shoulders. The man's six pack had a six pack. He was absolutely stacked. My mouth fell open and I suddenly felt incredibly intimated, when I heard a derisive snort from behind him and Hollis said, "Jeez, put a freaking shirt on, John. This isn't *Survivor*."

And with that sarcastic snipe, my heart bloomed anew.

"Hey," Hollis said, shoving the meaty man blocking the doorway aside and darting out as if relieved to see me. "What's up? How's the boat?"

"Oh, good. I . . ." I spied Wren uphill giving me a thumbs-up and cringed again. "Want to go for a walk?" I suggested, wanting to avoid my little sister's prying eyes. "There's something I want to ask you."

"Sounds good," Hollis replied, swinging her arms as she slipped her flip-flops on and we wandered downhill. "I'd very much like to stay gone until John decides to put a shirt on, thanks."

"Do you want me to say something to him? Send out another staff email?" She arched her brow at me. "And by that I mean, would you like me to ask Hawk to say something to him or send out a staff email?"

"Ah," she said with a knowing nod. "I was wondering if that message about inappropriate staff conduct had something to do with him. He stopped mentioning women by going like—" She held her hands over her chest, and I guffawed. "A vast improvement, which I appreciate. But no need for another email on my account. I just ignore him."

"Roger that," I said, and she laughed.

We wandered through the zoo, meandering into the rainforest walkthrough. We were halfway through the marmoset exhibit when she looked at me and blurted out, "Did you know that your brother-in-law slept with a Madigan?"

My mouth fell open. "I did . . . . How did *you* know that?"

"I was eavesdropping," she blurted out, grimacing. "I'm sorry. I was out in the rain at Kangaroo Point watching your boat be towed back in." I grinned at the fact she'd been worried about me. "Also, you and I need to have a conversation about rope tying before the next storm because you clearly don't know enough about nautical knots, but I digress." Now I was full-on beaming. To most, she was monosyllabic, but with me it was different, and damn I loved when she got on a roll. "Your mom and Hawk came up the path below the hill and they obviously didn't see me, but I couldn't move because I was being very important shelter for a water-logged wallaby—"

"Naturally."

"And so I overheard their whole conversation." She winced. "I'm sorry. Don't tell your mom, please?"

"Why are you telling me?"

"I don't know." She shrugged. "It's you. I feel like I tell you everything."

My smile widened. "I feel like I tell you everything too."

I couldn't believe this was the same person who I'd thought hated me only a few weeks ago. I loved the way she lit up when she spoke about things she was passionate about—her energy was infectious—loved the way she was excited to hear all the things that lit me up too. How could anyone not want to be near that kind of glowy personality? Everything about her was just incandescent.

We started wandering again. Hollis swung her hands back and forth, loose instead of the normal tension she carried. "So what did you want to ask me?"

"I was wondering . . . you know the gala?"

"Yeah. I'm planning on taking the chameleons out for the visitors first. And then the blue-tongue skinks. Or did you think I should do skinks first? I was thinking to finish with whoever was most likely to poop on me so I didn't have to walk around with poop on my dress all night."

"You have a dress ready?"

"It's the day before the event," she said as if I were crazy. "Of course I do. I had one prepared as soon as I saw we needed formal attire for the gala in the onboarding packet. It's a great thrift store find too. Very shiny, magpies would love it. What are you wearing?"

"I don't know." I hedged. "Something boring probably. Normally, I just do a suit."

She narrowed her gaze, considering. "Do you like wearing a suit?"

"I don't know."

"Say more."

I sighed wearily. "I've never really quite figured out formal wear," I admitted, feeling like maybe she would understand. "I feel like I'm the most myself in khakis, honestly. Wearing suits and ties feels dysphoric, but I don't see myself in full glam, heels, and a dress either. Khakis make sense. That's how I see myself: laidback, part tomboy, part flower child."

"I definitely get those vibes."

I grinned, glad to have the way I saw myself affirmed in the way she saw me. "But when it comes to dressing up, I struggle. I don't know, I feel like suits have always been my default and I kind of retreat into what I've done before even if it doesn't feel great. The most I've figured out is maybe a fun print or a colorful blazer? And even though I feel like I lean more trans fem, a dress doesn't really feel like me either, and I just don't know how to be . . . me." I hung my head, my long hair spilling out of the ever-present bun atop it.

"Could I try?"

I peeked at her through my long tresses. "Could you try what?"

"Could I try to dress you for the gala? See if you like what I pick out for you?"

I blinked at her. "What do you have in mind?"

"Something that feels more you," she suggested. "Something that feels like the way you feel to me, at least. I've brought a few other pieces that I think would really suit you, and I saw some other items down at the shops that would fit your build. I'll bring a couple different options down to the boat, and if you don't like them, we can always go back to a fun-print suit, okay?"

"Okay." I couldn't hide the surprise in my voice. I liked the way she'd said "we" as if we were going through this sartorial experiment together.

"Yes, awesome, I'm excited." She beamed at me. "Is that what you wanted to ask me?"

I realized we'd stalled out halfway down the path, and when she turned to keep walking, I reached out and grazed her elbow with my fingertips. It was the barest of touches but still, she stopped. "No, actually, I was wondering if you wanted to, uh, go to the gala together? Like as my date?"

She held my gaze for a long second, and I lost myself in the ocean blue of her eyes. Nerves like I'd never known clawed their way through my gut before she gave me the softest smile and said, "I'd like that."

Fireworks exploded in my chest, the feeling of relief and excitement so elating that I thought I might pass out. I'd taken big swings in past relationships, had had my heart broken a few times even, and never had I felt more of a buzz than a simple "I'd like that," and it was probably because for once it had come from the right person.

"Okay, great!" I said a little too enthusiastically.

"We can get dressed at your boat and head up together," she offered. "I'll bring the different clothing options down a couple hours before the event if that sounds good?" She bounced on her toes, her excitement evident all the way through her body.

"It's a date."

With that, I whirled around and headed up the hill, practically levitating with my feet-sweeping, gibbon-level feelings.

Chapter Twenty-Five

Hollis

I floated through the next day, wondering how often it was that Heron had anyone fuss over them. They deserved someone to fuss over them, someone who made them feel seen and special. That thought propelled me through the next day as I went about gathering outfit options with all the mischievous whimsy of a parent sneaking a tooth fairy coin under a pillow.

Heron seemed too laid back to ask for help, and if I hadn't brashly offered, they'd probably never have even considered it. It felt like they were *constantly* pulling me back together, protecting me from my blunders, and lifting me up again. I was glad I finally had the perfect opportunity to return the favor.

We'll take turns.

With a giddy smile on my face—that I permitted only a select few to see—I wandered down from Kangaroo Point to the wharf below. Heron had given me a key that morning to the barbed-wire gate at the end of the dock so that I could meet them at their boat. I wore my backpack laden with my carefully curated "dressing up" toolkit, which consisted of mostly unopened beauty products that I'd purchased on a whim after scrolling through MUA videos. I carried a clothing bag with five hangers draped over one arm and a bouquet of sunflowers in the other. Still in work overalls and splattered in mud from the day, I figured we'd doll up together over tea and music.

As I sauntered down the wharf, excited for the evening, I once again eyed the poorly positioned boat, one rope too tight, another too slack, and tried to make a mental note to teach Heron the ABCs of mooring before the next storm rolled in.

But when I swept around toward the foredeck, I found Heron pacing with a bouquet of flowers in their hand. They froze when they spotted me, a surprised look on their face.

"You brought me flowers?" they asked, their smile stretching wide.

"And you got me flowers?" I asked, allowing them to see my giddy grin as we swapped bouquets.

"I did."

Mine were beautiful and dramatic, black roses and purple snap dragons. "These are gorgeous," I murmured, taking a deep inhale of their beautiful aroma. "I thought sunflowers might look good on your table," I offered. "They reminded me of you."

"I'll put them both in a vase so they don't wilt. Come on in," Heron offered. "Or aboard, I guess I should say."

"You have a flower vase on this thing?" I asked quizzically.

They laughed as they dug through a basket of miscellaneous items. "I'm sure I can scrounge something . . . Here!" They victoriously hoisted an empty ceramic pitcher aloft and declared in a jaunty British accent, "I shall hither forth to fill it with fresh water."

They disappeared down the steep steps, leaving me

standing on the wharf with a ridiculously giddy grin on my face. I had to nearly do a split to climb aboard, arms wheeling for a second to regain my balance.

Heron re-emerged, setting the pitcher on the table and putting our two bouquets in side by side. "This should work."

"As long as it's not filled with sangria," I teased.

"I still fall asleep cringing about that moment," they admitted with a shake of their head. "What a terrible way to welcome you to the zoo. I'm so sorry that happened."

"Water under the bridge," I said with a wave of my hand. "It was certainly a memorable initiation to Prickle Island."

I took another side step toward them as we admired our two bouquets side-by-side. One earthy and bright, the other dark and mysterious. We silently grinned at each other, at the perfect display of our two personalities in a single pitcher.

The blaring sound of a microphone receiver made us both jump and look up the hill.

"Testing, testing, one, two," a voice echoed faintly in the distance.

We could see the peeks of vaulted canopies, the reflection of party lights being set up, and a trail of catering vans idling as they waited to be signed in at the side gate.

"Right, the gala," I said aloud. "Before we get too lost talking about that pangolin study—"

"We *have* to talk about that at some point tonight though," Heron cut in, eyes alight with excitement. "Did you see—"

"Not yet. Here." I held out the garment bag. "Try the first set. I brought some backups if you wanted to go a in a different direction with it too. And once you're changed, we can accessorize."

Heron's eyebrows lifted toward their hairline. "When did you suddenly become a fashionista?"

"I'm not," I replied simply. "I'm an observer. I just feel like I absorbed different styles and patterns, ways of expression so that I could catalogue them in my brain and better understand them and how I want to present myself to the world." I realized that sounded insane and rubbed the back of my neck. "I mean, I feel like I was made to perform this role—"

"What role?"

I hadn't realized they'd taken a step closer until I looked up, having to crane my neck a little farther to meet their gaze. "The role that neurotypical people expect me to be," I said with a shrug. "I had to kind of study them and learn how to reproduce what they were looking for, if that makes sense."

Heron's shoulders lifted and fell with silent laughter. "You are certainly speaking my language," they said, waving a hand up and down their body. "You've got to learn all the expectations in order to break them."

"Exactly," I confirmed, waving them off. "Happy expectation breaking. If we like it, we can talk hair and makeup." Heron arched a brow at the mention of makeup, and I grinned. "Do you trust me?"

"I do," they said instantly, like it was the easier than breathing. "And I like the way you see the world." They wore a secret smile as they turned toward the stairs before pausing and looking back over their shoulder at me. "And when it comes to this, I think I trust you more than I do myself."

"As you should," I said smugly, and they climbed below deck to get changed.

I waited until they were out of sight to do a happy dance.

Chapter Twenty-Six

Heron

Up until that very moment, staring at myself in the mirror, I'd convinced myself that I would only ever feel like my true self in work boots and khakis with my long hair up in a bun. It was my comfort blanket, my go-to, and even when I wasn't working, I rarely deviated from my uniform. Why develop a sense of style when I'd already had one issued to me? But now, standing in front of the narrow wardrobe mirror, I had a feeling I would be deviating from khaki more often.

I scanned myself from my toes to the top of my head: sleek black leather boots with chunky heels, a high-waisted, pleated charcoal-gray kilt, a silver satin button-down, black double-breasted blazer with shimmering silver buttons, chunky silver chain necklace, and matching rings. Hollis had braided my hair back at the temples, and the smudge of black eyeliner and nude lip made me feel edgy and, dare I say it, hot.

This wasn't zookeeper Heron. This was fashionista Heron. And I loved them.

I just kept staring and staring at my reflection. What sorcerery had Hollis performed?

I took me a long time to form any words. "I can't believe this is me."

"Believe it." Hollis nervously chewed her lip in the reflection behind me. "You like it?"

"I..."

How did I even begin to describe this feeling? This elation. Not just because of the outfit, which was perfect, but because of her, because she had seen these things and knew they would work, because she saw me like *this*. And I felt so seen and known and... *loved*.

That was what this felt like. Like love.

I'd told Hollis that I didn't know how I wanted to present myself and she'd said "I got you" and had created an outfit that felt like the perfect heightened representation of myself and my gender identity in a way that I didn't think I'd have the bravery to have done on my own. But she made me feel brave.

"Thank you," I said to her reflection, my voice getting hoarse. "It means more to me than you know."

She wandered up and hugged me from behind like it wasn't the first time, like she did it all the time. I turned into her hold and dropped my mouth to her hair. Her touch was endlessly comforting. Her smell, spicy and rich and delicious. Everything about her just made me want to hold her closer.

A knock on the hull of the ship had us both jolting.

"Ronny!" Crane called. "Do you have any of those sticky tack things? I tried to raid Mom's cupboard and I—"

"Coming!" I called, racing up the stairs and throwing a, "Be right back," over my shoulder to Hollis.

"I should get changed anyway," she said, tipping her head to the wet bath behind her.

"It's super cramped in there. Take the room," I offered. "I'll keep wrecking ball above deck."

She chuckled. "Okay."

As I climbed up, a sudden flash of nervousness hit me. All it would take was one wrong microexpression from my twin and I knew all my elation would burst. Was this too much? Would he laugh at me? Would he get it?

I barreled ahead, trying to summon my newfound bravery, and emerged onto the top deck.

"Whoa," Crane said, mouth falling open when he saw me. "Holy shit. Look at you."

Nerves clawed up my throat. His opinion shouldn't have mattered to me, but he was my twin, my best friend, and I immediately started spiraling, but then he continued.

"Listen, I really don't like that you've forced me to relinquish the mantle of hottest twin," he started, straightening his skinny tie with a frown. "But I have to concede defeat. You look hot as fuck."

A smile bloomed on my face, stretching wide. "You like it?"

"What in the Shonda Rhimes?" Finch barked as she trekked down the wharf. "Holy moly, Heron, wow! Talk about a glow up!"

"It's just so you," Crane gushed, shaking his head and looking me over with befuddlement. "Like, I would've never picked it for you before seeing it on, but now . . . this whole vibe has Heron written all over it."

"It's like your sexy secret twin version of yourself," Finch added.

"Hey, *I'm* supposed to be the sexy secret twin." Crane pouted, and Finch rolled her eyes.

"Let them have this, Craniac." Finch wore a sparkling burgundy suit and a black bow tie, short hair gelled to the side giving her masc gangster vibes, and I was grateful once again to my older siblings who'd paved the way and made it easier for me to be myself.

"Hey, I wanted to talk to you about the donor thing before the gala," Finch said.

My eyes bugged and I made a cutting motion with my neck.

"What?" She looked between Crane and me. "Are you choking? What does this mean?"

"Hollis is here," I mouthed, dramatically pointing below my feet. "She's getting changed."

"Ooh." Finch gave a delighted conspiratorial look to Crane.

"Don't make that face at each other!" I whisper-hissed.

"Heron's got a girl below deck, wrecking ball," Finch teased with a laugh, slinging her arm around Crane. "I couldn't be prouder."

I rolled my eyes. Of course Finch thought this was about sex. "Can we please talk about it later?"

"Okay, okay," Finch said with a shake of her head. "You have fun, kids. Let me know if you need a restock of condoms—"

"Finch!" I hissed.

"Safety first." She laughed and shrugged, dragging Crane back off *The Farrier*.

I hoped Hollis hadn't heard my older sister's taunt and I started racing through my mind, trying to recalibrate what I would say to her if she had, but as she emerged from below deck, all the words tumbled out of my brain.

She was stunning, wearing a satin pewter dress that I all at once realized matched my button-down shirt. It skimmed and skirted every curve, showing off her gorgeous body. She was so beautiful, it stole the air from my lungs.

Everything seemed to get fuzzy on my periphery until I was only taking her in as she, in return, took me in. And in that moment, it felt like we were two very different bouquets of flowers that seemed to perfectly fit in one vase.

Chapter Twenty-Seven

Hollis

For a small zoo on a private island, the gala was a stunning, star-studded event. I definitely felt more like a spectator than an actual participant. There were glitzy celebrities all flown in by Deacon Harrow, exquisite finger food catered by Chef Frankie, and opulent decorations that transformed the Peckish Peacock into a chic bar. I was grateful that since I was working, I didn't have to mingle so much as offer my reptile companions out for patrons to pet. It was much easier to make small talk about bearded dragons than myself anyway.

As I put the chameleon back, grateful that it hadn't pooped on my beautiful dress, Heron appeared from around the corner. I was struck once again by their beauty, those blue eyes limned in black, those curving lips and flowing hair. They looked like an androgynous *Vogue* model and a dark angel all wrapped in one.

When they didn't immediately speak, I began to wonder if their sudden appearance was work related rather than a quick hello.

"Am I late getting the cockatoos out?" I asked with a cringe, checking my watch.

With their simple laugh, my nerves eased. God, that smile. I didn't know if there was such a thing as a smile coach, but Heron Lachlan should be one. I swore a heavenly chorus started singing out every time they flashed those pearly whites. Then they took my hand and my pulse instantly ratcheted up again.

"The animal experience list becomes more and more of a suggestion as the night goes on," they said with a wink, and my stomach did a somersault. "If Lark were here, she'd kill me for saying that."

"I think I like the sound of this Lark."

"I think you would be two peas in a pod," they replied with a laugh as they tugged on my hand, leading me away from the reptile house.

"Where are we going?" It was more of a hoarse laugh than a question.

We wandered down the back path to a staff corridor that led between the savannah exhibit and the meerkat enclosure. Surrounded in a circle of towering bamboo, only peeks of the back side of both enclosures came into view, and the rest was blissfully shadowed. The rustle of bamboo quieted my mind, the bustle of voices fading along with the music and bright lights.

My body sighed. I hadn't realized how overstimulated I'd gotten until we had this break in the swaying moonlight. Heron looked like they needed it as much as I did, tension melting off them as we both stood there and took a deep breath. Then another. But then there was a twinkle in their sky-blue eyes as they spun me in a circle around the pathway.

As we stalled, Heron lifted my hand to their lips and kissed the back. My heartbeat drummed in my ears, drowning out the rustle of bamboo.

Their voice was soft and earnest as they asked, "May I have this dance?"

My mouth fell open as heat crept up my cheeks. I'd always thought the description of hearts bursting out of chests was ridiculous until this very moment. Now, I thought the organ beneath my sternum might truly explode. What was this feeling? It was like my whole body was overcome. This was better than every fairy tale combined. Never in my life had I thought I'd be whisked away to a moonlit circle and asked, "May I have this dance?" but this was better than that because this was a moonlit circle at a zoo, surrounded by my favorite kinds of wildlife, and the person holding my hand was Heron, the sunflower to my black rose.

But instead of saying any of that, I only whispered, "I don't know how to dance."

Heron shrugged and switched their grip on my hand to hold it out like we were about to waltz across a ballroom. "Neither do I."

"And they're playing a Black Eyed Peas song."

Their hand found the small of my back. "Does it matter?"

I let out a surprised laugh. "No. I suppose it doesn't."

With that, my hand copied Heron's and I pulled them closer. We fit together, holding hands, our free arms wrapping around each other's back as I guided them into my best attempt at a clumsy waltz.

We laughed and stumbled over each other's feet as we danced around the hidden circle of bamboo. I was grateful that they let me take the lead. I liked being the one in charge, the one knowing which direction we were going, and Heron seemed happy to be led, blissful even.

"You know," I said as we settled into a gentle sway. "I always dreamed about being asked to a ball, but the reality of actually having a bunch of people watching me sounded awful. This is a really nice in-between."

"I like the in-betweens," they said.

"I do too."

"Thank you for the outfit," they murmured, pulling me closer until my chest pressed against theirs and we were no longer dancing so much as rocking side to side. "I don't think I've ever felt so, I don't know, like an elevated version of myself."

"It just seemed like the dressing up version of who you are all the time," I said with a shrug. "Actually, your shirt and my dress were thrifted together. I think they were meant to be one piece, but I thought it would look better as separates."

We slowed, barely moving as their eyes dipped to my mouth. Their warm breath was hot on my lips, their eyes lingering over my features as if drinking me in. A flurry of butterflies danced through my belly at the look in their eyes, replaced just as quickly by a flurry of questions.

Just ask them, Hollis!

I decided that sometimes my bluntness was a strength and leaned into it. Take the lead.

"How . . . do you feel about different types of intimacy?" I hedged, nervously sweeping a wavy lock behind my ear. "Kissing, for example? I like most kinds of physical affection, hugs, hand-holding. I like kissing—as long as it's not too sloppy. I have a lot of sensory things around overly wet kisses. Too much saliva is really gross."

I felt the hairs on my arm rise just thinking about it. When Heron didn't immediately reply, I panicked. Granted, I probably gave them a single breath before I wished I could instantly take it all back.

"Oh my god, I can't believe I'm just saying this to you." I groaned. "Sometimes I really wish I knew how to finesse these sorts of things." I tried to release Heron, but they held on tighter.

"No, keep going." Their eyes crinkled. "I like learning these things about you. What else don't you like?"

A flush crept up my neck and burned across my cheeks, but I kept going. It was better that they knew the full of it now, and I felt like if anyone was ever going to get it, it would be Heron.

"Okay, full transparency." I took a steeling breath. I'd never tried just coming right out with it before. This was new and terrifying. "I'm not interested in sex at all," I admitted. "I used to tell partners that I was into it sometimes for their benefit, but the truth is I wasn't and I'd really like to not go down that path again." I took another deep breath, unable to meet their gaze, but forced myself to keep going. "I don't mind bodily fluids in a clinical sense, like I can clean up after animals fine, but I don't think there's anything hot or romantic about it either. Sex always gave me so much sensory overwhelm and, to be honest, kind of made me feel sick. I felt like I *should* like it, but I didn't, even with partners who seemed really kind and understanding and accommodating. I guess I've always found the whole experience of sleeping with people incredibly over-whelming, and that was before I even began to crack the headspace of: Do I make noise? Am I making believable noises? Am I doing too much? Too little? Does my face look like I'm into it? The whole thing made me feel touched out and like a fraud, and I always wanted to hermit for a week afterwards."

My throat constricted as I took a deep breath, wishing I could reel the words back into my mouth.

"Hey." Heron reached out with their pointer finger and tipped my chin up to look at them. "It's just me. You don't need to be embarrassed to tell me how you feel. I want to know."

Just me. How wrong they were. When they were just everything to me.

"I'm sorry." I shook my head. "This was all deeply romantic. Dancing in the moonlight even with my clumsy feet. And I just kind of threw all of that at you."

"I asked you to."

"Leave it to me to rip the Band-Aid off."

"It's one of the many things I love about you," Heron replied, and that made me rock back on my heels. Did they just sort of kind of say that they loved me? Or at least they loved things about me? No. That wasn't what they meant. I was definitely overthinking this. "You make it feel a lot easier to say things I've normally found really hard too," they admitted. "I feel like even if I don't have all the words, you just get me."

I felt the same. Like I was constantly having to translate myself to everyone else, but Heron just heard me, no translations needed.

"I like kissing too," they offered. "I don't mind wet kisses. I enjoy sex but don't feel particularly attached to it in the same way that everyone else around me seems to be. I go through phases when I'm more and less interested. When I'm tired or busy with work or just focused on other things, I'm not interested at all. But even when I'm going through phases of being more interested, I don't mind just taking care of my own desires. Sex with other people is not something that I think about very often, and even when I do, it's kind of on par with any other activity, watch a movie, go for a hike, go out to dinner, you know? All of my past partners wanted it more than me and I was okay with that, but I think they eventually always wanted me to have more of a drive, and when I didn't initiate, things just kind of fizzled out from there."

They sighed, the sound carrying with it all of the heaviness of so many failed relationships and miscommunications for both of us.

I echoed out the same sigh. "Yeah."

"Yeah."

Wow. This was so incredibly refreshing. Even though we were coming to our sexualities from different angles, I'd never had this kind of honest conversation with someone who understood me before.

"Horny people are so exhausting," I joked, making Heron guffaw.

"No, but like, they really are so much work!"

They laughed harder, which made me laugh harder, and suddenly we doubled over, shaking with unrestrained belly laughter, releasing what felt like years of held in frustrations. Then we heard a clicking sound and looked over to see Beaky's face floating like a dismembered head, jutting through the bamboo beside us.

"You've got to be kidding me! How the hell did you get out again?" Heron exclaimed in exasperation. They looked at me. "Please tell me your romantic evening fantasies involve rescuing a stubborn, escaped ostrich?"

I looped my arm with theirs and grinned. "Well, they do now."

Chapter Twenty-Eight

Heron

We managed to wrangle Beaky back into the savannah exhibit with a bucketful of feed pellets. The ostrich seemed more than happy to be lured away. It was a common occurrence in zoos that instead of training our animals, they trained us, and I was starting to suspect our feathered friend had conditioned us to give these food rewards every time he escaped. I made a mental note to message Crane in the morning and have him add a new padlock to the gate. The escapes had been low priority since Beaky only seemed to do it after visitor hours and he wasn't categorized as a dangerous animal, but these bad habits had to stop. Fortunately, no partygoers were present at the savannah— too late in the evening and too plied with drinks to hike up the steep incline to witness the wayward bird.

Hollis and I took the long way back to the party, veering off the upper path as if not wanting to admit to each other that we didn't want to return. Apparently, we weren't the only ones. Because when we reached the top of the zoo, we ran into Finch, Frankie, Hawk, and Hannah, the two couples crammed into the Jeep that had been converted into a playground climbing structure for children.

"I see we're all hiding out," Finch declared as her eyes landed on me and then dropped to where Hollis and I were holding hands.

As if sensing the mark of her eyes, Hollis released our interlocked fingers and started fiddling with her hair. I wanted to tell her that there was no point trying to keep our romance a secret from my siblings, that they'd all sniffed it out before even Hollis and I had been aware of it, but I decided to let her continue to believe we were being stealthy about it.

"Don't tell Mom we're here," Hawk warned me, and I loved that a man closing in on the fourth decade of his life still uttered the words "Don't tell Mom" with surprising frequency.

"You didn't invite any of the others?" I asked as Hollis and I leaned against the Jeep and took one of the beef Wellingtons that Frankie offered us on a stolen silver platter.

So apparently, it was okay to steal platters of her own catering. I would remember this moment if ever she tried to accuse my twin and me of doing it again.

"Crane would've immediately gotten us discovered," Hawk said. "He was never one for subtly."

"And Wren would've immediately told Mom," Finch pointed out. "And Dove is too busy running interference for her famous husband, who is currently surrounded by all the tipsy, post-menopausal rich women like a pack of hyenas circling an injured gazelle."

I snorted. It was a startlingly accurate description.

"So this is where you all come to hide?" Hollis mused,

craning her neck up to look at the treehouse above the Jeep and the twinkling stars beyond.

"People tend not to make their way up here during the gala, too dark, not enough animals," Hannah said, pulling Hawk's blazer tighter around her shoulders. "Unless they're trying to hook up, so we come up here to cockblock any stragglers and prevent it from happening in the first place."

"Pot, kettle," Finch jeered, and Frankie elbowed her.

A sound rang out and we all stilled.

"Was that a moan?" Frankie whispered, and Finch held a finger to her lips.

We listened closer, and just as I was starting to wonder if it was one of the Amazon parrots, the sound repeated. My mouth dropped open.

Hawk leapt up. "Nope, that's definitely human."

Finch clicked her tongue. "Well, speak of the devil." She clicked on her flashlight. "Alright, cockblock patrol. The party's over. Let's go bust this up before we have to scoop condoms out of the crocodile moat again."

Hollis cackled at that, and we shot each other looks. "You don't have to come with us if you don't want to," I hedged, trying to give her an out. "They can handle it."

"Oh no, this is hilarious," she replied instantly. "I'm hoping it's a celebrity. If it's that Russian tennis player, I'm going to die."

I added "scandal lover" to the growing list of surprising things Hollis loved as my siblings shot off in the direction of the sound. We followed in a big walking caravan down the path toward the tiger lookout, where we presumed the sounds were emanating from. There weren't that many little hideouts for people to bone around the zoo, but the tiger lookout seemed the most likely.

"A classic," Finch murmured with a snort. "They always think that if they shut the door to the aviary, they'll have privacy, but half the walls are mesh and we still have ears, isn't that right, Hannah?" She elbowed our sister-in-law, who started blushing furiously.

"That was one time," she muttered back. "Okay, fine, a few times, but still, that was years ago."

"Well, it seems your late-night escapades have been replaced," Finch teased as she kicked open the aviary door and shouted, "Alright, lovebirds, both literal and metaphorical, break it up. Party's over." But then her words died on a gasp. "Mom?!"

The rest of us rushed in, stumbling over each other to see what was happening, only to find our mother hastily buttoning her blouse and wiping her smeared lipstick as she rapidly moved away from another person.

And that person?

Beverly fucking Madigan.

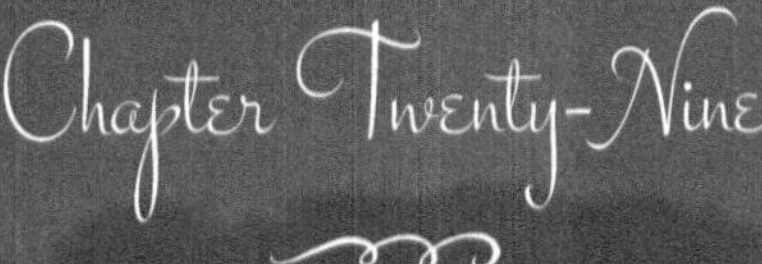

Chapter Twenty-Nine

Hollis

The group exploded around me as I watched two of my favorite conservationist matriarchs hastily adjust their clothes and wipe lipstick smears from their cheeks. From the amount of readjusting these two had to do, they'd clearly been really going for it.

Holy shit.

The two women, both of whom were in their sixties, looked like teenagers having just been caught drinking their parents' alcohol.

"Put the flashlight down, for crying out loud," Hannah said, smacking Hawk's hand. "This isn't an episode of *CSI*."

"You're fucking Beverly Madigan?" Hawk roared, his eyes bugged too wide as he looked accusatorially at his mother.

"I knew it!" Finch lurched forward, pointing an accusatory

finger at Evie. "I always knew it!" She looked back at her wife. "I told you. Didn't I tell you that they'd definitely hooked up?"

Frankie put a gentle hand on Finch, pulling her farther away, like a parent herding a sugared-up toddler. "You did, babe."

"And in front of the ringnecks too? Come on, Mom, not cool," Heron added, and Hawk and Hannah exchanged glances that told me Evie definitely wasn't the first Lachlan to use this spot as a hookup point.

I shuffled closer to Heron's side

"Okay, everyone, calm down," Evie said, trying to regain control of her wild horde of outraged children. "Bev, can you give me a minute to talk to the kids please?"

"Sure thing, Ev," she said, leaning in and giving Evie one last peck that had all of the Lachlan children gagging in disgust. She gave Evie a look like they'd always known it would come to this. She offered her a half shrug, winking one last time at Evie and pushing past us through the aviary.

"Ev." Finch gagged again. "No one calls you Ev."

"She does," Evie said with a sad sort of shrug that made me want to wrap her up in a big hug, even though I really wasn't a hugger. "She's called me that before any of you called me Mom, before Simon called me Evie even. I was her Ev first."

"I think it's time, Mom," Finch said, clearly knowing a little more to this story, or at least suspecting, than the rest of them.

"Okay," Evie said, pinching her eyes. "Family meeting in the living room after the gala. Round up the others, but"—she pointed a finger around the ring of her children and their part-ners—"no dramatics. I don't want to ruin this night. It's been going so well."

"Yeah, going so well for everyone but us," Hawk added with a grumble.

I instinctively reached out and rubbed a comforting hand down Heron's back. I couldn't imagine how strange this surprise must be for all of them, and I felt a responsibility to Heron's feelings first, but I felt terrible for Evie too. She looked like it pained her to share whatever she was about to, but from what I could gather, this seemed like it was a long time coming. Still, having all of your grown kids berating you for who you were sleeping with couldn't be easy.

The others filtered out as Finch added, "Go have a shower, or at least, you know, get the stink of sex off you or something."

Evie shot Finch a look like this was some kind of inside joke between them. "I appreciate the concern, Finch," she said sarcastically.

My mind was reeling as she added, "And I'd appreciate everyone's discretion." Her eyes landed on me. "This is private."

I nodded, miming zipping my mouth shut. I hoped I'd given Evie every reason to trust me, but she'd only known me since the start of the summer, and this was the juiciest of juicy gossip.

"I should go," I said to Heron, giving their arm a squeeze. "I'll help sweep out the last stragglers from the party. I'm sure your mind is elsewhere right now. Let me handle this."

"You could come with?" they offered, reaching out for my hand and lacing our fingers together again. We stalled at a halfway point around the tiger enclosure, and they tipped their head toward their mom's house.

"No, no, this is a family thing," I dismissed. "Let me help close things down so you all can go focus on . . ." I waved a hand. ". . . whatever conversation is about to happen."

"Honestly, I don't even know if I want to know," Heron admitted. "My mom is sleeping with Beverly Madigan and apparently has been for some time. What the hell? What does that even mean?"

"I swear the strangest things happen at zoos . . ." Heron nodded in agreement before I sheepishly added, "But I mean, I can see it."

"You can?" they asked incredulously, and I held up my hands in defense.

"I mean, I know you can't because it's your mom, but look how similar they are," I explained. "No one can relate to the life your mom has lived like Beverly Madigan can. They both are conservationists, running whole zoos, and big families too. They are probably the two most compatible people I've ever seen. I feel like in some strange ways, it makes sense that they'd be together."

"But we're supposed to hate the Madigans." There was no steel in Heron's voice, just confusion, like they were trying to get their thoughts to catch up to all this new information.

"I guess sometimes hate and love look a lot alike," I hedged.

"Not for me," they said with an adorable frown.

My insides lit up again as I smiled, lifting their hand and kissing the back of it. My lips lingered on their skin for a second, sending skitters of electricity across my own as I replied, "Me either."

"Thank you again for the glow up." They reached out and swept a lock of hair behind my ear, the gesture so tender it made me ache. I wanted to lean back into them, fold into their arms, and sway to the rhythm of our heartbeats until the sun rose, but I knew the night had to end, and Heron needed to be there for this family meeting.

"Tonight was wonderful," I said wistfully. "Thank you for asking me to be your date. Maybe, would it be too forward if I ask you out again?"

That furrow in their brow smoothed, their face brightening. "Not at all."

"Great. How about dinner at the Salty Dog on Wednedsay night?"

Heron nodded, unable to contain their smile. "It's a date."

"Okay." I gave their hand one last squeeze and took a

decided step back, a punctuation point to myself so I wouldn't reach out for them again. "Be brave."

"Yeah." Their smile softened as they turned toward their mom's house. "I've been hearing that a lot lately." They gave me one final wink and disappeared off to hear the story it seemed like Evelyn Lachlan had been waiting years to tell them.

And with that skippy feeling in my stomach, I danced off down the path, not even letting the horrified, haunted faces of the rest of Heron's siblings sully the moment. I was sure whatever Evie had to say to them would be fine. They could take the news like mature adults, right?

I grimaced even as I continued skipping. Yeah. That didn't seem likely.

Chapter Thirty

Heron

We sat crammed into Mom's living room in various states of undress like we'd all simultaneously stumbled home after a major bender. Half of us were in sweatpants, the other half still fully glammed up but looking worse for wear. Makeup was smudged, jewelry abandoned on the coffee table, and shoes and socks discarded in random heaps across the carpet. Whether we sat or perched or lounged or paced, every single one of my siblings had their arms tightly crossed, like we were waiting for the start of the worst Christmas morning ever.

Hannah kept squeezing Hawk's forearm in a silently signal to calm down from where they stood behind the couch. Meanwhile, Frankie, Finch, Dove, and Deacon all wedged into the couch and spilled over either armrest. Simon and Max were fast asleep on the armchairs that bracketed either side of the old sofa, and Crane, Wren, and I sat on the floor. At twenty-seven and twenty-four respectively, we were still the youngest of our generation, which meant we were relegated there.

Mom paced back and forth in front of the TV as if trying to find her words. She kept scrubbing her hand down her face.

Finally, Hawk said, "The night when we had that break-in at the monkey exhibit a few years back . . ."

"The one where you punched Fox Madigan in his stupid fucking face?" Finch asked smugly.

"Yep, that one," Hawk said, and Mom already looked exasperated. "You and Bev appeared from the same direction, coming from your office . . ."

"Oh snap," Crane whispered to me. "How long do you think they've been hooking up like that?"

Mom clapped her hands, pulling our focus back to her. "Okay, team, listen up," she announced, holding up her "quiet coyote" hand like we were five, but to her credit we all did quiet down and listen.

I braced myself for whatever she was about to say next, knowing that something would be forever changed when she was done. Not necessarily that she was seeing Beverly, but the lies she'd kept, how long she'd kept them, and the reasons why. We were all dancing around it, but I suspected from everyone's wary expressions that they also thought this secret was bigger than one illicit rendezvous.

Mom opened her mouth to speak and then chickened out and started pacing again. She let out a groan as she shook her head. "I don't know where to start."

"At the beginning," Wren offered gently as she peeked up from her anxiety knitting project.

"Right, well." Mom swung her arms back and forth, clearly struggling to get the words out. "I've known Beverly longer than

I've even known your father. We met when we were thirteen during a summer exchange program in Australia." Everyone shared surprised looks.

Crane leaned into me and whispered, "Did she ever tell you she did an exchange program as a kid? Or that she's ever even been to Australia?"

"No. You?"

"No."

"Shh!" Finch poked me with her big toe, and Mom continued.

"After I went home, she and I kept in touch as pen pals throughout our teen years. Even half a world apart, we were best friends. But time went on. Your father and I met, and it was love at first sight." She smiled, and something in me eased at knowing that at least that part of my parents' backstory was true. "Simon and I traveled all over together with nothing more than our backpacks, but when we ended up in Australia, something made us want to stay . . . or rather two people did."

"Gaz and Bev?" Dove surmised.

Mom took a deep breath and held it for a second as if willing the next words not to come out. "Yes. We spent a good chunk of our early twenties in far north Queensland, the four of us working conservation odd jobs and volunteering doing the field research no one else wanted to do. We were a unit, a team, and the four of us were also . . ." She wheeled her hands, implying plenty, and we all collectively groaned and gagged.

"You all slept together?" Wren screeched, her hands flying to cup her cheeks like a *Home Alone* poster.

"It was the seventies!" Mom erupted. "Everyone had multi-partner relationships or were polyamorous or whatever you call it now. Back then, we just were. We didn't think too much about it."

"So you guys were like the Fleetwood Mac of conservationists?" Hannah chimed in.

"Well, that's one way to put it," Deacon quipped. "That does sound very groovy, Evie."

"Don't high-five my mom for having an open marriage," Dove muttered, crossing her arms. "I mean, no shame to you, Mom, but Gaz Madigan, seriously?"

"Yeah . . . ," Mom said with a sigh. "He was always the one throwing a wrench in the works. Even back then. He was a fun, carefree, wild guy when we were young, but he always had that darker side too. I don't think anyone wanted to admit it, you know? You want to see the best in people. But even before all his latest antics, I never wanted Bev to end up with him," she lamented.

"So, were you two always together, even with . . . Dad?"

"Once your father and Gaz imploded," Mom explained. "We went our separate ways for nearly two decades. We'd write letters and eventually e-mails, send Christmas cards, you know, touch base, but it always had to be in secret because our respective husbands wouldn't tolerate knowing that the two of us never truly had a falling out like they did."

"Wait, wait, wait," Finch said, waving her hands like a referee. "You can't just gloss over the falling out part. What actually happened? We knew about Gaz stealing all of your ideas and—"

"They weren't just your father's and my ideas," Mom corrected. "They were *our* ideas, the four of us together. We were going to have children together and name them all after animals, we had them all picked out, and then we were going to raise our family at Prickle Island Zoo, all four of us together. At least, that was the dream."

"How very modern of you," Dove said with a bemused nod.

"Oh my god." Crane leaned forward as if he suddenly saw a ghost. "Did Beverly Madigan pick out any of our names?"

Mom grimaced. "I don't think you want to know the answer to that, Crane."

"No!" He crowed. "I was named by a fucking Madigan?"

The whole group erupted at that again, and Finch had to smack each of us one by one to get us quiet enough for Mom to continue.

"Gaz always really loved the idea of Prickle Island Zoo, probably even more than your father did at the time," she said, staring at the back wall as if staring through time. "I think Gaz was jealous that Simon had his family legacy, that there was a whole zoo out there that he'd one day take up the mantle of running. What to do with the zoo was always a point of contention between them. Gaz wanted what Simon had and resented him for not appreciating it enough. Honestly, your father might've never even returned to this zoo if Gaz hadn't encouraged him—"

"But Dad loved it," Hawk cut in, looking hurt and betrayed by that thought.

"He did," Mom assured him. "But without that push from Gaz, he might've never become the renowned conservationist he became."

"So what happened?" Finch pushed.

"There was a fight," Mom said, rubbing her weary eyes. "Gaz and your father were both drunk, both knew each other well enough to say the worst things to each other. Things got violent. It was . . ." The look in her eyes was haunted. "Bad. After that, we broke up. Simon's and my visas had expired, his parents were starting to need more help running Prickle Island, and . . . I wanted Bev to come with us. I was afraid to leave her with him. But immigrating to another country is complicated, and Bev was the one who wanted to stay in Australia anyway. She didn't want to leave Gaz behind either. Technically, the two of them were already married and your father and I—"

"Wait, you and the Madigans got married at the same time?" Dove barked, waving to a photo on the wall of our parents at the altar in an old New England church. "But the photos."

"We got remarried when we moved back to the States, around the time your grandparents were semi-retiring and your father and I needed to become more active in the zoo again. It was the year after Finch was born."

"Wait, we were born before you two got married?" Hawk asked.

"That explains a lot," Crane said as he skillfully dodged Finch's smack.

"We were married," Mom pushed. "We just got married again, not that any of that matters."

"What matters," Finch cut in, "is that you completely rewrote your timelines to take out all the Madigan drama and never told us any of it."

"I think the split was inevitable. We were all so young, and we knew our years in Australia wouldn't last forever," Mom carried on. "We thought Gaz and Bev would come with us, that had always been the plan, but Gaz got mixed up with the wrong people and . . ."

"What kind of wrong people?" I asked, the first thing I'd contributed to the entire conversation.

Mom's brows pinched together as she got that look in her eyes like she was thinking back through time. "You name it, drugs, gambling, loan sharks. He drove his parents so far into debt that he had to flee to a different state. He conned his way into starting Madigan Mountain Zoo. That place was always one step away from bankruptcy, and Bev was constantly bailing them out, finding new ways to make enough money to cover all of Gaz's wild indiscretions and ill-fated schemes."

Hawk blew out a long breath. "He sounds awful."

"He wasn't always," Mom said simply, and the thought of her ever sleeping with him made my stomach sour. "I think he hid a lot of it behind his charming, larger-than-life persona. I think Bev loved him and once they had kids, she had an even harder time letting go."

"Are we going to ignore the you four getting married together thing?" Wren cut in. "Where did you even get married?"

"In a crystal cave a few hours into the hinterland near where Madigan Mountain Zoo is now. We were part of an eco-commune—"

The room erupted again, and Mom's voice shouted over everyone, "It was the seventies!"

"You can't just excuse everything you did because of the decade it was at the time," I said with a laugh.

"So when did things between you and Bev . . ." Finch wheeled her hands. "Rekindle?"

"I don't know if I want to know that," Hawk said, dropping his hands on his knees and looking at the carpet like he might vomit.

"About five years after your father passed," Mom answered. "We were at a conference together, both of us speaking, and it was . . ."

She shook her head, her cheeks dimpling, and she seemed so young in that moment. Not our mother, not the headstrong, determined matriarch of the Lachlan clan, but just a woman feeling the first blushes of love again. I knew then I couldn't be mad at her for it, wouldn't, even if the rest of my siblings were. I'd defend her because I knew that look in her eyes, recognized it in myself. She was in love with Beverly . . . just like I was with Hollis.

"How can you be into her after what Fox did to Hannah?" Hawk growled.

Hannah leaned into her husband and hissed, "Don't you bring me into this!"

"No one was angrier at Fox than Bev," Mom countered. "He may be his father's son, but I swear to you, she straightened him out after that. I think once he really saw all the things his father put his mother through, he tried to take it back and make things right."

"Psh! Not to us, he didn't," Finch scoffed.

"Beverly was going to buy Prickle Island Zoo out from under us," Hawk pointed out.

"I *asked* her to help us buy the zoo for ourselves," Mom pushed. "Before Dove came in with a better plan." Deacon slung his arm around Dove and kissed her temple. "Bev was always good with finances. Well, she was forced to be, considering how terrible with money her ex-husband was. She'd been saving money to buy out Gaz from all of their show IP before everything erupted. She was going to use that money to divorce him and protect the family's zoo and still, she was ready to drop all of that to help us." A tinge of anger rose in Mom's voice. "So stop treating her like she was trying to sabotage us."

"Daw, look at you defending your girlfriend," Finch jeered.

"I don't think you're allowed to say girlfriend after the age of sixty-five," Wren countered. "Say partner or something."

"I can't believe you've been dating Beverly Madigan without telling us for . . ." Dove started doing the math in her head. "Seventeen years? Holy shit."

"We thought we'd keep it a secret until all of her kids were adults. We didn't want to make anyone uncomfortable—"

Hawk guffawed. "We're still pretty damn uncomfortable, Mom."

"And," Mom continued. "We were so busy with our own lives that we didn't know when we'd ever really have a chance to be together more than the occasional star-crossed meetings."

"Star-crossed meetings is code for banging at the tiger lookout," Finch announced.

Mom ignored her. "And that's not to mention the Gaz problem. We always knew he'd be trouble." She looked tired and exasperated, clearly more going on with that than she was ready to hash out.

Finch's pocket started vibrating. "Oh shit," she said. "I texted Lars. It's like the middle of her day." She clicked answer phone and Lark's face appeared with the sweeping New Zealand countryside in the background, the wind whipping her face.

"Mom is sleeping with Beverly Madigan?!" she screamed, and Mom covered her face in her hands as Finch turned the camera around so that Lark could see everyone. "Oh. Hi, guys," Lark added sheepishly.

"I'll catch you up in the chat." Finch propped the phone in her lap so that even Lark was facing Mom, who now stared down all seven of her children and their partners.

"Well, that's it," Mom said with a shrug. "The cat is finally out of the bag. I didn't want to hurt the memory of your father by dredging up our past like that, and he was determined to make you all hate the Madigans because of that falling out and all of Gaz's subsequent problematic and illegal behavior. But this is the truth. And like all truths, it's messier and more complicated than a simple good and bad."

"Do you love her?" Wren asked, and Mom's face softened. It was all she needed to do.

"Yeah," she said softly.

Half of us—the romantic half—melted at that. The other half still looked like they were picking up tiger diarrhea.

"Just no more secrets," Finch implored.

"Keep some," Crane cut in. "I really don't need to be thinking about Dad and Gaz Madigan boning."

The whole group cringed, and Dove threw a pillow at Crane.

Mom made a "time-out" gesture and said, "The two of them didn't *bone* that often. It was normally—"

"Yup!" Hawk's hand shot out, cutting Mom off. "This is the

exact kind of secret you should be keeping. We don't need to hear all of your stories, even if it was the seventies."

"Okay." A smile tugged Mom's lips, as if she were supremely relieved to finally have spilled her guts. "But if any of you have any questions, I'm here." The group seemed to loosen for a second before she added, "Oh, and I should probably tell you, we're engaged."

Everyone leapt to their feet again.

Chapter Thirty-One

Hollis

After stumbling upon the conservation scandal of the century, the rest of the evening was a blur. I helped pack up, double-checked that there were no stragglers or lost attendees, even pitched in with the catering cleanup for an hour just because I wasn't ready to go home and stare at the wall and think about what had transpired with Evie and Beverly. The fact that the two of them had been shacking up in the tiger hut had been one thing, but it was the way Beverly had reached out to Evie, brushed a kiss on her lips, her hand finding the small of Evie's back like she did it all the time that had told me plenty about how long the two of them had been together. That sort of inti-macy wasn't born out of a single passionate fling, and I had a feeling their story had been transpiring over a matter of years, not moments.

By the time the last catering vans disappeared through the zoo gates, I was boneless and exhausted. All of the feelings I'd absorbed from the Lachlans had been wrung out by my tiredness until I didn't feel like a hot cloud was tumbling through my mind anymore. Part of me wanted to go find Heron, make sure that they were okay, see if they needed a hug and a listening ear. But by the time I finished working, the zoo was silent. I went to Kangaroo Point to peek down at their boat and the lights were off. Heron was probably already asleep after a long—and wild—evening, so I stumbled back to the house and instantly fell into bed.

The following day, I slept in, and by "slept in" I meant I woke up at 6:50 am and gave myself all of ten minutes to get dressed before starting my shift. I always needed extra sleep after a big night of people-ing. But as I went about my day, the most interesting behaviors in the zoo weren't coming from the animals, but rather from the family of zookeepers that looked after them.

The Lachlan siblings seemed to be having many and varied responses to the news that their mother was sleeping with a famous former reality TV star. Wren knitted an entire sweater in what felt like three hours, Crane had started a new construction project at the converted garden shed he lived in, Dove and Deacon had immediately helicoptered off the island and were somewhere across the Atlantic back to France, Finch was helping Frankie overhaul the entire restaurant menu, and Hawk had decided that he would be holding one-on-one staff meetings at the end of each day for "feedback," though I suspected it was probably to occupy every last second of his mental energy.

And then there was Heron, who, from a distance, seemed to be handling the news the best out of all the siblings, but it wasn't until my lunch break that I finally had a moment to confirm it.

"Is this seat taken?" they asked, sidling over to my picnic table outside the Peckish Peacock.

Their blue eyes popped against the remnants of black eyeliner that still hadn't completely washed off. I made a mental note to buy them a nice brand makeup remover . . . one that I liked the smell of, just in case our faces ended up being really close again. It was such a random thought, but I felt my cheeks blushing anew.

I moved my plastic lunch tray back so they had enough space to set theirs across from mine. "How are you?" I asked, an inescapable grin tugging my lips. "Is it weird that I feel like I haven't seen you in ages?"

"Logically, I know it's been less than twenty-four hours," they said with a cheeky smile as they opened their can of soda. "But same."

"At least our lunch breaks align for once." I unwrapped the cellophane on my egg salad sandwich and eyed their tofu burger and fries. "Unless you're a loud chewer, in which case I will be banishing you to a different table."

"I promise to chew quietly," they vowed, taking a careful sip of their soda. "Which will be a new challenge for me considering our entire household eats like feral, half-starved animals."

"Seven siblings. That makes sense."

"Do you have any siblings?"

"Two younger sisters," I replied. "Twins, actually."

"Ah yes, I'm familiar with the concept." They said it with such a straight face that I nearly snorted passionfruit sparkling water out my nose. "How old are they?"

"Eighteen," I said.

"Nine years apart. You probably helped raise them."

"I helped, poorly. My parents are . . ." I circled my fingers through the air.

"Pedantic?" Heron offered.

"That's a nice way of putting it, yes. So they had strong opinions of what I should be doing to help out with my younger sisters. You know, there's a right and wrong way to do everything, and I, apparently, could only do things wrong." I took another bite of my sandwich, bobbing my head as I let that omission float between us. "My sisters somehow managed to get the more lenient version of my parents. This is their first year at Tufts and my parents couldn't be more proud."

"That must be hard with your family all the way out in Wyoming," Heron replied. "Having all of you on the East Coast. Or maybe that was the reason you all chose to be out here?" they added with a chuckle.

"Yeah," I hedged, having a sudden twang of guilt that I still hadn't told them the truth. But it was a small lie, right? A white lie. I knew the longer it went uncorrected, the worse it would be, but what if they were angry? What if I ruined the first good thing I had in a long, long time?

It didn't matter how big or small the lie was. I needed to tell them. They knew me instantly like no one else had. If anyone would understand why I'd decided to lie and forgive me for it, it was Heron Lachlan.

I smiled down at my food. God, I couldn't stop smiling. It didn't matter that it was way too fast, if it defied the social norms of the appropriate amount of time to fall for someone. I looked at Heron and knew. They were my person. Simple as that.

And maybe that fact would never amount to anything, and maybe we both had more than one person who could be that special to us, and maybe it was just a nice thing to feel, belonging with someone else, but it didn't matter. It was true. I'd claimed Heron the moment they'd told me about that skink research study. We were meant to be something more and it was terrifying.

"Actually—" I started my confession, only to be cut off by

Frankie and Hannah emerging from the Peckish Peacock and waving exuberantly in our direction.

"Oh hey, Hollis!" Frankie called, bounding over to our table. "We were looking for you."

Heron and I exchanged confused glances.

"We're going to go do WAGs drinks at that little vino spot by the Westworths' tonight," Hannah said. "Do you want to join us?"

"I didn't understand half the words in that sentence," I admitted. "What are WAGs?"

"Wives and girlfriends," Frankie explained, gesturing between her and Hannah and then frantically adding, "or like, it can be friends of the family, too." She darted a look between Heron and me. "It doesn't need any specific label."

"What are you two up to?" Heron asked suspiciously.

"Nothing!" Hannah's voice went way too high, as if she were clearly lying. "We just know that you two are close and we wanted to invite you, that's all."

So this was their attempt to suss out what Heron and I were to each other. Got it.

Heron looked more than a little pissed off at the two of them for that. We had barely gone on a single date and already everyone was swooping in and trying to put a label on us. Not that I necessarily minded being considered Heron's girlfriend. In fact, I liked that idea quite a lot. But did Heron like the idea of having a girlfriend?

My spirits wilted. It didn't matter how many relationships I'd had before Heron. I was suddenly transported back to being a "butterflies in the pit of my stomach" teenager, afraid to ask the person I had a crush on if I was their girlfriend or not.

But as Frankie and Hannah leaned over the table, acting like they could surmise our relationship from intensity alone, I simply offered, "I can do drinks tonight, thanks."

"Great!" Hannah replied merrily. "Hawk seemed more than

eager to have a night in with the boys after all the gala drama," she added with a laugh. "Heron, I think maybe you should see if Crane wants to do something too. He seems equally traumatized about . . . the engagement."

"The engagement?" I shrieked, shooting to a stand and clumsily smacking my legs on the underside of the table.

"Shh!" Frankie gave an apologetic smile to the other restaurant patrons.

"Your mom is engaged to Beverly Madigan?" I whisper-hissed. "Holy shit, no wonder you all are freaking out so much. I thought they were just drunkenly hooking up in like, a secret affair over the years, but they're getting married? Like *married* married? Are you all going to their wedding?"

Heron let out a groan. "I forgot that engagement meant there was going to be an actual wedding until right now."

I grimaced. "Sorry."

"I'm trying really, really, *really* hard to be happy for her," they amended as Hannah placed a conciliatory hand on their shoulder. "I never wanted her to be lonely. I always wondered if she'd move on someday, but . . ." They shook their head and rubbed a hand down their face. "I'm working on it."

"Working on it," Frankie echoed. "Sweet, well, maybe you can work on it over tequila with your twin because Craniac seriously needs help. I think he is spiraling right now."

"Look at you calling him Craniac," Heron said with a click of their tongue. "You're spending too much time with Finch."

Frankie shrugged. "It's why I married her. For the puns."

I watched the dynamic between the three of them, normally feeling like an outsider to these interactions but for once feeling included, welcomed to participate, knowing when to jump in with a comment of my own, the give and pull so much more natural than it usually was.

Often, being around people made me feel the same way I did when I was doing wildlife observations: as if I were looking at them through a pane of glass and they me. But with this group, I wasn't thinking so much about being perceived. They never made me feel like I needed to perform. I didn't need to suit up in my usual armor. I hadn't realized how much of my energy had gone into interacting with all of my past coworkers, acquaintances, hell, even the grocery store cashier, until a group of people had come along and made it easy.

It was the closest I'd ever felt to home.

Hannah gave me another wave as she and Frankie peeled off back to the kitchen. "We'll swing by your house at six and head off from there," she called.

"Sounds good," I called back.

Heron leaned in and whispered so they couldn't hear, "If you want me to help you bail on them, just say the word. I was silently brainstorming escape strategies while they were talking."

Damn, are we two peas in a pod?

My lips curved, and I once again felt like they could read my mind. Helping me escape an awkward social situation was honestly the sweetest gesture, but I actually liked Frankie and Hannah, and I wanted them to like me too, wanted to imagine what it would be like to be a part of this zany crew.

"I think I'm actually going to go," I countered, matching Heron's surprised expression with one of my own. "I know, right? Look at me. I'm growing."

"You're perfect just the way you are," they replied and then bit their lips together, like they hadn't meant to say it aloud. "Well, you definitely need to report back to me with any interesting gossip you acquire."

I saluted them. "Roger that."

That only made my smile stretch wider until we were beaming at each other like two heart-eyed fools, and for once, I didn't care who saw me.

Chapter Thirty-Two

Heron

My mind drifted back to Hollis throughout the day, but I decided whatever zookeeper baptism Hannah and Frankie were about to give her, she could handle on her own. My meddlesome warnings and advice would probably only make her anxious. So instead, I decided to take my sister-in-law's advice and go check on Crane.

My twin and I sat at the edge of the wharf, feet dangling over the choppy water below. The wind had picked up throughout the day, and I suspected another summer storm would soon be arriving. I peered out at the comforting sight of the blue and gray horizon. A bottle of rum sat between us, courtesy of Kirby, along with two bottles of old-fashioned cola from Johnny's Rockin' Candy Emporium. The two of us were too lazy to mix them together, so we just drank the rum with soda chasers like we used to do when we'd been teens sneaking drinks.

"That is a team building game, not one you do with your twin," Crane muttered after I suggested we play two truths and a lie. "Besides, I already know all of your secrets."

"Most of them," I hedged with a hoarse laugh. "Not all of them."

"Yeah right." He snorted and added sarcastically, "And you don't know all of mine either."

"I don't believe you."

"Oh yeah?" He let out an incredulous laugh. "What about that time I thought I'd shit myself but it had been actually baboon poop that was aerially dropped into my underwear—"

"When you were going through that baggy, low-rise shorts phase and decided to clean under their lookout?" I finished for him and took another swig of rum as he gaped at me. "You literally radioed me to tell me that there was a little yellow turd in your underwear and sent me a photo from the bathroom."

"Oh yeah, I forgot about that." Crane cackled. "That was a one-in-a-million shot though, don't you think? That Loki would poop right when I was bent over and it would land straight down my shorts?"

"Talk about a trick shot," I replied with a laugh that sounded nearly identical to his. "And the weirdest installment of it's feces but what species."

"Thank God you confirmed it was, in fact, baboon poop 'cuz I had a ten-second freakout there," Crane said.

"You only waited ten seconds to send me a photo?" I asked and then sighed. "Yeah, that tracks."

"And then we had to figure out how the hell it got there." Crane shook his head as he stared out at the horizon.

"What are twins for if not helping you solve embarrassing poop mysteries?" I teased.

He snorted and grabbed the bottle from me to take another

drink. "Okay, fine, you know all my secrets." He passed me back the bottle. "You were always better at keeping them than me. Tell me yours. I need cheering up." He moped, shoulders drooping.

"The Mom and Bev news happened to me too, you know."

"Yeah, but you're all chill and happy because you have heart eyes for Hollis."

I huffed out a laugh. "That obvious, huh?"

"I'm your *twin*," he reminded me. "I knew *long* before the gala. I probably knew before you did. But I didn't want to nudge you. I knew you'd tell me when you were ready."

He took another long sip, and I pulled the bottle away before we were both regretting a wicked hangover in the morning. Nothing like pressure washing a room filled with screaming birds and monkeys to punish you for your overindulgence.

Crane was full-on pouting like a toddler as he said, "I'm not calling her Mom."

"What?"

"I'm not calling Bev, Mom."

"As if that were even a possibility." I guffawed. "We're all grown ass adults. No one is asking you to call her *Mom*. You probably don't ever even need to talk to her. I mean, between the two of them there are fifteen freaking kids. If she even remembers we exist, that would be a surprise to me."

"Then what will we call her?"

"Bev, probably," I said. "Beverly when you're feeling formal."

"It's weird though, right?"

"It's so incredibly weird," I confirmed. "I didn't even have the tiniest sneaking suspicion. Did you?"

"Zero," he admitted. "I don't think we can face any of those Madigan kids without turning their wedding into a full-blown brawl either."

"The reception will certainly be interesting," I conceded. "They can't all be that bad, though. There's got to be at least one good Madigan in the rotten bunch."

"Fox tricked Hannah into spying on our zoo, Lynx slept with Deacon and then called the paparazzi for clout, and one of them, I'm pretty sure, is running a jewelry MLM now, and that's just all off the top of my head."

"Okay, yeah, maybe they are all that bad," I lamented.

"I really hope Mom plans her wedding while I'm in Borneo or Botswana or something doing this conservation show so I have a good excuse not to go."

"Have you heard if you've gotten in yet?"

"No," Crane muttered. "Dove said the team will be sending out all the invitations next week. Apparently, a producer will call me if I get it."

"Ooh, a producer," I said, waggling my fingers. "Fancy." I had no idea what a producer did, but it sounded important. "So, she didn't even give you an inkling?"

"Nope, such a ballbuster. I even had Lark read over my application and give me notes!"

"Whew, I bet they were brutal."

"They were!" he exclaimed, his gestures looser with the rum. "But that's how much I want this. It's going to this once-in-a-lifetime kind of adventure."

I sighed. "Yeah."

"Thank you for your enthusiasm," he snarked.

"Sorry. It's just that I miss Lark. And Dove. And I'm going to miss you while you're gone too," I admitted. "That's a secret."

Crane dramatically rolled his eyes. "That is *not* a secret, and I'd be really offended if you didn't miss me."

The wind whipped up the waves, and all was quiet for a long time before I capped the rum bottle between us. I straightened, attempting to steel myself for what I was about to say. If ever there was a time, this was it.

"I think . . . No, I know," I started a little more resolutely, the bravado dying before the words were even fully spoken. "I'm asexual."

Crane stared out at the water for a long time as anxiety clawed up my throat before finally nodding like a builder checking over his work. "Yeah, that makes sense."

"What?"

Crane shrugged. "I mean, we went through puberty at the same exact time," he said with a half-laugh. "And we shared a bedroom and only one of us was sneaking off to jerk off in the shower all the time."

"Mom's water bill was crazy for a few years there." I shook my head with a rueful laugh. "You suddenly had a very vested interest in bathing."

He smiled. "Yeah, it was pretty clear, too, when we first started dating people that I thought about sex almost all of the time and you didn't. I didn't know if you had a label or term associated with it. Finch and I are certainly on the hornier end of our family's spectrum."

"Yep."

"And you were coming out as enby at the time, so there were a lot of things going on and I wasn't really keeping close tabs on your libido," he said with a chuckle. "I just knew it was different than mine. I figured you were being you, whatever that meant, but yeah, ace, that's cool." He clapped me on the shoulder. "I dig that for you."

"You dig that for me?" I asked him incredulously.

"I don't know." He chortled, his words slightly slurred. "Insert whatever more appropriate and supportive comment you'd like. Just know, I've got your back. Always."

In that moment, my mind flashed back to Hollis's parents at our kitchen table, at how little they'd welcomed or accepted or even *seen* her for the awesome person she was. I thought about how few people had a family as open and loving as mine. Every year, I was even more grateful for them.

Crane started laughing, and I eyed him. "What?" He laughed harder, and I started laughing too without even knowing why. "What?" I asked again through belly laughs.

"No, it's just that—" He could barely get the words out, he was cackling now. "I always thought Mom and I were the token straight ones in the family, and now it's just me . . ."

I started cackling right along with him, and the two of us keeled over toward the lapping ocean waves at our feet. All of the confusion and fear and worry for our mom suddenly evaporated as we laughed out to the sea.

It would all be okay because I had a twin who had my back. And I had his too. Always.

Chapter Thirty-Three

Hollis

The fact that we could walk pretty much anywhere on the island was incredible. But since the skies had darkened early and the wind was whipping up off the sea, we decided to take one of the zoo golf carts down to the boutique restaurant at the easterly end.

We were certainly the most underdressed people in the place, still in our work boots and cargo shorts, but Frankie seemed to know the owner, and he swept us to a back room. We were served the most delicious dinner that I was worried would cost me the entirety of my summer wages before Frankie assured me that it was "on the house."

Each course was paired with a small glass of wine, the fanciest degustation I'd ever partaken in. And even though I wasn't the most adventurous eater, I had to admit that I could get used to this whole fine-dining thing. I wasn't convinced of the point of flavored foam yet, but I could get there.

Hannah, Frankie, and I all got along surprisingly well, too, even without Heron, who felt like my conversational safety blanket. We chatted about life in the blissfully quiet, private room where the music wasn't blaring on the speakers overhead and I didn't have to read lips to understand what people were saying over the general din of chatter. I wasn't one for loud, crowded restaurants, especially with the bougie patrons who all reeked of perfume, half of whom were old enough to have hearing aids but clearly weren't using them as they shouted over the tables to each other. Talk about sensory overload. But this—fancy food in a quiet, plush room with two fellow neurodivergent people who had a special interest in wildlife? Yep. This I could get used to.

"Alright, I think dessert at Johnny's," Hannah suggested. "He's got the best gelato on the island, and the peanut butter cookie dough is to die for."

"Agreed," Frankie added. "But first." She turned to me and splayed both hands on the tablecloth like she was about to announce to me I was her bridesmaid or something. "We've got a surprise for you!"

I looked between the two of them, not wanting to ruin the mood by saying that I wasn't a big fan of surprises. "What is it?"

"We happen to know one of the grooms at the Holloway estate, and he agreed to let us borrow their horses for a sunset ride on the beach!" Hannah exclaimed like she'd just bought us all tickets to Paris.

My mouth fell open. Oh no. Red alert. This wasn't good.

"You both ride?" I asked, shifting in my seat.

"We do," Frankie answered with a too-wide smile. "All the time."

The hair on my arms stood on end. Well, this was one way to very quickly learn I'd never ridden a horse in my entire life, except a pony at a petting zoo once when I'd been seven. And if they rode horses all the time, they would definitely spot my ineptitude immediately. Hell, I had more experience around giraffes than I did horses.

Why had I done this to myself? I knew I shouldn't have bought that cowboy hat! What was wrong with me?

"We figured it would feel like home," Hannah said, which under any other circumstances would've been a really thoughtful thing to say. "Since you grew up around horses, we thought you might miss it."

"Psh. I don't." I awkwardly waved the sentiment away.

Hannah seemed to ignore that comment entirely. "You'll be fine to saddle your horse up and everything, right? I mean, Western and English riding styles are different, but you must know enough to get by, surely."

"I . . ."

"I bet you can give us some pointers," Frankie said, blotting the corners of her mouth one last time and standing. "Tell us about all your tack." What the hell did that mean? "Come on, let's go."

"I don't know anything about horses!" I blurted out, my cheeks burning in embarrassment. "I'm not from Wyoming, and I'm definitely not a horse rancher."

"I knew it!" Hannah said victoriously, slapping a hand to the table. "You lie about as well as I do, which is like, honestly really, really bad."

My mouth fell open. "You knew?"

"Yeah, you're not the first person to lie about who you are around here," Frankie revealed, giving Hannah a look.

"Or lie about who you're in a relationship with," Hannah shot back, and I knew there was a lot more of a story there that they had yet to divulge.

"Touché," Frankie said, turning back to me. "So what's the deal, Hollis? Why lie about that?"

"I picked Wyoming because it was the name of my dad's boat and I used to fantasize about growing up somewhere remote and magical and nothing like my actual childhood, so I picked there," I admitted, anxiously tucking a strand of hair behind my ear. "But no, I've never ridden a horse in my entire life and I am not from Wyoming."

"No one's from Wyoming," Hannah added. "I mean, except for people from Wyoming, but like statistically, not that many, and statistically fewer ones who live on a horse ranch. And you knew way too much about New England native wildlife and the Atlantic Ocean to be a transplant from another region."

I hung my head. Dammit. I had gotten excited around them and let my guard down and started blabbering on about right whales. "So you knew."

Hannah shrugged. "We suspected."

I dropped my head in my hands. "I'm sorry I lied. I . . ." Nervous tears pricked my eyes, and I grabbed my wine glass and swigged back the last dregs. Maybe I should ask the sommelier what paired well with tears. "I was just so mad at my parents when I was filling out my job application, and I didn't want to be associated with them anymore."

"Having met them, I'd say that's understandable," Frankie muttered.

I scrubbed a hand down my face. "And I thought I could just skate by under the radar and no one would ever really talk to me or get to know me well enough to ask more."

Hannah's lips curved down. "I hate that's how you thought this summer would go."

"That's how every workplace goes for me . . . until here, and by the time I fell in love with this place, it was too late and I'd dug this hole deeper than I knew how to climb out of."

Frankie blew out a slow breath. "That is something both of us can heavily relate to."

"You can?"

Frankie winked. "Story for another time."

"Are you going to tell Evie? Do you think she's going to fire me?" My eyes widened as I looked between them.

"I think Evie has enough of her own drama on her hands." Frankie gave a sarcastic smile. "So I wouldn't worry too much about her."

My throat bobbed. "Are you going to tell Heron?"

"No," Hannah said. "Not unless you don't."

"I will," I vowed. "I want to. I just, I'm trying to find the right time."

"Take it from two perpetual fuckups," Hannah started, folding her arms.

"Hey," Frankie cut in.

"There is no 'good time.' The sooner you tell Heron, the better."

"I know." I frowned down at the crumpled linen napkin in my lap. "I just, I really like them and I'm afraid of ruining things, and it's all still so new, and what if they don't feel the same way about me after they find out or . . ."

Great, now I was definitely almost crying.

Thunder roiled overhead, the windows tapping with a sudden spat of pre-storm rain.

"Oh yeah," Hannah said, elbowing Frankie. "Those two are the real deal."

But instead of admonishing me further like I'd expected, the two of them swarmed around me and gave me a two-sided hug—one I was surprised I actually didn't mind. And while I thoroughly didn't appreciate their ambush, I did appreciate that they were protective of Heron. They had a good group of people looking out for them. I wanted to be a part of that group.

The sound of the whipping wind snagged my attention, and I suddenly remembered that I hadn't told Heron to retie their boat. If a big enough gale rolled in, it might become untethered again, and then they'd be drifting out at sea, motorless. Sudden panic flared in me as I thought about their boat being dragged out of the harbor by the storm.

"Okay, I'll tell them." I shoot to my feet, surprising both Hannah and Frankie. "Right now. I'll tell them right now. Can you drop me off?"

Chapter Thirty-Four

Heron

Even though my boat rocked with unprecedented vigor, my stomach was finally used to the rolling motion. At least the marina was sheltered from the prevailing winds. No storm had hit this side of the island too badly before . . . but there was a first time for everything.

I decided instead of worrying too much about it, I would turn my music up louder and went about finally unpacking my clothes out of the suitcase I'd been living out of, deciding which of the built-in drawers should house what. Part of me wanted to FaceTime Lark because she would definitely have strong opinions on where I should put everything, but I'd also probably get an earful about how I hadn't unpacked in the month I'd been living aboard too. Plus, with the storm, the reception would be terrible, and there was only so many times we could play "can you hear me?" before we eventually gave up.

Fortunately, I didn't have much in the way of clothing. Mostly zoo uniforms that I shoved in the drawer beneath my bed. This boat had a clever amount of storage hidden in almost every available space. I honestly didn't need that much of it. I wore khakis every day.

The only thing hanging in my closet was the outfit Hollis had brought me from the gala night. She'd insisted that I keep it, and when I, in turn, had insisted I would pay for it, she'd requested I take her out to dinner instead. I grinned to myself as I found a place for my two pairs of work boots.

A tapping sound interrupted my rocking reverie. At first, I thought my song was clicking, then I thought the sound was the tapping of a line hitting the deck up above, but when I turned the music down to a sensible level, I realized it was someone knocking on my bedroom door.

Knocking? In a storm?

Panic flared in me, a list of increasingly catastrophic emergencies flashing through my mind. Was someone hurt? Had an animal escaped? How long would it take an emergency helicopter to reach a hospital during a storm like this? Could they even land? But then, I threw open the door and found Hollis standing there, drenched.

She gave a sheepish wave. "Hi."

I blinked at her for a second, wondering if I was hallucinating—a phantom in a hurricane. But as water bucketed down on her, I came to my senses, pulling her inside and shutting the door.

"What are you doing here? Are you okay? Is something wrong?" The questions came out in rapid succession as I scanned over her waterlogged body, looking for injuries. Her wet hair clung to her face, and she might as well have jumped into the ocean for how dry she was, but I didn't see any blood or bruising. Judging by her pink cheeks and pinched brow, she seemed more embarrassed than panicked, but . . . something had to be wrong.

"You retied the boat," she stated, as if that were enough information to glean what had propelled her to a marina in the middle of a storm.

"What?"

"The knots," she clarified, as if that meant anything to me. "The ones you were using to tie up your boat . . . I thought you might get blown away in the storm and like, shipwreck somewhere in the night."

"So you decided to come get shipwrecked with me?" Water dripped off her clothes and pooled around her feet, but I couldn't move my eyes from hers.

"Or retie the lines. But, uh, yeah."

I let out a surprised laugh, and she followed suit, the humor of the situation finally cutting through the surprise. I took another step back, allowing her to move farther into the tight quarters, trailing water as she went. "Okay."

"Okay," she echoed.

I reached into the top drawer of my dresser, pulled out a towel, and passed to it her.

"Thanks," she said, accepting it and blotting her face and wet hair.

We just stood there for a second, her soaked to the bone, me taking her in. She'd braved a storm to come check on me. I was "run out in the middle of a dangerous storm" level important to her. And while it had been an incredibly foolish thing that I'd have choice words with her about later, a dam broke inside me, an emotion I could no longer temper. I loved her. Simple as that. Simultaneously the easiest and most thrilling thought of my life: I loved her.

But instead of proclaiming anything of the sort, I just

nervously tucked a strand of hair behind my ear and asked, "Want to watch a movie?"

"Sure," she replied instantly before frowning down at the towel.

Finally, the part of good host caught back up to me and I realized she was standing there shivering and dripping wet.

"Let me get you some clothes," I offered and darted around the cabin to find an old, baggy hoodie and zoo-branded sweatpants.

Hollis accepted them gratefully and ducked into the head to change. When she re-emerged, she was drowning in my clothes, the sleeves covering her entire hands, the legs bunched up to the knees so that her feet could protrude. But she looked happy and warm, and I had the sudden thought that maybe I wouldn't fill my clothes in every single drawer of the boat. Maybe she'd want a few drawers of her own too. That was definitely putting the cart before the horse. We'd only had *one date*. But it was like a switch had just flipped and I knew. I didn't want to be coy about it. I wanted her to have a drawer. Hell, I wanted her to move in.

Okay, Heron, one step at a time, I coached myself, letting my exuberance catch up with me.

I propped up all my pillows to form a makeshift couch on my bed, which consumed 90% of the room.

"I've lost Wi-Fi with the storm," I said. "Do you want to pick one on my hard drive from Lark's old DVD collection?"

"Perfect." Hollis settled into the pillows beside me, close enough that one whole side of our bodies touched, and I knew there was still plenty more space on the other side of her, that she'd chosen to lie right beside me.

I didn't know what this sensation was, like my heart was skipping a beat, nerves dancing along my spine, and yet at the same time, it was calm and deep and steady too.

I passed her the laptop, and she began scrolling through the titles. The storm rocked us, jostling the boat back and forth, and to her credit, Hollis wasn't the least bit seasick. She dropped her head onto my shoulder as she scrolled, and another bout of warmth spread through my chest, my lips pulling up.

Chapter Thirty-Five

Hollis

We ended up getting more and more horizontal as the night wore on, melting into the pillows as the storm rolled over and past. The rocking had thrown us together a few times before Heron wrapped their arm around my shoulders and we bundled into one heap, them murmuring about how we wouldn't jostle as much this way and me replying how that was very sensible, even as I snuggled into their shoulder.

The roller coaster of undulating waves settled to a gentle, easy rocking by the time we finished *Austenland* and decided to pick another since we were far too comfortable to disentangle ourselves by then—another very sensible suggestion on my part.

And every once in a while, my conscious mind would flare for a split second with sudden awareness. *Is this how it felt to be at ease with someone?* Why had it never felt like this before? Why wasn't that little voice in the back of my mind looking for an exit strategy? Why was I, for once, the one instigating the contact? But then everything was warm and womblike, the softening wind, the steady rocking, and my anxieties were too boneless and placated to kick up any further fuss.

It was well past midnight when the waves slowed and the wind began to quiet enough that we could hear each other's whispers, but by then we were both half-asleep. The only light was the blue glow of Heron's laptop, the second movie long over and the start of the BBC's *Pride & Prejudice* beginning.

I could repeat the movie with my eyes closed. Austen adaptations had been the soundtrack to my youth, a profound comfort in the repetition. I never thought I'd have something so sweeping and romantic, but now I was beginning to think real romance came from small moments, quiet whispers and sleepy touches, the feeling of not needing to translate myself and the safety of simply being.

I folded myself further into Heron's shoulder, the sleepy rise and fall of their chest lulling me to sleep.

"I'm glad you retied the lines," I murmured, and they hummed, the vibration rumbling through my chest.

"Petey did," Heron admitted with a yawn. "But you showing up here in the middle of a storm because you were worried about me was an incredibly romantic gesture."

Maybe it was. Maybe all those Austen novels had taught me a thing or two, or maybe Heron was just worth running out into a storm for.

"Who would I hang out with if you blew out to sea?" I teased, but secretly I was pleased that they thought it was romantic. I hadn't really thought of myself as a romantic person before, despite craving it, but now it just seemed to happen without any thought. They deserved big gestures. I liked that I could be a big gesture person, too, that there was a care and reciprocity to our affection, that I felt like we both wanted to take big swings for the other.

Heron hummed again, their fingers trailing up and down my back in soft circles—the sort of light touch that I often found irritating and now found soothing because they were the one doing it. I turned my forehead into their neck, delighting in the way we fit together. It was even darker in that position, the light of the computer not reaching my eyes as sleep tugged on me.

"You're right," they said, their woozy words a little slurred. "If I was lost at sea, you'd be stuck with all the rest of them."

I was too tired to fully laugh. It was more of a puff of air as I said, "I really like the rest of your family. But they're not you." I felt the stretch of their cheek as they smiled. Sleep pulled me in its heavy undertow. "I think I get it now though."

"What?"

"Why people like their families," I murmured. "Why anyone would choose to stay close to home. Why someone would fly back from France because their mom was hosting a party. Hell, I'd even get excited for Christmas."

"Christmas at the zoo is seriously magical."

"Dammit," I said with a hoarse laugh. "I knew it. I hope I get the job and can stay."

"I hope you get the job and stay too," they murmured. "I'd really, really miss you. I don't know if I could bear it." They started to shift. "Sorry, that's too—"

As they pulled away, I tugged them back, turning into a rabid koala to keep them in my hold by slinging my leg over theirs and making them laugh. "It's not too much," I countered before they had a chance to. "I'd really, really miss you too." They hummed. "But I also want to deserve the job. I don't want to be picked just because we'd really, really miss each other."

"Mom and Hawk would never let that happen," they assured me. "You'll get the job because you're the best person for it. They'd be fools not to hire you. You're smart. You work hard. You fit right in with the rest of us."

That last one made my chest tighten. My eyes might've watered if I wasn't nearly asleep.

"Good," I said, letting out another sleepy yawn, the words coming out slower and slower. "My name isn't Hollis," I murmured, the confession spilling from my lips without thought. I was starting to wonder if maybe I'd already fallen asleep and this was all a dream. "My name is actually Holly. I just always liked the name Hollis better. It felt like it suited me more."

"Then you're Hollis to me." Heron's hand went slack, circles abruptly halting, sleep pulling them under. I took a deep breath, and then another, and a third before finally committing to it and saying, "I didn't grow up in Wyoming on a horse ranch."

Now it was my turn to squirm away, to flee before the other shoe dropped, but as I tried to inch off the bed, Heron bicep-curled me back into them.

They dropped their sleepy lips to my hair and murmured, "I know, cowgirl."

Chapter Thirty-Six

Heron

There were a lot of firsts in my life that had been forever cemented in my mind: the first time I'd held a lion cub, the first time I'd tried pumpkin spice ice cream, the first time my family had used my new pronouns . . . but this was one like no other. The first time I woke up with Hollis in my arms, I wanted to mount a plaque above the bed with our names and the date. That was how important this quiet, little moment felt.

At least, I hoped it was only a first and not also a last, that this was the start of something that would repeat again and again until I looked back on this first with all the fondness of something that was now a well-worn routine. The first blush of something world changing.

I snuck into the galley—that doubled as a closet and storage cupboard—and boiled water to make us coffee. Hollis yawned and stretched like a cat in sunshine as I walked back into the room.

She peeked one eye open, sniffing the air like a cartoon character. "You are a saint," she said, her other eye still closed as she reached out with grabby hands for me to pass her a mug.

She barely lifted her head to taste it. It took several bracing sips, her head ratcheting up an inch with each one, until she finally sat up and leaned against the curved hull of the boat. Her tousled hair circled her head, poking out at odd, wispy angles. I waited until the mug was half-empty before I spoke.

"So, where did you actually grow up? New Hampshire, I'm guessing?" I asked, perching on the built-in bench across from the bed.

I saw her mind whirl for a second as she remembered that she'd confessed what I'd long suspected.

"You already knew?" She swept a hand down her hair, attempting to tame it. "How?"

"Hmm, let's see." I tapped my chin, taunting her as her lips quirked. "Maybe the fact that you know nothing about horses or Wyoming? Or that both you and your parents have New England accents and your parents use 'wicked' as an exaggeration for everything?"

"They do not," she shot back.

I grinned. "Your mom literally told Wren she was 'wicked talented' *twice*. Shall I go on?"

She groaned and pinched her nose. "Fine."

"Your dad seemed to know a lot about lobster fishing and sailing," I added. "And he had a Mount Monadnock sticker on his phone case, and your mom had a lot of opinions about 'massholes' on the I-95 and wished your sisters had gotten into a college closer to Portsmouth?"

"She said all that?"

"Yep."

"Ah." She gave a weary nod. "Yeah, that would do it."

"*And* they told my mom they didn't like animals, so horse rancher was definitely out."

"She told you that?" She groaned, grimacing as she cradled the mug in her hands. "I'm sorry I didn't tell you sooner. I don't know why I picked Wyoming, apart from that it was the name of my dad's boat. There was a farm down the street from me growing up and they had two horses, and sometimes I'd go down to their paddock and sit on the fence all day dreaming about living on a big ranch somewhere and riding bareback across the prairie and roping cattle, and everything felt just so big and open and free in a way that I'd never felt in my little townhouse, with twin sisters and overbearing parents who always made me feel like I was . . . broken."

My heart cracked a little at that confession, but anger rose in me too. "I hope you don't take offense to this, but I hate that anyone ever made you feel broken, and I really don't like your parents."

She laughed. "I really don't like them either," she admitted. "But you know, I think they're just in denial about a lot of things. I still love them. They're still my family."

I nodded. "Yeah, I get that. I just hate the idea of anyone making you feel lesser than when you're spectacular."

She snorted. "You don't have to do that."

"What? You don't believe me?"

"I'm not spectacular. I'm strange," she retorted flatly. My eyebrows shot up as I pointedly set my mug to the side and steered my way to her.

"Oh no, they put their coffee down," she narrated as I crawled onto the bed beside her. "This must be really serious."

I leaned into her until my face was inches from her own. "You are strange," I said, and her brows knitted for a second before I continued. "And I am strange. And my family is strange. And this job is strange. And this island is strange. And the life I hope to live one day will be a wildly strange one too.

But I never thought I'd meet someone who made me feel like the best kind of strange, and that's all down to you. Smart. Beautiful. Brave. Witty. And extraordinarily strange."

She laughed and shook her head, turning to set her coffee on the raised lip of the bedside table.

"Oh no, she's setting her coffee down," I whispered.

And when she turned back to me, she grabbed me by the cheeks and kissed me. It was the sweetest, softest kiss of my life. It made my insides melt and my heart race, and I rose up on my knees so I could thread my fingers into her hair and kiss her back.

Chapter Thirty-Seven

Hollis

I was buzzing the entire shift, floating an inch off the ground as I went about the day's routine. I had no more secrets weighing me down. Heron and I had shared our first kiss, and it had felt like the spark of only bigger and better things.

Everything was finally coming up Hollis.

The icing on the cake was being on the reptiles team. Crane seemed just as excited by my enthusiasm for his animals, and we fell into easy conversation, talking about all of their different personalities. The massive boa constrictor in the rainforest exhibit, Matilda, and the albino python, Daisy, were two of my favorites. And I'd admit, I definitely spent more time than I needed to fussing over their enclosure humidity and substrate density just so I could be around them a little longer. To be fair, Crane seemed to do the exact same thing at the chameleons. Definitely kindred reptile nerd spirits, the two of us. And if Crane was selected for the Simon Lachlan Conservation Trust's new reality TV project, he'd need someone to look after his animals whom he trusted, right?

Okay, maybe finding a romantic partner and a dream job over one summer was too much to ask for, but it could happen. Anything felt possible now.

With that thought, I was buoyed throughout the day despite the late night, forgoing the afternoon slump as Heron found me humming a tune while washing buckets.

"Do you take requests?" they asked, and I looked up and grinned. And who could resist that megawatt smile? I couldn't help myself. I lifted on my tiptoes and gave them a peck on the cheek.

"Only for my favorite people," I replied, carrying on humming KC and the Sunshine Band.

"Hey, I was wondering . . ." They rubbed the back of their neck, and I loved the way their cheeks pinked with nerves. "Would you like a redo of Sunday Funday Fondue Day? Maybe you could join me tonight?"

"I can't believe you say the whole Sunday Funday Fondue Day every single time," I replied, too hung up on the thought to answer their question. "This is a zoo. We abbreviate things. It should be like SuFuFoDa or something."

"I will bring it up at the next committee meeting," they teased, a hand mindlessly sweeping down my back in a casual touch, like I was theirs and they did it all the time. "So? Fondue? Tonight? Yes?"

I loved how eager Heron was, like a kid begging their mom for a sleepover, but when I didn't respond with an enthusiastic "yes," they gave me a quick out. "Or we could do our own thing instead? Another movie night?"

"No, no, I don't want you bailing on your FoDaDay." I

paused, considering, and they chuckled. "I'll workshop it. But I want to be there, thank you."

"You're thinking it's pretty chaotic and kind of overwhelming," they replied, "but you don't know my secret weapon."

"You have a secret weapon for surviving family dinners?"

They produced a clenched hand from their pocket and unfurled their fingers to produce two sets of ear plugs in their palm.

I guffawed. "Oh, I see. *This* is why everyone thinks you're the chill one, huh?"

"Yep," they said proudly.

"Okay, deal." I plucked the earplugs from their outstretched hand. "What time is dinner again? Seven?"

"Six," they relayed. "We're all asleep by eight normally."

"You stayed up later last night," I countered with a grin, rocking back and forth.

"Because a really adorable zookeeper was keeping me awake."

"I am really adorable."

"You are." They leaned in and kissed the top of my head. "Also, I'm pretty sure the show paused and we fell asleep before the lake scene, so I think maybe you should come back to my place after dinner and we should finish the series together."

"We can't miss the lake scene," I replied.

Normally, hearing "come back to my place" was an immediate red flag, but this time I knew that we were actually on the same page. It felt so incredibly freeing. I didn't realize how many guards I'd constantly been holding up against the weight of other people's expectations until I was with someone who simply got me. And the idea of being rocked to sleep on a boat to the sounds of the ocean sounded far more appealing than lying in bed awake with my own thoughts as Diego's chainsaw snores echoed around the house. Crane had clearly done a good job renovating the place from what had once, apparently, been an old monkey exhibit, but the place still had a lot of concrete and was too echoey for my liking. Neither of my housemates seemed to mind though.

I finished my shift and went back to the house, getting ready to head to dinner. I mindlessly breezed through the kitchen, until I pulled up short at the sight of John leaning against the island, arms folded as if waiting for me.

"Where are you going?" he asked, the question more accusatory than curious.

"Dinner," I replied, confused, unable to read the meaning behind his surly tone. Normally, he was like a ball of annoyingly positive energy, but right now he seemed seriously perturbed by something.

"Dinner where?"

I gave him a quizzical look. That was none of his business.

"Dinner with the Lachlans?" he supplied, and when I didn't reply, he let out a deep, threatening laugh. "I have to give it to you. You might be quiet, but you're a clever one."

My cheeks flushed. "I don't know what you're talking about."

His eyes narrowed to slits as he said, "Of course you don't."

I moved faster to the door, suddenly feeling a little unsteady as the hairs on the back of my neck stood on end. He was angry at me that I was going to dinner with the Lachlans? They invited people all the time. Diego had partaken of Frankie's artisanal pizzas at their house two nights ago. They adopted everyone, well, apart from John. But it wasn't my fault that his personality was about as soothing as a cheese grater.

"You know," John added when my hand was on the doorknob, forcing me to pause. "I decided to start work early today. Did some raking up at Kangaroo Point, and guess who I saw leaving a certain zookeeper's boat at the crack of dawn?" He clicked his tongue and shot a finger gun at me. "Classic walk of shame."

"You don't know what you're talking about," I muttered.

"No?" John asked. "So you wouldn't mind me telling the gift shop girls that I saw you sneaking off Heron's boat at five am?"

"The gift shop women," I snapped. "And I wasn't sneaking. And yes, I would mind because I don't like people gossiping and spreading rumors about me."

John shrugged. "They're only rumors if they're not true."

My whole body burned with anger as I pushed past him, storming up the hill to the Lachlan house. How could John think that I was sleeping my way to the top? That I was only using Heron? My gut plummeted. How could he not? He didn't see the way Heron and I were together. He didn't get my personality at all. And Heron and I *were* sort of dating, but it was because I loved them, not because I wanted the job.

I nearly walked right into the hedge in front of me, arms wheeling at the sudden impact of that feeling.

Well crap.

I loved Heron Lachlan. Definitely. Completely.

So I rolled my shoulders back and lifted my chin and decided, if people wanted to talk, let them. I was finally happy, and I wouldn't let John or gossip ruin it for me. *I won't let John faze me,* I assured myself as my legs wobbled like a baby giraffe's. Nope. Not fazed at all.

Chapter Thirty-Eight

Heron

Hollis seemed more than a little flustered when she arrived at dinner—cheeks pink, knee bouncing, staring straight down at her plate. I didn't know what had happened between washing buckets and now, but something was definitely up. It took twelve times of her reassuring me she was okay before I decided to let it go . . . well, for now at least. I had six siblings, after all. I knew "okay" was code for "definitely not okay but too stressed to talk about it right now." Whatever it was, I knew she'd tell me when we weren't amongst my chaotic horde of siblings.

The ear plugs seemed to help though. With our hair down, no one seemed to notice us bobbing along, nodding in unison as people spoke. We kept shooting each other little conspiratorial looks like we were sharing an inside joke. I only heard the vaguest comments but was able to get the basics from my siblings' overly expressive hand gestures. Dinner table topics varied wildly, but the big hitters were always animal and visitor antics, and judging by Wren's dramatic brachiating arm swings, the current topic was the gibbons.

I smiled at my arm-swinging little sister as I took a bite of Frankie's garlic knot and did a little happy dance, rocking back and forth at the taste. Honestly, these knots were a highlight of my week, second only to every moment I stole with the woman sitting beside me. When Frankie had joined our family, she'd definitely elevated Sunday dinners, but the old fondue pot came out every time too. You'd think over an entire lifetime, my family would get bored of the same meal every single Sunday, but actually, I found the routine of it comforting and the food was always delicious, perfected over many years and evolving over time.

Kind of like our family, I thought as I looked around the table, taking stock of all the new members and new food dishes they'd brought along with them. Even the little butter sand-wiches and fruit salad that had emerged from the presence of my young nephews. It was all expanding year upon year ... and I kept thinking about how nicely Hollis rounded out our group.

Whoa! I dropped my foot to the brake pedal of my ridicu-lously premature, heart-eyed thoughts.

My mind echoed with my mother's proclamation that she'd placed on us like a curse so many years ago: Lachlans fell hard and fell fast. It had certainly been a pattern thus far: Lark and Logan, Hawk and Hannah, Finch and Frankie had all fallen in capital L love over a single summer. Technically, Dove and Deacon had had heart eyes for each other as kids, but when they'd reconnected as adults, yep, they'd fallen hard and fast too.

But I wasn't like my siblings. Nope, not at all.

It was far too soon to be thinking about Hollis and me like

that. We'd gone on all of *one* date. We'd had *one* sleepover. We still had several weeks until the end of summer, and I didn't even know for certain that my mom would be offering her a permanent job. *Although, she would be a fool not to hire Hollis.* I highly doubted Hollis wouldn't get the position, but still. Here I was, imagining what it would be like to have her sat across the table from me in another year, another decade, how the food might have changed and the people surrounding it crammed even fuller with nephews, nieces, and niblings, spouses, partners, and friends . . . and Hollis. Hollis was in every single iteration of the future. In a blink, she'd secured herself a spot in my every damn daydream.

It was the sort of wistful thinking the rest of my family teased me for, always having my head in the clouds. Where I was a daydreamer, Hollis was practical, and where she was whimsical, I was a realist, and we balanced each other so perfectly, I got lost thinking about all the ways we fit.

So lost, I barely noticed Finch was talking to me until she threw a piece of bread in my direction. It pinged off my forehead and clattered onto the plate of salad in front of me.

I turned my head to pull an earplug out without the room seeing, playing it off like I was tucking a strand of hair behind my ear. "What did you say?"

"Finch," Mom admonished her. "What kind of example are you setting for your nephews?"

"The cool kind," she said with a roll of her eyes. "Obviously."

Hannah let out a cackle of a laugh. "Oh, I'm going to really enjoy when you two have kids," she said with a knowing shake of her head. "We'll see how you feel about all of that then. We still need to pay you back for that light-up drum set you gave the boys last Christmas."

"Speaking of which," Frankie cut in, leaning across the table to look at me. "I just wanted to thank you again. We've made an appointment with the clinic for you next week, and if all the tests look good, we should be able to make another appointment in September."

"Tests?" Hollis asked, looking between us, and I noticed she held a single earplug in her hand too.

"Heron's going to be our sperm donor," Frankie offered, a grin stretching her lips in clear excitement.

Hollis looked directly down at her plate. "Oh."

She strung out the sound as if a gymnast bailing on a flip mid-air, changing from surprise to excitement but not quite sticking the landing.

My gut clenched. I tried to infer a million things from that single "oh." That lone word left me reeling, trying to figure out how Hollis felt about it. This was the sort of thing you talked about with partners, right? But we weren't partners yet, not officially at least, but we were dating . . . Then again, it felt strange to flag something so serious with her if she wasn't thinking about being in my life long-term. Asking her what she thought might've freaked her out even more. And it wasn't like we'd had an abundance of time to share our life's stories with each other.

Plus, there wasn't any guidebook on how to casually broach the topic with your new girlfriend that you were going to be your sister's wife's sperm donor, was there? Maybe the fantasies of decades passing with Hollis still sitting at this table with me were completely one-sided.

Shit.

As if sensing I was spiraling out, Frankie cleared her throat and caught my gaze. She looked like she'd bit into a lemon. "That was something I definitely should've let Heron tell you for themself," she told Hollis as she gave me a deeply embarrassed, apologetic look. "Sorry," she mouthed to me.

Mom immediately jumped in with a story about the cheetahs, and the table roared back to life, quickly jolted from its standstill, but I could tell that all the wheels in Hollis's mind were still turning. She fidgeted with her spinning ring under the table, her knee bouncing as she zoned the conversation out.

Being a sperm donor wasn't something I'd been trying to keep from her. I'd been planning on telling her at some point. It just hadn't come up and . . . now I was wondering if this would be weird for her. I felt like this conversation was on par with talking about if you wanted children one day. It wasn't a one date and one sleepover sort of thing. The thought jarred me. What if she wanted kids? I hadn't even thought about what I would do if she wanted children and I didn't. But one person wanting kids and the other not was a pretty giant relationship hurdle to get over. There was incompatible like wanting the same sides of the bed, and then there was wanting your futures to look completely different.

I realized I was bouncing my knee and fidgeting right alongside Hollis, both of us lost in our thoughts.

"You know, I think I'm tired," Hollis finally said after an appropriate amount of time had passed, clearly waiting for a lull in conversation, and I wondered if she'd just been waiting for a good exit this whole time.

"Yeah, I should get the kiddos to bed too," Hannah chimed in, clearly missing the subtext, as she started giving hugs and Hawk gathered the boys' things.

"I'll walk you back to the house," I offered.

I moved to stand, and Hollis held her hand out. "No, that's okay. I'm just really sleepy and think I'm going to hit the hay." She retreated another step. "You enjoy your family time."

I would've rather she punched me right in the chest. With a surprising amount of certainty, I knew she was pulling away from me. I might be losing her. The thought threw me into a panic, the eagerness to fix it rising in me and cresting like a wave. But the logical part of me forced me to sit back down. She needed to think. Bombarding her now with all of my fears was the worst thing I could do. Maybe in the morning, everything would calm down again and we could talk. I knew I didn't like to be ambushed before I'd had a chance to think things through either. I needed to give her some space.

But for once, there was someone I never wanted space from, especially not like this, feeling like it might be permanent.

Chapter Thirty-Nine

Hollis

It had suddenly all become too much. Embarrassment burned through me at the way I'd fled, but I couldn't stop myself. I'd freaked out.

I stood in the shower, the hot water beating down on me, the steam circling around as I tried to catch my breath. I'd already been thrown off by John accusing me of sleeping my way into a job, and then the dinner and the way Heron had looked at me and all at once it had felt like we were just living this life together. The reality of it had caught up with me. I didn't know what had happened. It was as if I'd blinked and I was there forever. But that wasn't what had made me panic.

I *liked* the idea of being there forever. Being a part of the Lachlan family. Being another Hannah or Frankie and just slotting right in. It was how badly I wanted it to be true that had made me flee. This feeling burning through my gut wasn't like me. I wasn't the sort of person who just stumbled into forever. I needed to pick each decision apart, turn it over in my mind, analyze every in and out until I'd figured out every possible outcome.

And then Heron was going to help Finch and Frankie have a child and another little khaki-clad baby would be brought into the world to be some kind of future kick-ass conservationist or award-winning chef and it had all been too sweet. It had been too joyful, too good, and I'd run for the hills because . . .

I leaned my forehead against the steaming tiles of the shower. Because why? Because I didn't feel like I deserved it? Because it was too good to be true? Because I might never survive if it wasn't?

It all felt like a cruel trick, an illusion about to be shattered, a rug about to be pulled out from under me. It had happened to me so many times before. Things I'd only gleaned in hindsight, maybe because of my brain and the fact that I'd been wired differently. Shame and guilt burned through me still at all the times I'd missed it: people who didn't actually want to be my friends, people who pitied me and weren't actually interested in what I had to say, relationships and jobs that I thought were going well and then they fell through. And every single time, when the other shoe had dropped, it had been devastating.

And here I was, everything going well, and I was freaking out that maybe this was like every other time when people said one thing and meant another. Maybe it was all an elaborate ruse and I was about to find out I was wrong again.

I stood there for far too long, the scalding water washing over me. Diego and John were probably annoyed at me for wasting all the hot water, but I couldn't summon an ounce of will to move. So I just stayed there, trapped in my own thoughts, crying when I should've been smiling. Terrified.

I had an emotional hangover the next day. Embarrassed that I'd bolted from the dinner, I went about most of it without being able to look anyone in the eyes. It was my rostered day off anyway, so I decided to flee Prickle Island on the early morning ferry and spend time wandering around the mainland.

The beaches weren't as nice, the vibes weren't as good, there was far too many people packing the shops, but at least I wasn't going to bump into anyone and no one was going to bump into me.

As I wandered down the esplanade, my phone vibrated. I looked down to see a text message from Heron and my pulse quickened as my eyes scanned over it.

"If you want some space, feel free to ignore this, but I'd really like to talk about everything that happened last night sometime? I'm sorry if the whole donor thing was weird for you. I feel like it was kind of sprung on you, and neither of us are big fans of surprises."

Ugh, why did they have to be so sweet and understanding? I read the subtext there, though, too. I knew they were freaking out that I was mad at them, and I decided I couldn't let them think that, even if the truth was far more embarrassing. That was the problem when two people knew each other so implicitly. I didn't want to leave Heron panicking while I figured out what to do with all the feelings exploding through my chest.

So I replied, "I think you being a donor is a really nice thing. That's not why I freaked out, sorry. I was just overstimulated and had to think about some things."

Oh man, way to be vague, Hollis.

At least they knew it wasn't about the donor thing.

The dots appeared and disappeared three times before the

line went silent. They probably thought I was breaking up with them or something. We weren't even really dating. But I wanted to be. Even if it was the scariest thing in the world, I didn't want it to stop. I was pretty sure they wanted that too, but we were just dancing around and saying all the big truths in our hearts because the stakes felt too high.

It was then I realized that I was the Band-Aid-ripper of the two of us and I needed to just tell them. Everything. A deluge of word vomit and half-baked thoughts would freak them out less than these short, vague texts anyway. One of the best things about Heron was that I knew I didn't have to contort my words for them to hear me. So I had to just say it. But I couldn't do it via text.

So I wrote, "Still on for our date tomorrow night? I was thinking maybe beach picnic instead of Salty Dog if that's okay with you? I'm feeling a little over-peopled after that record-breaking visitor number the other day."

"Beach picnic sounds great," Heron instantly replied. Then they added, "Can't wait!" as if the first reply weren't enthusiastic enough.

I could practically feel their relief lifting off the screen. I grinned, knowing that they were probably smiling at their phone with eagerness, and felt even more lucky that I got to be the person that made them smile like that. But the lightness was clouded with nerves too. I needed to tell them all of my fears. I needed them to know where my head was at. Every other relationship now felt small in comparison to the enormity of what I felt for Heron.

Suddenly. Surprisingly. Irrevocably.

And just when I thought my anxiety couldn't be any worse, my phone pinged and a calendar invite from Hawk popped up for tomorrow morning, Diego and John also cc'ed in.

This was it. The internship was nearing an end, and while there were no guarantees that two of us would be offered permanent contracts, I was really hoping I would get the job. And the self-sabotaging part of me hoped I didn't because then I could flee Prickle Island with my tail between my legs and never have to face the fear that my heart would be broken. But I knew it was too late. I'd already jumped into the water, and now I just had to wait with bated breath to see if I'd sink or swim.

Chapter Forty

Hollis

The nerves for my date with Heron that night were overshadowed by the swing team meeting that morning with Hawk. If I didn't get the job, then what? I hadn't planned that far. I hadn't expected to fall in love with someone. And now, summer was almost over and if I didn't get a permanent position, then—no, I couldn't think about it.

John flexed his muscles in a wrestling pose like something on of the cover of a WWE magazine and said, "Carnivores, here we come."

Diego and I shot each other looks, a single glance containing multitudes. John seemed to think he and Hawk were now best friends, something I didn't think Hawk had been made aware of nor wanted.

The three of us stood in a line, leaning against the stainless-steel workbench of the food prep kitchens, waiting for Hawk to come down from his office upstairs.

Aya was humming across the echoey room along with her radio, wearing a knife-safe glove as she wielded a meat cleaver. She was busy quartering half-frozen fish, tossing them into the otter diet buckets. A few other keepers popped in and out as the tension mounted—Wren, Hannah, and Crane in rapid succession—shooting us quick glances or thumbs-ups— knowing the three of us were collectively freaking out as we waited for our fates to be sealed.

The kitchens were the central hub of activity: picking up food buckets, dropping off dirty ones, making enrichment, prepping diets, and coordinating with each other on the notice boards. The sterile scent of metallic tables and industrial-grade cleaners filled the room. The heavy doors of the walk-in fridges were constantly being slid open and closed, coating my skin in cool air before it went back to beading with sweat on the humid summer's day.

I was too nervous to make small talk, especially not when a group of volunteers came through and set up on the workbench in front of us to make toilet paper roll foraging tubes for the meerkats.

The buzz of activity just made my nerves rise and rise as we heard the upstairs door open, and Hawk walked down the echoing metal steps.

He gave us a tight smile, and my stomach clenched.

Diego leaned over toward me and whispered, "Good luck."

"You too," I whispered back.

"Alright," Hawk said, folding his arms and leaning against the bench across from us. "I would invite you up to the office for this meeting, but the AC isn't working and it is hotter than Satan's ass crack in there, and I think waiting has already tortured you enough." We all laughed tightly. The tension was thicker than the humidity in the air. "So we're just going to talk here, cool?"

We all nodded like reprimanded school children.

"I was going to offer two of you a job." Hawk looked between the three of us, and all of my muscles tightened as I nervously picked at my fingernails in my pockets. "But after further discussions, I'm only going to offer one."

Concern etched Diego's face as Hawk's eyes landed on him, and he pointed at Diego with steepled hands. "I've been made aware that you've also applied for a job at Logan County Zoo?"

Diego's eyes widened. "I-I . . ."

Hawk held up a hand, and Diego snapped his mouth shut. "It's absolutely fine. I actually just got off the phone with Maddie, and she really wants you on her team. They have an extensive painted dog breeding program over there, and I know from our time on shift together how eager you are to work with them."

"I am," Diego hedged, eyes darting everywhere, wondering what that meant.

"Well then, congratulations, Diego, you've got a full-time job offer, just not at Prickle Island Zoo."

Diego laughed, pumping the air with excitement.

I gave his forearm a squeeze. "Congratulations!" I whispered.

"Thank you!" he whispered back.

The group of volunteers filtered out again, and we were left with only the echoing hum of the radio and the occasional thwack of a meat cleaver on a chopping board.

"Now, this was a tough one," Hawk continued, his face getting serious again after the momentary levity. "But sometimes we feel like people fit the culture of our workplace better than others."

My gut sunk at that. I had many strengths, but fitting in wasn't one of them. John's smile widened as he pushed off the counter, ready to claim his victory, but before I had a chance to wallow in the fact that maybe the belonging I'd been feeling was one-sided, Hawk continued.

"Which is why we will only be offering Hollis a permanent job," he said. "I'm sorry, John. It was a pleasure working with you this summer, and we wish you the best of luck on your future endeavors."

I blinked, not sure I was hearing correctly.

"Hollis?" John asked incredulously, clearly wondering the same thing as I was. "You're hiring *Hollis*, the one who swore on the radio and told people they were too sensitive when the tiger decapitated a fucking seagull? The one who got trapped in a hedge on her first day? You're hiring *her* and not me?"

"That is correct," Hawk confirmed, expertly threading a very delicate needle between being firm and gentle.

"But I have more years of experience than she does, and . . ." John's brows knit together, and he looked at Diego like he might get some backup. "You were going to offer two jobs at the start of the summer, so why not just offer me the other one?"

Hawk's jaw clenched. "Unfortunately, it's not a good fit, John."

I was incredibly impressed by how even-keeled Hawk was. If it were me, I'd have been in tears. Thank God I never had to work in management.

"This is ridiculous!" John exploded, pointing at me. "You only picked her because she's fucking your brother!"

My eyes started pricking with sudden tears at his outburst and I had to look up to the skylights high above to keep them from welling. My cheeks burned with embarrassment.

But not Hawk's. No. Hawk's eyes darkened.

"Heron's my sibling, not my brother," he growled. "And whatever their relationship is with Hollis is none of my concern. That is not why you're not getting hired."

I noticed Aya had turned around, meat cleaver still in hand

like she might chop John's dick off if he misgendered Heron again.

"That is the only reason why!" John shouted, his voice bouncing around the cavernous space, and Diego took a half step to position himself between John and me, looking like he might punch the guy square in the jaw. "I'm more qualified. It should be my job."

"Tell me, John," Hawk said tightly. "How many milligrams of glucosamine does Kita need?"

John's brow furrowed. "What?"

"Hollis?" Hawk asked.

"500 milligrams with her morning feed," I replied instantly.

Hawk nodded, keeping his eyes on John. "What enrichment does Henry get on Wednesdays?"

John let out a little growl. "That doesn't mean anything. I could just check the calendar."

"Hollis?"

"Trick question," I said. "He is in the education room for school visits on Wednesdays. Although technically, visiting a bunch of children could be considered his enrichment."

"John," Hawk continued. "Why is the building next to the lion exhibit called the Harrison Centre?"

John didn't answer, and Hawk's eyes darted to me, inviting me to speak.

"It's the name of your paternal great-great-uncle, who built the original lion exhibit in 1902. Parts of the original structure have been built into the modern redevelopment, to honor the history of the zoo." I looked at John and added, "It was in the handbook. And on a plaque that we walk past thirty times a day. And said on the microphone by the tour guides every lunch break as they pass by the Peckish Peacock."

Apparently, those weren't enough opportunities for John to learn why the building was named that. The fact that it was also in the information booklet that they'd needed to learn a brief history of the historic buildings on site also seemed to go over John's head.

"You expect me to have a history lesson now?" John threw his head back and laughed. "That's not part of my job."

"It's literally in the description," I muttered, but John was only focused on Hawk.

"I expect you to be a representative of this zoo and be able to communicate the history and legacy of this place to its visitors," Hawk countered.

"That's bullshit," John blustered.

Hawk took a menacing step toward John, and I was satisfied to see John cede a step back and bump into the table behind him. "And that sort of attitude is exactly why I'm hiring Hollis and not you." Hawk's eyes darted to Diego and me. "Thank you, I won't take up any more of your time." John moved to leave with us, and Hawk held up a hand. "John, hang back for me."

Diego and I slipped out of the room as Aya saluted us with a meat cleaver. Diego intertwined his elbow with mine and leaned in, whispering, "That was the hottest thing I've ever seen." I rolled my eyes. "Also, how did I miss you and Heron being an item? You have to tell me everything."

Chapter Forty-One

Heron

We sat atop a tartan blanket on the western beach, watching the late-evening sun go down. It was clear a careful amount of thought had been put into everything, from the blanket's orientation to the food Hollis had selected. But instead of being charmed by her meticulous effort, I felt nervous. Things still lingered in the air between us, unspoken.

I knew that Hawk had offered her the job and she hadn't declined, but... she had wanted to talk in person about something and I didn't know what. Surely she wasn't about to break up with me over a romantic dinner at the beach? Hollis was the queen of exit strategies. There were more strategic ways of ending things, ones with quick getaways, so it couldn't be that. Still, nerves clawed through me. Would I be able to survive working so close with her if she didn't feel the same way about me as I did about her? I guessed I'd have to find a way. Or maybe I'd see if I could go with Crane on his conservation trip like he'd wanted all along…

My thoughts spiraled out of control as I picked at the fine fare Hollis had laid out atop the blanket. A picnic basket sat between us, the contents all made by Frankie. A charcuterie plate, finger sandwiches, and chocolate-dipped strawberries, which seemed too romantic for a breakup, right? Thank God for the sparkling wine. I'd downed three glasses trying to quell the fears spiking through me.

As we ate, I forced myself to try and enjoy the moment, even as worries ping-ponged in the back of my mind. We sipped on bubbles and stared out at the setting sun as it dipped lower on the horizon, the sky lighting in shades of pink and gold. We made easy conversation throughout the meal, animals, TV shows, books we were reading, but still that little seed of doubt wormed its way into my belly. As things were winding down, I was braced for it.

"Okay," I finally said. "I can't wait any more. What is it you're going to tell me? I'm kind of freaking out that this was your way of really gently setting me up for a letdown."

"No," she sputtered, setting her wine glass down and turning fully toward me. "Well first I was going to tell you about John being a massive asshole, but that isn't really the most pressing topic right now, seeing as you're freaking out." I put finding John and murdering him on my mental to-do list. Hawk told me he fired the guy, but that didn't feel like enough all of a sudden.

"We're definitely going to be returning to this topic," I muttered, but as she wrung her hands, my murderous thoughts were put on the back burner.

"Shit, all of the things I've been practicing saying have just left my mind."

I reached out, hand hovering in the air between us for a

second before touching a finger to her chin. "I don't need rehearsed speeches."

"But it might not make sense if—"

"You make sense to me. Just talk to me," I encouraged, practically vibrating with nerves now.

"I, uh, I wanted to explain about the other night. I kind of fled dinner and had a . . . *moment* after." Her eyes scanned the horizon, and I instinctively took her hand in mine. She squeezed it back tightly, as if the contact were grounding her. "I kind of panicked." She took another deep breath and muttered to herself, "Okay, just say it." She met my gaze. "I know this is all really new and it feels like way too soon to talk about the fact that I don't ever want to have kids, and I just felt like it was suddenly all a lot and things were moving really fast and maybe we weren't on the same page about a lot of things, like deal-breaker things, and . . ."

"I don't want to have kids either," I said softly. "But I do really like being Heihei to all of my siblings' kids . . . well, and I suppose one day I'll have children with Crane—the bird, not my brother—if co-parenting chicks with a critically endangered species isn't a deal-breaker?"

Hollis laughed, sucking in another sharp breath, and her eyes welled with tears and mine did as well. "Sorry, I cry sometimes when I'm feeling—"

I squeezed her hand tighter, waving up to my eyes, showing her that mine were just as glassy as hers. "I wish you'd stop apologizing for having feelings." My chest swelled. "I love that about you. You make me feel like it's okay to be the sensitive, emotional person I am, too, without needing to be embarrassed or feeling like you'd judge me for it. I feel like with everyone else, I'm just too much or not enough, and I don't always have the words to explain myself but—" My voice hitched. "But you just see me as I am."

I wiped a hand to my eyes, blotting away my tears before reaching out to swipe the stray one that trailed down her cheek.

"Look at us," she said with a half-laugh, half-cry. "I feel like we fit together so well, and that feeling, that hope, it . . . it really scares me." She released one of my hands to wipe a tear with her sleeve. "I didn't think anyone could ever break my heart, Heron, but you could. I've never loved anyone the way I love you." She bit her lip as if the words had just accidentally spilled out. "I love you."

My eyes stung with tears, emotions clogging my throat, and I released her hands to kiss her. "I love you," I murmured against her salty lips. "And it scares the shit out of me too."

She kissed me again. "Well, at least we're not alone in that either. I always thought I wanted to get away from everyone," she admitted. "But now, I only want to be alone, together, if that makes sense? You're the only person I've ever felt lonely for. I miss you when you're not around." The way she looked at me was like staring right into my soul. "You're kind and funny and beautiful and smart and . . . I just want to be with you. I never thought I'd want to do life with someone else like the way I want to with you."

"Maybe we could start with doing life together?" I suggested, blinking back tears. "And maybe go from there?"

"Yeah," she said with a watery laugh. "Let's go from there."

"We're going to have to find a better boat," I admitted with a laugh, sweeping a lock of her hair behind her ear.

She pursed her lips and looked off to the side in that cheeky way she did when she had a mischievous idea. "I've already been scoping out the ones in the marina."

"Of course you have."

"Not that we could ever afford any of them, but just in case another rich person decides to abandon one there."

I grinned. "Crazier things have happened."

And with that, she leaned in to kiss me again as the sun set.

Chapter Forty-Two

Hollis

"A package for you," Evie called as the entire Lachlan clan crowded around the lawn of Kangaroo Point.

She tossed me a small, padded envelope, and I caught it before she made her way over to the blanket, where Simon and Max sat gorging themselves on misshapen animal cookies from Frankie's test batch.

The zoo was now officially closed for the summer, but it was still open for school groups and private events, a slower but steady pace for the rest of the year. We'd decided to celebrate the autumnal change of season with a movie night. Hawk had hooked up a projector so that we could watch a kids movie across the smooth wall of the kangaroo barn—the perfect makeshift movie screen.

I already knew if Simon picked, it would be *K-Pop Demon*

Hunters, and if Max did, it would be *Moana*. But this time Hannah picked *Mulan*, a throwback and another family favorite.

Even I got a turn in the rotation—although with so many of us, mine wouldn't come up until after Christmas. It felt both surprising and inevitable how quickly the Lachlan family had welcomed me into the fold. It was as if I'd always been there, the family I'd never known I needed, slotting into this crazy and loving life in a way that felt effortless.

Heron and I sat snuggled on a blanket toward the top of the hill. Most of the macropods who called the enclosure home during the day had all turned in for the night, leaving the perfect open field for us to have an outdoor movie night—apart from the occasional smattering of kangaroo poo, but none of us really minded that. Thank the zookeeper gods for herbivore poop.

We all sat bundled up in our blankets and hoodies as Frankie passed around mugs of hot chocolate heaped with marshmallows.

"What is it?" Heron asked, nodding to the envelope that Evie had tossed to me.

I frowned at the label, my stomach jolting as I recognized the handwriting. "It's from my mom."

"What do you think it is?"

"No idea. I've barely so much as texted her since she was here this summer."

I pulled out the Leatherman from on my hip and opened the overly taped package. Inside was a letter and a red leather, bracelet-sized jewelry box. My mom wasn't one for jewelry, and I doubted if we had any family heirlooms, that she'd give them to me over one of my sisters. She also wasn't one for sentimentality and care packages, so I really had no idea what this sudden ambush was.

I opened the letter first.

Hollis,

I've always struggled with the right words to say. I thought making you feel less different would make you feel more included and stronger. I've been doing a lot of reading lately, and I'm working on learning everything. I wish I'd started sooner, but you know how I am. I think I'm seeing a lot of myself in these books too, and that's a little scary for me. I know I won't get all the jargon right, but I just want you to know that you are incredible and we're very proud of you. I'm sorry we ever made you feel like you were lacking. We'd like to maybe try to come visit again at a date and time of your choosing?

Until then, we've been keeping up with the zoo on the Instagram. Congratulations on the permanent job offer. I hope you get on the reptile team. I know they're your favorite. Your staff photo looks great. We heard from Evelyn that you are living on an old motorboat and we decided that was just unacceptable.

Love you,
Mom

"Well, that was a jarring way to end an otherwise lovely letter." I arched my brow even as tears misted my eyes from the things she'd written. "She ended by telling me that she disapproved of my living conditions?"

Heron took the letter and read it silently, laughing to themself a few times before saying, "It's hilarious to me that she's only now realizing that she might be neurodivergent, but I guess we all come to it in our own time." They set the letter down and squeezed my hand. "It's nice to see her actually making an effort though, right? How are you feeling about it?"

I shrugged. It was an attempt at reconciliation. "I appreciate it regardless, I guess."

"What's that?" they asked, tipping their head to the present that had accompanied the letter.

"I have no idea," I replied quizzically. "Jewelry? Not very practical for a zookeeper but . . ." The hinge groaned as I opened the scuffed leather box. I gasped when I saw what was inside, tears instantly welling in my eyes before it was even fully visible.

There, in the box, was an old red plastic key fob, one that had bite marks on it from when I chewed it as a child. A golden key hung from it along with a silver tag that said: *The Wyoming*.

"This is my boat, our family's boat. I . . . I don't understand why he sent this to me."

I looked at Heron, who just shrugged, as bemused as I was. But when we looked up at Evie in unison, she nodded out to the chain-link fence and the marina below.

Heart racing, I leapt to my feet, sprinted to the fence, and whirled to look down at the bay. There, moored next to Heron's little boat, was my happy place, the site of all my favorite memories apart from the ones I shared with the person standing next to me. Now they'd been combined into one. It was here. *The Wyoming*.

Heron's arms wrapped around me from behind and we stared down at the gorgeous ocean clipper together as they kissed my hair. I couldn't believe it. My dad's pride and joy. Something I'd always thought he cared about more than anything. And he'd given it to me? How? When? Judging from Evie's knowing look, she'd been in cahoots with them this whole time.

My father was a man of few words, but this was a big

gesture, as big as my mom's apology letter. Bigger. He'd given me his boat. He'd given me my happy place.

I beamed down at *The Wyoming*, thinking I might blink and she'd vanish, a daydream. But no, she was there, glistening in setting sunlight.

And she was seaworthy, which meant Heron and I could sail around Prickle Island and all the other little islands dotting the shoreline. Go fishing and swimming in secret, little alcoves. Explore the shoreline with enough space to bring the whole family with us. And, of course, escape all of the family when we needed alone time together, just the two of us, feeling so small in a vast ocean. A lifetime of adventures stretched out before me, the final star pulling into alignment, and everything felt so right.

I dropped my head to Heron's shoulder and said, "Looks like we're home."

Chapter Forty-Three

Heron

We crammed around the kitchen for SuFuFo, or Sunday Funday Fondue Day, as it was still called by everyone except for Hollis and me. At some point, the abbreviation would stick. Hollis and I had offered to do the dishes, enjoying our little alcove of quiet amongst the chaos, me washing and her waiting with a dish towel to dry them. It had become our Sunday evening routine.

Wren sat with Max on her lap in her rocking chair, a skein of yarn in a bowl at her feet as she knitted yet another Christmas sweater, determined to make ones for the entire family. Hawk and Hannah sat laughing at the table with Mom, playing a round of cards, while Finch and Frankie entertained Simon with a dramatic retelling of a children's book by the fireplace, doing all of the silly voices and sound effects.

And Crane held court entertaining the dual screens of Lark and Logan and Dove and Deacon, both having video conferenced in to dinner, late at night for Dove and Deacon, early in the morning for Lark and Logan, but still, they always made it.

I enjoyed the cool autumn evenings on Prickle Island, the days getting dark out earlier. Soon, it would be Halloween and we'd have our Boo at the Zoo event for all the shoreline kids to come carve pumpkins and trick-or-treat around the zoo following a treasure map with little conservation fun facts hidden along with the candy. Hollis and I had already coordinated our matching pirate outfits and were planning on sailing *The Wyoming* around to the western bay to be a part of the island-wide treasure hunt, hoisting a skull and crossbones flag. The smoke machine and red laser lights had already been tested. It would be quite the show. And bonus points, it meant we didn't have to be crammed in the throng of sugared-up children either.

As we settled into our post-dinner activities, a strangled gasp caught us off guard, and we turned to see Crane had minimized the Zoom screen and was looking at an email. "I got in!" he declared triumphantly. "I'm going to be on the conservation show!"

"Congratulations, wrecking ball," Dove's voice echoed through the computer as Crane frantically scrolled to read the rest of his acceptance letter. "Don't get too excited reading through all the competition rules and disclosures, but you're in. Looking forward to seeing you on the small screen."

Everyone cheered, moving over to the laptop to congratulate him. Hollis gave my shoulder a little squeeze, as if she knew it was bittersweet for me. I'd miss my twin, but I was happy for him to go on his amazing worldwide adventure.

"And who are you going to be paired up with?" Finch asked, crowding in front of the screen. "The Abbot to your Costello. The yin to your yang."

"Please let it be someone from Singapore Zoo. Or Australia Zoo. Or San Diego Zoo or . . ." He prayed to all the conservation gods as he scrolled to the name of the person he'd be paired up with for a whole year of traveling around the world. Then his head reared back, his chair tipping, and Finch barely had time to catch him before he toppled onto the linoleum. "You've got to be fucking kidding me!"

"Language!" Evie and Hawk called in unison.

Hollis and I raced over at his exclamation, trying to see over the pressing crowd. "What is it? What's wrong?"

"No, Dove! No. No fucking way," Crane exploded. "How could you do this to me?"

Hawk swatted him over the back of the head. "Stop fucking swearing in front of my kids."

Hannah pinched the bridge of her nose and shook her head as I pushed to the front and saw the photo of Crane's partner for this conservation challenge. A pretty blonde woman in her mid-twenties beamed back at the camera.

And the name next to it?

Cricket Madigan.

Chapter Forty-Four

A few years later

Hollis

There was nothing like rocking a baby to sleep on a boat. It worked every time.

The Wyoming had rocked me to sleep for most of my childhood. It had been my parents' failsafe whenever I'd been too fussy. Always taking me out on the boat whenever they'd wanted to guarantee I'd have a good night.

And now I sat at the bow, watching the setting sun with Maisie fast asleep on my chest, strapped to me in her carrier.

Finch and Frankie's daughter was the cutest, chubby-cheeked thing I'd ever seen, and that was saying something considering I got to work with baby animals for a living.

And whenever Finch and Frankie needed a break or just a

simple Hail Mary with a fussy baby, Heron and I took her out on the boat. We got all the best bits of cute baby snuggles, and then we got to give her back and get a full night's sleep. It was honestly perfect. Cool Heihei and Leelee forever.

I'd been anointed as Leelee by Simon, who struggled with the name Hollis, and I was forever grateful that he didn't call me "Ho" for the rest of my life instead. I loved being an auntie. It felt like there was an adult for every sort of situation in this family, someone who always had an idea or could lend a hand or had the right skill set to fix a problem. I had never realized how beautiful it could be to live in community with other people until I'd met the Lachlans. I guessed I'd just needed to find the right people.

Life was good. I'd secured myself a permanent spot as the head reptile keeper and I'd even managed to deliver the animal talks consistently without any swearing blunders. Well, almost. It got easier as time went on.

Heron had become quite the sailor too, now that I'd whipped them into shape. I'd taught the whole Lachlan clan how to sail, something they should've known how to do long ago in my opinion, considering they all lived on an island. Heron had taught me horse facts in exchange, and somewhere we'd met in the middle, swapping fun facts and hyperfocuses, having the sort of interest-focused minds that always had more to share with each other.

"Alright, babysitters!" Finch called from the stern as she and Frankie rose from the daybed they were snuggled on. "I'd like to reclaim my baby now, please."

"Just five more minutes," I called in mock protest, getting my squats in with the rock, crouch, bounce rhythm that I had perfected.

"Five minutes," Finch echoed, giving me the "I'm watching you" eyes as she stretched and breathed in the fresh sea breeze.

I grinned at Heron, and they winked back, the sharpness of the world softening to a blissful sort of calm.

Heron

We sat on the log at the meerkats, looking out over the zoo. The cold winter wind cut through our fleeces, which were currently lined with foraging meerkats eager to explore up our sleeves and burrow into our warmth.

"I'm thinking toast for dinner," I declared in a faux fantasy voice. "What say you?"

"Toast!" Hollis cheered with a pleased hum, as if she'd forgotten that was the best meal in the world. "I am so pro-toast for dinner. I have zero spoons left after that Christmas market."

I smiled down at out intertwined red and green painted fingernails. "It was so good though."

"It was," she agreed. "Wren really shines at Christmas."

I bobbed my head. "Yeah, that's her season for sure. I was thinking," I hedged, studying the flurries of snow that blustered across the hillside. "We should take all the niblings sledding tomorrow now that the snow is finally sticking."

"Ooh, yes." Hollis beamed at the meerkat sniffing her vanilla gingerbread lip balm, careful not to move too suddenly lest she get a new lip piercing. "Frankie already offered to make her spiced hot chocolate afterward."

"Of course she did." A smile caught the edges of my mouth as I sighed, my breath whirling steam around my face. "I don't think life could get any better." I licked my finger and checked the wind. "Yep, the conditions are perfect. There's nothing more that I want."

"There's one thing that could make it better," Hollis added, and I looked over to her as she was fishing around in her pocket.

I arched a brow as she crouched off the log and kept searching, then began frantically patting the ground. "Where the hell . . . ?" She looked all around, her eyes landing on something. "No!"

I followed her line of sight across the enclosure to see a meerkat with a golden wedding band in its mouth.

She rose from what I now realized was one knee and darted across the exhibit, nearly tripping in a newly dug burrow. "Give it back, you cretin! You are ruining the moment!"

She broke out into a fit of laughter as she whirled, chasing down the meerkat as I grabbed for the bucket of mealworms and started sprinkling them around the burrows to entice it to drop the ring.

With the distraction, the meerkat thankfully released his new treasure, and Hollis picked it up, wiping the meerkat saliva on her fleece. Both of us were laughing so hard that tears streamed down our faces, instantly cooling on our wind-chapped cheeks.

"You know, I thought this was going to be really romantic," she admitted between gasps of laughter. "I should've known better than to include wild animals in my attempt."

"It is romantic," I assured her. "You know, I've thought about this. Doing this." I nodded at the ring. "But I know you don't like surprises, so I was going to warn you first."

"Good," she said, bouncing on her toes with delight. "Warn me before you propose."

My face scrunched as I tried to contain my smile. "I still have to propose even after you did?"

"Oh yes. We take turns, remember?"

"Deal," I said, beaming, my heart practically levitating out of my chest. "So . . . was there . . . something you wanted to ask me?"

"Oh!" She dropped back down to one knee with a laugh. "Right." She held up the ring again, little waves carved around the band inlaid in gold, swirling up to hold three square cut diamonds across the top. My smile widened. It was so perfectly her, perfectly us. I wasn't going to tell her that her ring had already been picked out and hidden deep in a drawer aboard *The Wyoming*. Also gold and diamond, it would match perfectly.

"Heron Lachlan," Hollis said, her voice wobbling with emotion. "You have been the biggest surprise and greatest gift of my life, and I have loved every second of our time together. Before you, I didn't believe that there was any person for me. I was too much of a realist to believe in something as silly and whimsical as soulmates. But you make me feel silly and whimsical and happy and safe and loved. You are my soulmate, and I want to spend the rest of my life being the same kind of strange as you. I want to be your person forever. Will you marry me?"

Warm tears steamed down my cold cheeks as I nodded and blubbered out the word, "Yes."

She rose on her toes, wrapping her arms around my neck, and kissed me.

"My proposal speech is never going to top that," I said with a rasping laugh.

"It will," she countered. "Because it's coming from you. I love you."

"I love you too, fiancée," I replied as she slid the ring onto my finger. "I feel grateful every second that we found each other. Every day, just when I think I couldn't love you more, I do. Endlessly."

"I think you'll do just fine at that proposal speech," she said through tears and rose on her toes to kiss me again.

I leaned down to continue our kiss as a meerkat climbed

onto the top of my head and used me as a lookout. Well, I guessed I'd have to stay there kissing my fiancée for a little while longer then. Couldn't stop a meerkat from his sentinel duties.

My radio scratched to life at my hip, and a bunch of cheering echoed through it. "Champagne at the Peacock!" Frankie called from wherever she was hiding around the zoo. "Congratulations, you two!"

Hollis pulled back with a laugh. "I only told one person."

"Which means you told everyone," I countered.

"Yep."

"Come on, cowgirl," I said, slinging my arm around her shoulders. "Let's go to our engagement party."

We headed off into the snowy quiet, a ring on my finger, my heart full, and just as we rounded the corner, we ran head on into Beaky, foraging through a sparse hedge.

Hollis guffawed, threading her arm through mine. "After we escort this ostrich back to his home."

The End

FOR ZOO
NEWS

Ali K. Mulford Books:

The Prickle Island Zoo Series:

She's a Keeper

Easy Tiger

Party Animal

Crocodile Tears

Hold Your Horses

Monkey Business

Oh Deer

Maple Hollow Series:

Pumpkin Spice & Poltergeist

Curses & Cold Brew

Lycans & Lattes

Acknowledgments

Thank you to all of my amazing readers for coming on this new adventure with me. I am so humbled by your support and all the ways you champion my books out in the world!

Thank you so much to all of my Patrons! I love writing new stories, commissioning spicy art, and getting to connect with you on Patreon! A very special thank you to Aleah, Morgan, Ashley, Samantha, Stacy, Lauren, Naiomi, Latham, Jaime, Krista, Ciara, Linda, and Katie! Thank you for being on this bookish adventure with me!

Thank you to Norma from Norma's Nook Editing

Thank you to Enni from Yummy Book Covers for designing the gorgeous covers for this series

Thank you to Holly Dunn for designing the Zoo Map

Thank you to my amazing assistant Shae for all of your creativity, enthusiasm, and support on this crazy journey

Ali K. Mulford (also known by their bestselling fantasy pen name A.K. Mulford) is a rom-com author and former wildlife biologist who swapped rehabilitating monkeys for writing novels. A US and NZ citizen, Mulford now lives in Australia rearing two human primates, writing lovable characters, and making ridiculous TikToks (@akmulfordauthor).

www.akmulford.com